"I think you care about me," Zane whispered.

He knew he shouldn't be so honest with her. Glory's rose scent tickled his nostrils, making his stomach churn with equal parts need and premonition.

She gasped.

"And I think you want to kiss me as much as I want to kiss you," he whispered. Her soft lips parted and her eyes widened. The need to taste her was a magnet, drawing him in, making his lips tingle in anticipation. He bent his head down, moving closer inch by inch, giving her time to move away.

She didn't. His palms itched to touch her, but he sensed that it would be a step too far. The heated air between them was thick with tension. "Say yes to me."

For a moment, the only sound in the room was their breathing mixed with the ticking of the clock on the mantel. "Yes." The soft whisper burrowed inside him, grabbing something deep within him and pulling him to her.

His lips touched hers.

Author Note

Gold was discovered in Helena, Montana, in 1864, and for the next three decades it was a town flush with wealth and those looking for power. For a brief time, the town boasted more millionaires per capita than any other place in the world. This is the main reason I chose it as the setting for my Outlaws of the Wild West series. I loved the idea of such opulence set against the backdrop of a rough and sometimes lawless territory.

In researching the town, I came across a couple of prominent women who helped lay the groundwork for the character of Glory Winters. Josephine "Chicago Joe" Hensley was one of the wealthiest people in Helena. She owned a brothel, a saloon and a variety theater, along with other commercial investments. Mollie "Crazy Belle Crafton" Byrnes owned a famous brothel known as "the castle." She and the women who lived there were quite charitable, contributing to those in need at Christmas.

I hope you enjoy getting to know Glory and Zane. I absolutely loved writing their story. Please visit my website, harperstgeorge.com, to sign up for my newsletter for sneak peeks and contests.

HARPER
ST. GEORGE

An Outlaw
to Protect Her

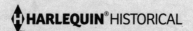

ISBN-13: 978-1-335-05178-3

An Outlaw to Protect Her

Copyright © 2018 by Harper St. George

All rights reserved. Except for use in any review, the reproduction or utilization of this work in whole or in part in any form by any electronic, mechanical or other means, now known or hereafter invented, including xerography, photocopying and recording, or in any information storage or retrieval system, is forbidden without the written permission of the publisher, Harlequin Enterprises Limited, 22 Adelaide St. West, 40th Floor, Toronto, Ontario M5H 4E3, Canada.

This is a work of fiction. Names, characters, places and incidents are either the product of the author's imagination or are used fictitiously, and any resemblance to actual persons, living or dead, business establishments, events or locales is entirely coincidental.

This edition published by arrangement with Harlequin Books S.A.

For questions and comments about the quality of this book, please contact us at CustomerService@Harlequin.com.

® and TM are trademarks of Harlequin Enterprises Limited or its corporate affiliates. Trademarks indicated with ® are registered in the United States Patent and Trademark Office, the Canadian Intellectual Property Office and in other countries.

Printed in U.S.A.

™ www.Harlequin.com

Harper St. George was raised in rural Alabama and along the tranquil coast of northwest Florida. It was these settings, filled with stories of the old days, that instilled in her a love of history, romance and adventure. In high school she discovered the romance novel, which combined all those elements into one perfect package. She lives in Atlanta, Georgia, with her husband and two young children. Visit her website, harperstgeorge.com.

Books by Harper St. George

Harlequin Historical

Outlaws of the Wild West

The Innocent and the Outlaw
A Marriage Deal with the Outlaw
An Outlaw to Protect Her

Viking Warriors

Enslaved by the Viking
One Night with the Viking
In Bed with the Viking Warrior
The Viking Warrior's Bride

Visit the Author Profile page at Harlequin.com.

Chapter One

Being the madam of the most notorious brothel in Montana Territory came with certain privileges. Financial security and independence rode high at the top of that list for Glory Winters. In fact, she would go so far as to say that those were the only benefits that really mattered. For they allowed the other freedoms to exist. Without them, she'd never have been able to open her home to women running away from unfortunate situations. Nor would she have had the resources to purchase nearly an eighth of the town of Helena, making her the single most prosperous female landholder.

Unfortunately, those very same privileges that she so enjoyed came with some definite negatives. One of those negatives sat across the table from her now. He grinned, giving her a flash of the gold crown capping his left bicuspid as he tossed back the remainder of his brandy. Glory suppressed a shudder as he swallowed, making the beginnings of what would soon be a double chin wobble as he did so. He brought his handkerchief up and pressed it to his mouth before wiping it across his sweaty forehead.

"Excellent beefsteak as usual, Miss Winters."

Drawing on the impeccable manners she'd been taught at her mother's knee, Glory offered him a dazzling smile. He was a guest and she wouldn't insult him, but making conversation with him made her skin crawl. "Thank you, Mr. Harvey. I'm so pleased you enjoyed your meal." She intentionally drew out the vowels to make her Southern drawl more pronounced. It never failed to charm even the most cantankerous gentleman. Though she used the term *gentleman* loosely in the case of William Harvey. The only thing noble about him was his dress. He was a snake in the trimmings of probably the most expensive suit she'd ever seen on a man. For a town that had made millionaires out of humble miners, that was saying a lot.

"You've done quite well for yourself here." He sat back in the chair, leather creaking as he laced his hands over his lap.

Glory kept her smile in place. The words hung heavy in the air between them, filling it with silent tension broken only by the hushed conversation at one of the other tables across the dining room. Harvey always had something up his sleeve. She recognized this as the moment before he would strike and she tried to prepare herself for how bad the bite would be. One thing she had learned in her years here was to never underestimate the greed of men, especially when they saw a woman who had something they wanted.

Harvey wasn't the first to want a stake in her business. He wouldn't be the last.

"You're too kind," she said.

"And you're too humble. I remember when this place was little more than bare floorboards and straw mattresses."

She tried not to wince. Victoria House had never been quite that shoddy. When she'd arrived with her dear friend Able, the place had been a neglected mansion that had seen better days, but it certainly hadn't been a hovel. They had slowly transformed it into the grand club it was today. She'd hired a proper chef, and they had several dining rooms and parlors where gentlemen could come to relax surrounded by opulence. There were plenty of saloons down the road where they could go to get a whiskey for half the cost with cheaper buy-ins for poker and faro, but they came to Victoria House because they liked the atmosphere. The dust of sophistication that coated the mansion fed their need for luxury.

These men had pulled gold, silver and copper from the earth to make themselves wealthier than they'd ever dreamed possible. The social salons of New York and London might not welcome their new money, but Glory was happy to give them a taste of that same opulence right here in Helena. Even her gowns came straight from Paris. The men were more than willing to hand over a portion of their riches for a taste of that life.

"Well, I've always known the value of a little hard work. As do you." She wasn't above pouring on a little flattery.

He inclined his head as if it were quite the task to lord over the men who did the backbreaking work of maintaining his gold mines. "It'd be a shame to see all of this hard work go to waste." He raised a hand and indicated the room with its silk wall coverings, Persian rugs and brass finishings.

Ah, and there it was. He *was* after her wealth. Now to figure out his game before he could lower the trap. She'd perfected her poker face years ago, so she managed not to reveal so much as a flicker of her lashes. "Hard work rarely goes to waste."

His smile faded, replaced by cold calculation. "You are aware that statehood is just around the corner for our humble little territory? Helena is in the running for state capital. Thanks to the railroad, nice Christian folks are moving here and they don't want to see an establishment such as this in our midst. Surely you can see the benefit of having a *friend* like me."

Rumors were that Harvey would be elected to the legislature; it was the main reason she tolerated his odious presence. She couldn't afford to alienate anyone with political clout. "But I thought we *were* friends," she countered.

He shrugged, his cold gaze sliding over her exposed shoulders and down farther in a slow glide that made her want to scrub away the filth he'd left behind. "We could be closer, Miss Winters. Much closer. I could help you keep everything you've worked for, and you could help me."

She didn't even want to entertain the thought of what helping him would entail. "I think the fine people of Helena will come to understand how much good I do for the town. My taxes and personal donations have contributed to the school that was recently built."

He laughed. "Money only goes so far. The reputation and honor of our fair city is at stake, particularly when it comes time to vote for statehood. Why, a notorious place such as this might not be able to exist in a law-abiding state."

"Then the fate of Victoria House is sealed either way," she said with a shrug of her shoulder.

"Ah, but I have friends, Miss Winters. And soon I'll have influence. If we were…*friends*…I could extend that influence to you." He licked his lips, leaving them wet and shining in the light of the candle flickering on the table between them.

She swallowed past the bile that threatened to rise in the back of her throat, and opened her mouth to tell him in her sweetest voice that no way in hell would she ever be that sort of friend to him. Because she was a madam, men often assumed incorrectly that she was also for sale and she had to set them straight. Thankfully, Able intervened before she said something foolish and made an enemy they didn't need.

"Miss Winters." His large frame took up nearly the entire doorway of the dining room. "You're needed upstairs."

He had a sixth sense when it came to saving her. It had been that way ever since they escaped together twelve years earlier. She simply wouldn't have made it out of that house in the South Carolina low country all the way to Helena had he not almost literally carried her the entire way.

"Excuse me, Mr. Harvey. Duty calls. It's been a pleasure." She rose and nearly gasped audibly when the man leaned forward and grabbed her wrist. No one ever touched her. From the corner of her eye, she saw Able step into the room, ready if he was needed.

"Think about what I've said, Glory. You may not have that long to make up your mind," Harvey said. His eyes flashed with cruelty as he let her go just as Able came to a stop next to his chair.

"Is that a threat?" She bit the words out through clenched teeth.

"Not at all." He grinned, but it wasn't the least bit friendly. "Merely an observation of things to come."

"Good evening, Mr. Harvey." Without another word—as much as she hated him and all he stood for, she wasn't willing to make Harvey an enemy—she strode out of the room with Able close behind her.

"Thank you for intervening," she whispered once they'd walked far enough down the hallway to not be overheard.

Able made a grumbling noise in the back of his throat. "I've never liked that man. Don't trust him."

"You and me both." She opened the door leading to the servants' quarters in the back of the house and paused to make sure no one followed them. Closing the door behind them after Able had stepped inside, she said, "He wants Victoria House."

Able drew in a sharp breath through his nose. "He won't get it." The light of the electric wall sconce reflected off his medium-brown skin, revealing a brow that was smooth and not furrowed in worry. His dark eyes were calm. Quiet and sensible, he'd become the barometer against which she measured the scope of their problems. There wouldn't be reason to worry until he was worried.

Nodding her agreement, she said, "It's nothing we haven't faced before." A couple of years ago they'd faced a similar threat, only this one had been a group of investors looking to purchase the place from her at a value far below market. Little had they known that Able was part owner and any decision she made would have to be corroborated by him. Once they'd found out they'd resorted to force instead of seduction. In the end, they'd dealt with those men and she had confidence that Harvey could be handled as well.

"Is everything else going well?" she asked.

"Fine. We're a little busier because of the faro tournament across the road, but everyone is behaving themselves."

"In that case, I'll go get a little work done in my study and give Harvey some time to leave. Let me know if I'm needed." Able agreed, and Glory took the back stairs up to her study on the mansion's third floor. The top floor was private. Her apartment was attached to her study and the other ladies who lived at Victoria House full-time had rooms there. It wasn't decorated quite as ostentatiously as the rest of the house. The wall color was a soft cream with a blue-and-gold runner softening her steps in the hallway. Each door boasted a wreath or some other decorative trinket that reflected the resident's personality. In short, this floor felt like home and was a respite from the bustle of the rest of the house.

Up here the William Harveys of the world felt far away. Glory let out a breath, already anticipating the nice long soak in her bathtub she'd take when the evening was over. It seemed like the nights were getting longer, or maybe she was simply getting older. She'd be thirty in a couple of years, which didn't seem particularly old, but this wasn't where she'd imagined herself at this point. Life was strange in that way. Nothing ever seemed to happen the way she meant for it to happen, but she'd learned that it could still be good. She had about a million things to be thankful for, not the least of which were security and independence. It was more than she'd had a decade ago.

She was smiling when she approached her study, but the smile faltered when she realized that the door wasn't latched. A gentle nudge revealed that her assistant's desk sat empty. Glory turned on the wall sconce to reveal that no one was in the antechamber at all. How odd. Charlotte, her assistant, always closed up when she finished her work for the evening. A stack of correspondence ready to post the next morning sat on the corner of Charlotte's small desk, exactly as she'd left them. It was possible that Charlotte had forgotten to lock up, but a strange sense of foreboding made her stomach tumble.

Glory took in a deep breath, consciously avoiding looking across the room at the door that led to her study. Glory was the only person with a key to that door. If it was open then it meant that someone had broken in and she'd have to face that her sanctuary wasn't really a sanctuary at all. But she was being silly. Of course it was locked. To prove it to herself she put her hand into the hidden pocket of her skirt and wrapped her fingers around the warm metal of the key. It was still safely with her. Charlotte had simply forgotten to close the door to the hallway.

Her heart pounding, she turned toward her door. It was mercifully closed. An exhale of relief left her feeling deflated and weak. She put a hand on the corner of Charlotte's desk to keep her balance. Even after all these years she was wary of any irregularity. She knew all too well how quickly life could come crashing down with very little warning.

There was no light coming from beneath her door and no sound came from within her study. No one had been inside. She knew that, but her heart resumed its pounding as she approached the door with her key in hand. The cool metal of the latch chilled her palm and she gave it a quick turn to test the lock. Her key held useless in her other hand, the door latch made a clicking sound as it unlatched. She gave a little push and the door creaked, swinging open to reveal the interior of her office. Moonlight flooded in through the windows facing the street, spilling onto the carpeted floor. No one was inside, but nevertheless she moved forward cautiously.

As soon as her feet crossed the threshold she saw it. It was a square piece of parchment sitting in the middle of her tidy desk, and it seemed to have a nearly ethereal glow in the moonlight. It had not been there when she'd left earlier in the evening.

Turning on the electric sconce on the wall didn't help. The white parchment lost its glow, but it didn't seem any less dangerous. It hadn't been sent by post. There was no envelope, no markings at all. She crossed to her desk, watching the note as if it were a living thing that could jump out and grab her at any moment. Blood pounded through her head, filling her ears with its roar. Somehow her life would change when she read that letter. She just knew it. Good things rarely came along unexpectedly.

Her fingers trembled when she reached for it. The stiff paper was cool under her touch, barely crinkling as she sucked in a deep breath and flipped it open. The first five words on the page jumped out at her, sending a shard of terror straight through her heart.

I know who you are.

Chapter Two

Zane Pierce tossed back the last of the whiskey in his tumbler and rose from his stool at the bar. The woman tending the bar gave him a smile as she picked up the glass and wiped the mahogany beneath it to a shine. "Fancy some company later tonight?"

Penelope was naturally pretty in a quiet way that wasn't very outrageous. Even with the kohl lining her eyes and her reddened lips, she gave off an air that was almost wholesome. As if she could just as easily be teaching Sunday school at a church across town instead of working at Victoria House. Some men seemed to like that. Since Zane had been around for the past week, he'd noticed a few of the patrons asking to take her upstairs, but she'd turned them all down. Maybe she didn't "work upstairs," the code he'd learned referred to the prostitutes who worked on the second floor. Hell, he might've even been interested at one time.

He glanced across the length of the dining room to the door through which Glory had recently disappeared. She'd made it clear when she'd allowed him to have a room a week ago that taking refuge in Victoria House meant that her women were off-limits. The castration that would result probably wasn't worth it, he mused.

"I don't think Miss Winters would appreciate that." That was only part of the reason. In reality it was a gentle way to let Penelope down, because the only woman he was interested in was Glory. The truth was that Glory Winters was the only woman who'd caught his interest in a long time.

They'd known each other for a couple of years now and had spent that entire time circling each other. He could probably count on one hand the times they'd spoken. He might've thought she wasn't interested in him except that he heard the way she caught her breath when he passed too close. He caught the looks she flashed his way when she thought he couldn't see her.

One night earlier in the week he'd caught her staring at him in the lounge at Victoria House. He'd been sitting at the bar drinking a whiskey before returning to his room for the night. She'd been standing just outside the doorway at an angle that should've obscured her from view. He only saw her because the mirror above the bar had caught her reflection just right. She'd stood there for a solid two minutes staring at him with a look that he could only describe as pure longing on her face. When he'd turned to talk to her she'd taken off running. He hadn't followed her because he'd hoped to give her time to come to him.

"Oh." Penelope nibbled her lip and offered him a shy smile. "I didn't mean that I'd charge you anything. I don't work upstairs."

Something about the woman's softly worded admission tugged at him. For the first time he found himself wondering what life was like for the women here. Did Penelope want to be a farmer's wife or was she happy at Victoria House? Was she lonely? He lowered his voice to soften his rejection. "Maybe some other time after I've moved out."

Which could be as early as tomorrow since their hunt for Buck Derringer was over. The search had consumed them for the past few years. Zane had been working on a ranch down in Texas owned by his friend Castillo's grandfather. Derringer had come around offering improved ranching methods and expertise, and pretty soon he'd swindled Castillo's grandfather out of his life savings. When Castillo had tried to collect, Derringer and his son, Bennett, had blown through the ranch one night, killing Castillo's grandfather and leaving destruction. The ranch had burned to the ground. The scar Zane carried on his face was a lifetime reminder of that horrible night. Zane had vowed to help his friend get revenge.

They'd been joined by Castillo's half brother, Hunter, and had soon become known as the Reyes Brothers. After years of searching from Texas to Montana Territory, Derringer had found them in Helena, Hunter's hometown. Last week they'd been in a shoot-out with Derringer's son and killed him, and Derringer had gone into hiding again. Two days ago Derringer had come out of nowhere, shooting at Castillo from an alley. He'd been wounded, but Zane had managed to come to his aid and together they'd killed the bastard.

The years of searching were over, but Zane wasn't

ready to leave Victoria House just yet. He'd taken a room here to root out Derringer and while their enemy had fallen, Zane hadn't moved one step closer in uncovering the mystery of the brothel's madam. No one was willing to talk much about the madam or her past. It was as infuriating as it was intriguing.

Penelope gave him a smile and a disappointed shrug before moving on to help another customer, while Zane turned back to the dining room. William Harvey had stood from the table he'd occupied with Glory and was making his way out of the room. Zane couldn't stop himself from glaring. He'd nearly come off his stool when Harvey had grabbed Glory. He'd have gone over to stop the son of a bitch from touching her if Able hadn't intervened.

Zane followed behind Harvey to the front door, making sure the man didn't try to find her. He had no idea what they'd been talking about, but it had been apparent that she had left their conversation upset. Harvey stopped to talk with a man Zane recognized as a banker and frequent guest of the house, so Zane paused in the shadows, unwilling to let Harvey out of his sight as long as the man was in the house. After a few minutes, Harvey said his goodbyes, retrieved his hat from the doorman and left.

Zane breathed a sigh of relief and made his way to the servants' hall and out the back door. Some time ago Glory had purchased the property that adjoined Victoria House in the back. It had been a boardinghouse hastily built to accommodate the influx of miners. At some point it had fallen into disrepair, so she'd restored it. The second floor was now a temporary home for women who needed it. Women who were abused or abandoned and often had nowhere else to go. The first floor had a set of apartments occupied by Able and his wife on one side, while the other side had been turned into a makeshift clinic for her ladies that he'd heard was better equipped than the town's hospital.

That's where he was headed now. They'd taken Castillo there because the hospital's doctor was a known drunk. He had a reputation for killing as many as he saved, and the gang hadn't been willing to take the chance on their leader's life. Castillo was still there recovering from his gunshot wound, and they needed to discuss what to do next. His boots clicked on the cobblestones of the courtyard and a few lanterns lit his way across the fenced-in enclosure. The second- and third-floor windows of Victoria House were boarded over with decorative shutters to preserve privacy. A few of the ladies who weren't working were taking advantage of that privacy and the mild summer night to play a game of dice.

"Evening, ladies." He gave them a nod as he passed. They returned his greeting and a few watched him with interest. None of them had approached him in the entire time he'd been in residence. He'd discovered that, due to his size and the nasty scar that covered part of his face, women tended to be afraid of him. Penelope had probably only warmed up to him because he'd had a drink at her bar each night before going to bed and maybe she'd realized he was harmless. He almost laughed at the description. Well, harmless for a wanted outlaw.

A few minutes later Zane walked into Castillo's room, where Castillo's new wife, Caroline, was busy fussing over him. She fluffed Castillo's pillow and stroked his cheek as his friend looked up at her, clearly besotted. The fool. Zane had to stop himself from shaking his head. He'd learned his lesson about women and love with Christine. Even the thought of her made his scar tingle.

Although Zane hadn't let his feelings be known about the matter, he was of the opinion that Castillo would've been paying more attention to his surroundings on the morning he was shot had Caroline not been with him. He might've noticed Derringer sooner. Instead, Derringer had gotten the best of him and left him with a bullet wound in his abdomen. Caroline, who was studying to be a physician, had stitched him up. Though Castillo seemed to be on the mend, they weren't out of the woods yet as infection could seep in at any time. It just proved the point that men like them had no business with women. Well, not for more than a casual affair. Anything more intense would be too risky.

"How are you feeling?" he asked, jarring the couple apart.

"Like I got shot in the gut," Castillo said in his slightly accented English. "But I'll live thanks to the doc here."

Caroline grinned and brushed back a strand of black hair that had fallen across his forehead. "Not a doctor yet, but soon."

She was being too modest. She'd spent her childhood apprenticing under her father, and Zane had seen firsthand how efficiently she'd worked on Castillo. She knew what she was doing. "We're thankful you were here," Zane said, walking farther into the room to stand with a hip leaned against a bureau.

Hunter sat in a chair beside the bed. "Caroline says he'll be stable enough that we can move him to the town house in the morning."

Zane nodded his agreement. The town house was more secure, and they'd be able to post their men around it. So far it seemed that Derringer had been alone and no one would come to avenge his death, but they needed to take precautions just to be sure. Not to mention the fact that the clinic was essentially attached to the brothel. The Jameson name and wealth could only protect Caroline's reputation for so long. If she had any hope of showing her face in polite society again, they needed to get her away from Victoria House soon.

"Let's move him before dawn then," Zane said. "Less people around to worry about."

As they made plans for moving Castillo, Zane realized that this really would be his last night in Victoria House. His last night close to Glory. His last chance to explore the strange attraction between them. But she'd been so careful to never let him get close, he didn't know how he was going to make that happen. She never let *anyone* get too close. As far as he could tell, Able was the only one she trusted. At first, he'd been able to respect that. He knew how it felt to keep others at a distance. He'd done it himself most of his life. But staying at Victoria House for the past week had made him want things with her that were better left unexplored.

If only he could heed his own advice.

Part of him knew that he should let it go, but another part, a *stronger* part, of him wondered if there was something holding her back. Some reason that she wouldn't approach him even though she was clearly interested. Damn, he'd give anything to know her secrets. She kept herself so guarded they were impossible to figure out. One night wouldn't be nearly enough time.

"Glory?" Hunter's voice made Zane jerk his head up. He found Glory standing in the doorway as if his thoughts had somehow conjured her. She wore the same emerald green gown from earlier. Her deep red hair was piled impeccably atop her head. She was easily the most beautiful woman he'd ever seen. It was more than her looks though. It was the way she held herself, the way she ran the brothel with confidence and competency. She was like a queen.

Only when he looked closer did he notice the tension lines around her mouth and the worry lines creasing her brow. She seemed pale. He pushed away from the bureau, ready to chase Harvey down for whatever he'd done to her, but her voice stopped him.

"How are you feeling, Castillo?" she asked, doing her best to put on a calm facade.

"Much better, thank you," Castillo answered.

"Thank you so much for opening your home to us." Caroline came around the foot of the bed. To her credit, she extended her hand toward Glory as if she didn't care the woman was a brothel madam. "I've never seen the hospital in town, but the stories make me fear what would've happened had we taken him there. Your setup here is one of the nicest I've seen. It rivals my father's own practice back in Boston."

Glory smiled and shook her hand. "Please don't thank me. It's the least I could do. I'm happy everything's turned out well."

Hunter added, "We're indebted to you, as usual. If you ever need anything—"

"Actually, I do need your help," Glory said, turning her attention from Caroline to Hunter. Zane noted she managed not to look at him even though he stood close to Hunter. He couldn't help but feel she did it purposefully.

"Anything. What do you need?" Hunter asked as he came to his feet.

"If you and Mr. Pierce could come to my study as soon as possible, I'd be grateful."

Mr. Pierce. She'd only called him by his given name once. It had happened last week when he and Castillo had captured a man who'd been following them and brought him to her storeroom to interrogate. She'd been so angry at them for daring to endanger her ladies, and she'd forgotten her resolve to only use his last name. It wasn't much, but he'd decided to call it progress and he'd made it his mission to get her to call him Zane again.

"Has something happened?" Zane asked.

She finally looked at him, her eyes going slightly wider as she took a deep breath. He couldn't be sure with the low lighting but he'd bet that he could see the pulse in her throat flickering. Her tongue came out to moisten her lips and something deep inside him clenched.

But aside from the anger, he saw fear in the depths of her eyes and it raised the hair on the back of his neck. "Are you in danger, Glory?" he asked.

"Please come to my study. I—I'll tell you both everything." She turned and left without giving him a chance to say anything more.

Now there was an invitation he couldn't refuse.

Chapter Three

Glory rushed across the courtyard toward the sanctity of her study as fast as she could without rousing suspicion. Only she couldn't really think of it as her safe place anymore after someone had broken into it. As she fled she could still hear the echo of Zane's deep voice reverberating within her. She didn't just hear his voice, she *felt* it, bouncing off the hollows inside her and smoothing out their edges. He'd been wreaking havoc on her emotional state all week without even realizing it. She wanted him to leave so that she could stop thinking about him, but the thought of possibly never seeing him again made her feel bereft.

It wasn't his fault she couldn't stop thinking about him. Glory couldn't even figure out why he affected her so. It had simply always been that way and she couldn't stop whatever he did to her as much as she wanted to. Instead of trying anymore, she simply ignored it.

Grabbing the key from her pocket with more force than was strictly necessary, she shoved it into the lock of her study door and pushed it open, half expecting someone to pop out at her. It was as empty as it had been before, and that damned letter was still on her desk except this time it was open just as she'd left it. From across the room, her gaze caught on those five little words.

I know who you are.

They were ominous. Able was the only person in the whole world who knew her true identity. No one else knew her real name or where she had come from. She'd made up several stories and told them all at various times with a wink and a smile. The wealthy patrons of Victoria House didn't care where the madam was from. All they really wanted was a bit of intrigue, so she told them she was a runaway countess, or the long-lost granddaughter of the famous pirate Jean Lafitte. Once, a rumor had started that she was an illegitimate Russian princess, and she hadn't bothered to refute it. If they believed the stories it was because they wanted to. Because of her accent, most assumed she was a Southern belle whose family had been displaced during the war. She never confirmed or denied anything. The stories were good for business, because they kept her mysterious.

The truth would not be good for business. As a matter of fact, the truth could very well get her and Able killed. The shock of that settled into her bones as she walked to stand behind her desk, staring down at the letter. The words written in black ink on the parchment sent cold tendrils of fear curling down her spine. She shivered and forced a deep, even breath to keep the terror at bay. She refused to allow one simple note to paralyze her with fear.

But it *was* jarring, because she'd never received a note like this since her escape. It was certainly plausible that someone from her old life had tracked her down, even after all this time. It was also true that she'd made many enemies in her line of work—namely men who wanted the fortune she managed—and would relish bringing her past rushing back to meet her. Harvey came to mind immediately. Had he somehow had a hand in this? Was this a move to push her into accepting his *friendship*?

Well, she wasn't a sixteen-year-old runaway anymore. She had ways to fight back now.

Able walked in with a wary expression on his face. She'd sent word for him to meet her here before she'd gone to talk to Hunter and Zane. It was unusual for her to call a meeting with him this late at night, especially when they were so busy.

"Is there something wrong?" he asked, his gaze searching her face.

She waved her hand to the empty chair across from her. Some part of her wanted to hold off the sharing of the letter as long as possible to keep things as they were before she'd found it. Her peace of mind might be shattered, but that didn't mean she had to involve Able. Only she *did* have to involve him. The letter affected him as much as her, so it was only right to tell him. He took in a deep, fortifying breath as if he knew what was coming and unbuttoned his coat as he sat down.

"I thought you should know that I received this today." She held up the letter. "Someone is claiming to know who I am."

His jaw clenched and his dark eyes hardened. "Who sent it?"

She shook her head. "It's anonymous."

He held out his hand and she gave the letter to him, dropping the parchment as if it had burned her the second he took it. His brow furrowed as he scanned the letter and tightness squeezed her chest. Glory realized that she was holding her breath, hoping against hope that he'd find something she had missed that would tell them the letter was a hoax, so she let it out and felt her muscles relax.

A knock on the open door drew her attention. Hunter came in followed closely by Zane. Hunter was tall at just over six feet, but Zane towered over him by a few inches. His large frame was strapped with lean muscle, matching Able in sheer powerful strength. If not for Zane's darker coloring marking his native heritage, she'd imagine there was at least one Viking ancestor in his lineage.

Despite his size, his appearance wasn't the most striking thing about him, at least not for her. It was his eyes. They were so dark they were nearly black and looked at her with an intensity she didn't know how to interpret. It was almost as if he could see past the role that she played. As if he was the only one who could look through the brothel madam costume and wonder at the real woman beneath.

The longer she was around him the more she craved that. He was looking at her now as he closed the door behind him. She couldn't stop herself from staring at the pink scar that started just above his right eyebrow, went down over his cheekbone, before drifting off into his hairline. Time and time again she'd wanted to ask him about it but hadn't. She knew what it was like to have scars you didn't want to talk about. Luckily hers were hidden, but she could only imagine how she'd feel if someone questioned them. So she stayed silent on that point out of both respect and self-preservation. The less she knew about him the better. He was an outlaw and she was the madam of a brothel. There was no future for either of them, especially not together.

"Thank you both for coming," she said, returning her attention to Hunter. He was always the one out of the band of brothers who'd taken the lead in dealing with her. "Please sit down." Noting there was only one chair available since Able occupied the other, she added, "There's an extra chair in Charlotte's office."

"There's no need," Zane said, crossing his arms over his chest as he came to stand behind the empty chair. He gave a nod to Hunter, and his friend sat down in the chair.

"I've asked you here because I've received a rather disturbing letter." The paper crinkled as Able finished reading it and handed it back to her. A glance at his face told her nothing of how he felt. If he was worried he was careful not to show it. "Well, perhaps I should simply read the letter so you'll understand."

At Hunter's nod of encouragement, she took a deep breath, loath to read the words again. There was no help for it though, so she plowed forward.

"I know who you are. You will understandably doubt my claim, so allow me to elaborate. It is my preference not to give too much away in the event someone else

finds this letter, so I will simply say that I know you are from South Carolina. I know that you arrived in Helena in 1876 with nothing but the funds you managed to steal, along with your grandmother's quilt.'"

Her voice trembled, so she paused to clear her throat. Those were details anyone could guess, she reasoned.

"It's common knowledge among the staff that I sleep with my grandmother's quilt and anyone could guess about the South Carolina bit," she said.

Able nodded in agreement. "Keep reading."

She took a fortifying breath and continued. *"'I know your true name. I know the details that caused you to run away. I know from whom you ran.'"*

She paused as that vile man's image came to mind. Justin Dubose. Every day that passed she resisted thinking about him, but he was always there lurking in the shadows of her memory. She feared that he always would be.

When she paused, Hunter said, "It's a clever attempt at extortion, but there's no solid information to prove they do know who you are."

His handsome face revealed no hint of alarm. Perhaps that meant she was overreacting, or perhaps it meant he simply didn't understand the severity of her danger.

Biting her lower lip, she read to the end. *"'Please do not misunderstand my intention. I was hired to find you. I have no personal stake in your recovery. My goal is simply to give you the opportunity to stay hidden. Should you choose to take that opportunity I will disappear with my payment, never to be seen again. Should*

*you refuse, then I have no choice but to report my find-
ings to my employer. The choice is yours. If you wish to
stay hidden, have five thousand dollars directed to the
account number and bank below. You have one week.'"*

There was no signature, only an account number and
the address of a bank in Chicago.

The room was silent as she laid the letter on her desk.
A myriad of emotions played out in her mind: fear, disbelief, frustration, anger, resolve. In the blink of an eye,
she went from uncertainty to somehow knowing exactly
what she wanted to do. "We have to find this person."

"Are the details in the letter accurate?" Hunter asked.

"Close enough." The waver was gone from her voice,
thankfully.

Able stood, his hand going up to the back of his neck
to massage away stiffness. "It doesn't say much, but the
things it *does* say…" His voice trailed off and he walked
to the window that looked out over the mansion's im-
maculate front stoop and the street beyond, his unfocused gaze taking in the night sky.

Zane walked around to take Able's vacated chair. Sitting down, he leaned forward, forearms on his knees.
"Did you run from someone, Glory?"

She blinked, her body instinctively tensing in reaction to having that old wound prodded. "I'd rather not
get into my past. That's why I want the person caught."

Zane stared at her, his gaze touching every inch of
her face. Maybe he thought if he looked hard enough
he'd find the answer there. God help her, a part of her
wanted to tell him everything. To share the secret
that only Able knew because he'd been there when it

had happened. She'd never told another soul, because she'd never trusted anyone enough. She didn't know Zane well, so there was no reason to trust him, but as she stared into the depths of his sympathetic eyes she wanted to tell him everything. Some small part of her hoped that sharing the burden would make it lighter, but realistically, she knew that wouldn't happen. Telling anyone else would simply open herself up to more situations like this. The world was ruled by greed. She'd learned that lesson the hard way.

Hunter intervened before Zane could reply. "We can find this person, but it would help if you'd let us know a little more."

"It's best that you know as little as possible."

Hunter frowned but the expression was mild. "If we're going to help we do need to know where to look for this person. And if a threat is coming, then we need to know who to look for to stop it."

She wavered and stared down at the letter again. What he said made sense, but there was no way she was letting anyone know where she and Able had come from. She didn't think that Hunter or Zane would intentionally betray her, but if the wrong person found out they could easily bring the devil himself to her door.

"Glory and I came here twelve years ago." Able walked over to stand behind her chair. "We have no contact with anyone we left behind. We can't tell you any more than that."

His brow creased in visible frustration, Zane said,

"You don't have to tell us who…yet, but we need to know… Is it possible that someone is looking for you?"

Taking a ragged breath, she nodded. "Yes."

"And what would happen if this person found you?"

She was silent as she thought about how much to tell him. Finally she went with the simplest version of the truth. "Very bad things."

He sat up straight, his palms running down his thighs as he visibly tried to control his anger. She was glad he was angry on their behalf. Maybe he and Hunter would be able to control this threat before it could hurt them.

"Able will be in danger as well," she added.

"We'll find the person responsible for this letter." Hunter stabbed at the letter lying on her desk with his index finger as he spoke.

Glory nodded. "It's not that I can't pay the five thousand dollars. It's that I'm concerned that this person will turn over the information to their employer anyway. I can't emphasize enough how important it is that Able and I stay hidden."

"Do you think the person you're running from would involve the authorities? Marshals? Congressmen?" Hunter asked. He was asking if they'd done something illegal.

"No, nothing like that. This is a personal issue," she said.

"Could it be Harvey?" Zane asked.

"How do you know about William Harvey?" she asked, surprised he knew when she'd only just realized that Harvey could be a potential, immediate threat.

His well-shaped lips tipped up into a semblance of what passed as a smile for Zane, giving her a flash of white teeth. "I saw you talking to him downstairs. He didn't seem pleased when he left."

"You saw him leave then?" she asked.

He nodded. "I followed him out."

"Well, then it wasn't him who left the note," she concluded. "I was with him from the time he arrived until I left him, and then you followed him out. He wouldn't have had time to come up and leave this."

"Wait." Hunter held up his arms and all attention turned to him. "The letter was left in your study?"

She nodded. "Right here on my desk."

"Does anyone have a key to your study?" he asked.

"No. The only key is here in my pocket where it's been all day." She felt its solid weight through the silk of her gown.

Zane moved so fast that she sat back in surprise as he drew a small revolver he kept in his boot.

She gasped but managed to keep her voice low as she said, "You know there are no guns allowed in this house, Mr. Pierce." Every man who entered was required to hand over his guns at the door to be returned upon his departure.

"Tell that to whoever broke into your study and could be in your apartment now. Go downstairs." He walked to the door that led to her suite of rooms, where he pressed an ear against the solid wood as if listening for movement within.

"I don't want to go downstairs. People are bound to get suspicious and I don't want anyone to know what's going on," she argued, staying where she was. "Besides, the keys to my study and my personal rooms are different."

He grimaced at her, clearly disapproving of her choice. Looking from her to Able, he said, "Stay here with her and keep vigilant." He tested the door latch and once he found it locked he motioned for her to hand over the key.

Glory sighed, but she handed it over.

"It's possible someone doesn't have a key so they picked the lock," Hunter explained. "Better to use caution and check it out now." He grabbed a gun from his boot and took up sentry at the door to her darkened apartment ready to rush to help should Zane need him.

Realizing they were right, but still not liking the additional invasion of her privacy, Glory turned her attention back to Able who was staring down at the letter. "What do you make of this?"

"It's blackmail." Able spat the word out as if it left a bad taste in his mouth and walked to the window again. The glow of the streetlights backlit him, making his medium-brown skin appear darker. He ran a hand over his head, his palm skimming right over his short hair. "I can't abide that cowardice."

"Do you think it's real? Do you think it's possible someone really knows who we are?" There was no doubt in her mind that if someone knew who she was that they'd know who Able was as well. She and Able had escaped together.

He looked back at her and even in the dim lighting she caught the flash of worry that crossed his eyes.

Solid, confident, levelheaded Able was concerned. The fear she'd felt earlier came back, only this time it wasn't creeping and cold. It came over her in a wave of panic that was cold and then hot, nearly sending her to her feet in a rush to do something. Anything.

"We need to find out where this letter came from," said Able. He paced over to lean a hip on the edge of her desk, clearly too agitated to stay still for long. "I'll start questioning the staff. There's an account number here where you're to deposit the money. We can have it traced."

Yes, there were things they could do. She wasn't defenseless anymore. She shoved the panic down again and held on to that one fact. "Right. That's the first place to start."

Able nodded. "I'll go out in the morning—"

"No," Glory interjected. "We can question the staff discreetly, but we can't let anyone know about the note. And we especially can't let anyone connect us to whoever owns this account." She pointed at the numbers written on the piece of paper. Turning her attention to the man guarding the door to her apartment, she said, "Hunter, this is the main reason I came to you for help. Your family owns shares in the bank." Hunter's father was one of the wealthiest men in town. The Jamesons had been major shareholders in the bank since its founding. "Surely you can make some confidential inquiries and figure out whose name is attached to this account without tying that inquiry back to us? I think if we could make some headway on that front, we can wrap this up quickly."

"I can make some inquiries in the morning," said Hunter.

She nodded, already feeling a little better now that they were making plans to deal with this. As if sensing her disquiet, Able put his hand on her shoulder.

"He won't be able to touch you here, Glory. You know that?" Able asked.

There was no need for Able to elaborate on who *he* was. *He* had been the dark phantom hovering over them ever since they'd escaped; the monster they both feared in the dark of night. She nodded and Able squeezed her shoulder. Here they were again after all these years. Trying to reassure each other that Justin wouldn't get them. To be honest, she wasn't quite sure she believed it fully. There were still times she woke up in the middle of the night expecting him to be there. If he found his way to them, she was certain that he would kill them.

Instead of putting voice to her fears, she squeezed Able's hand and took his offer of comfort for what it was. He'd become the family she'd had to give up. An older brother who would always be there to look out for her. Only now that was threatened and she needed to do something about it.

Chapter Four

Zane moved silently into the sitting area of Glory's suite of rooms. The only light came in through the window facing the street, casting the small space in shadow and shades of gray. Alert to any movement, he switched on the wall sconce. Yellow light filtered over the landscape paintings on the wall and the overstuffed, comfortable-looking furniture that made up the bulk of the room's decor. It was much cozier than he'd been expecting. All the furniture downstairs was elegant and chosen for fashion more than comfort. He'd been expecting more of the same in the madam's private rooms.

It wasn't a very large space, but it was relaxed and homey. A full bookcase sat on one wall and the other held what he assumed was a phonograph, though he'd never seen one in person. The large brass cone sat silently. Everything appeared well-kept and undisturbed.

On quiet feet, he glanced inside the tiled bathing chamber to find it empty before making his way to her bedchamber. A strange feeling came over him as he opened the door and switched on the light. A sense that he was intruding on her private sanctuary, the place she came to get away from the world, washed over him. It was a place he very much wanted to know. Her bed sat neatly made with a faded blue-and-yellow quilt. Given the understated elegance of the rest of the space, he'd expected something slightly more grand. Maybe something made of silk or satin. But it was an ordinary quilt. Her grandmother's quilt, he realized.

How many people knew about that quilt? The rumor was that she never entertained men privately. While that seemed to be true, rumors could be wrong. At the very least, it was highly likely that her staff had been to her private rooms. The list of people who knew that detail was endless.

He tried to imagine her sitting on the bed, reading the book that sat closed on the nightstand. Her bare feet peeking out beneath the hem of her gown with her hair down around her. He couldn't do it. He knew so little of the woman he couldn't imagine her as anything other than the self-possessed Glory Winters. Calm, elegant and always proper. Did she ever lounge in her bed without a corset? He grinned at the thought.

Stepping farther into the room, the soft scent of roses washed over him. Nervous energy moved through him at the same time his skin tightened, muscles deep in his gut clenched in pleasurable anticipation. The scent of roses had always filled him with wary trepidation, reminding him of the words of warning he'd been given as a child. Roses were a sign of death. Yet, ever since he'd met Glory, he'd associated the scent with her, leaving his body a mess of confusion.

A dressing table sat across from the bed with cosmetics and perfumes scattered across the surface as if she'd dressed in a hurry that morning. He felt like an interloper as he examined it. He should be checking the armoire and under her bed, but he couldn't make himself walk away just yet. He gently ran his fingertips over a handkerchief she'd left blotted with rouge from her mouth. The shape of her lips stared back at him.

A clouded glass bottle sat backed up to the mirror, and he picked it up. Bringing it to his nose, he closed his eyes as he inhaled the familiar scent of her perfume. It always lingered behind her, lying faintly in the air when she passed, sweetly calling him to his doom. The usual warning sounded in his head, warring with the desire that had flared to life within him. No matter how he reminded himself of the premonition, he couldn't stop himself from wanting to inhale that scent directly from her skin.

He shook his head at the thought. In all the years that had passed since he'd left his mother's people, he'd never quite been able to shake the words from his memory. His aunt had told him before she'd sent him away to his father that roses were bad for him because she'd seen it in a dream. That warning had stayed with him for years. He'd never even seen a rose before she'd told him that. She'd drawn a tightly budded flower in the dirt to show him, but he hadn't been able to tell much from it. He'd grown up avoiding every flower he came into contact with. Now that he was older, he couldn't decide if what she'd told him was real or something she'd imagined, but he still couldn't shake the premonition that came over him.

He put the bottle back and forced himself to walk to the armoire and look inside. Empty but for stacks of brightly colored silks and satins. It was the same beneath her bed. A couple of wooden boxes were stored there, and he realized that he'd give his eyeteeth to know what was inside—evidence of who Glory really was. But he wouldn't intrude on her privacy any further than he already had.

Turning the light off behind him, he moved back into the parlor. From his vantage point he noticed a wooden frame on top of a spindly table. The frame held a single rose pressed between two small panes of glass. He walked over and picked the frame up out of its little stand to examine it closer. The rose was dried, its petals various shades of faded pink.

A warning? It didn't matter. He wouldn't leave Glory to fight this battle on her own. The rose was a reminder that he could help her, but he needed to keep his distance. Setting the frame back down in its stand, he walked back to her study.

"It's empty. Doesn't look like anyone's been in there."

Glory gave a firm nod as if that was exactly what she'd expected him to find. He had to admit that he'd been a little brash, but the idea of someone hiding in her rooms ready to harm her had sent him barreling forward.

"We were talking about next steps," Hunter offered. "I'll check into the bank account tomorrow."

"And I can question the staff about who might have had access to this room," Able added.

"I can help with that," Zane said. It was no secret that most people were afraid of him. His height combined with the scar and his longer hair effectively kept most people at a distance. Over the years they'd been riding together as the Reyes Brothers, it had quickly become apparent that Zane was the most effective of the group when it came to interrogation. He always got the information he needed. His record was flawless, not counting the night they'd met Emmaline, but then she'd eventually married Hunter, so he didn't count her.

"No need, Pierce. I can handle it." Able gave him a firm look.

"Don't trouble yourself, Able. I'm happy to help." Zane smirked just to rile up Able's irrational distaste of him. There'd never been one incident that Zane could trace back to the origin of that dislike. It just was, like Zane's fascination with Glory.

"I can handle it." Able crossed his arms over his chest.

"I have more experience in these things than you," Zane countered.

"Gentlemen." Glory's voice cracked through the room. "There's enough staff for you both. The last thing we need right now is you two at each other's throats."

Able stepped back and dropped his arms, conceding her point. Zane gave a slight nod of acknowledgment. She was right. There was no need to make the task before them more difficult.

She sighed, calming herself. "I only ask that you

make your inquiries discreet. I don't want to give fuel to any rumors that may start." That seemed a simple enough request, but then she narrowed her eyes at him. "That means no dragging anyone into the cellar. No tying anyone up. No assaulting anyone."

Zane bit back a grin. She was referring to the man Derringer had paid to find Castillo. They'd caught him lurking around last week and brought him to Victoria House's cellar for questioning. "As you wish, but I can't be responsible for a lack of results with my methods inhibited." He was teasing her. Those methods he usually reserved for criminals or people actively trying to kill him.

She stared at him as if trying to determine if he was joking. He wasn't about to clue her in to whether he was or not, so he continued since he had her attention. "Until we know who sent this letter, I think it's best if you're never alone. We don't know who this person is, or if it's the very same person you both ran away from…" Zane paused because he knew what he said next would rile her. "I'll stay with you until we get this settled."

"Stay with me?" Her mouth dropped open slightly.

"Until we figure out who this is and if he or she is dangerous." He nodded.

She tensed to refuse, but Able interrupted her. "Pierce is right."

Zane stared at him, surprised that he'd so easily gotten the man's endorsement.

"Absolutely not!" Glory gaped at her friend as if he'd just sided with the devil himself.

"Someone got into your office," explained Able.

"What's to say that they can't get into your room to-night?"

She blinked as if she hadn't even considered the possibility and closed her mouth.

"But it won't be Pierce," Able added. "I'll stay."

"No, Able." Glory stood up and closed the distance between them. "What about Clara? She's due to go into labor soon, and she's on bedrest. She needs you around at night."

"Labor isn't likely for a few more weeks, according to the midwife." Able shrugged. "I can ask one of the women to sleep over while I'm gone."

Glory shook her head. "Whoever knows who I am, knows who you are too. What if they try to find you in *your* rooms, only to find Clara alone?"

Able frowned, the grooves on his forehead deepening. He ran a hand over his head, a tell that he was agitated.

Finally, after a tension-filled moment, Glory sighed. "It's too much trouble for something that's likely to amount to nothing more than you and Mr. Pierce being overprotective, but, in the interest of safety, we have no choice." She looked over at Zane, giving him the distinct impression that he was her second choice for the task. "Thank you, Mr. Pierce, for your offer. It pains me to admit it, but I'd feel better having someone around. Just in case."

Zane inclined his head and she gave him an impersonal smile as she retook her seat and focused her attention on Hunter. Hunter was smiling as if he'd enjoyed the little drama playing out before him. Zane sat down as they continued to discuss possible ways the account could be traced and took a moment to regather his composure. He was trying, but no matter how hard he thought of the possible danger ahead he couldn't stop dwelling on the fact that he'd be spending an awful lot of time with her in the coming days. Time that he could use to figure out the enigma that was Glory Winters, and to try to get to the bottom of their connection.

Able moved around Glory's desk, catching Zane's eye. He jerked his head toward the window, indicating that Zane should come over so they could talk. Curious, Zane rose and tried to seem casual so he wouldn't draw Glory's attention since Able seemed to want to keep this encounter private. Crossing his arms over his chest, Zane stared at the dark windows of the general store down the street. All the buildings in this area of town were humble and modest, except for Victoria House.

"I know what you're doing," Able said, he stood so close that Zane could smell peppermint on his breath.

"And what is that?" Zane asked without looking at him.

"I've seen the way you look at her."

Zane couldn't stop himself from glancing at the older man to see if that was jealousy in his voice. He'd always assumed that the relationship between Glory and Able was more of a familial connection. No, not jealousy. Concern and protectiveness were shining in Able's eyes. "And?" He couldn't help but prod.

"And she's not here for your amusement. Don't think you're the first one to come in here and leave a besotted fool. I've been told about the betting book at the *gentleman's* club across town." Able sneered as he said the term *gentleman* as if the word couldn't be further from the truth. Zane had to concede the man was right. He'd been in Helena a handful of times and never come across an actual gentleman, despite the fancy clothes some of the men wore.

The book Able referred to was notorious for having outrageous bets. They ranged in scope from the size of a heifer's first calf to the price of gold at some specified date in the future to the color of a particular lady's undergarments. Zane had heard of the particular bet Able referred to. A few fine upstanding men of Helena had wagered on which one of them would be the first to bed Glory. He didn't doubt it was real. Anger burned in his belly as he thought of them betting on her. "Let me ask you something, Able… You ever seen that book yourself?"

Able gave him a stony look. Zane held his hand up against the window. Dim light streamed in from the street, backlighting his hand so that his skin appeared very dark, though not as dark as Able's. Neither of them would be welcomed in that particular club. "I don't have a bet in that book."

"You don't have to have a bet in that book to see her as a challenge," Able countered.

"I've known her for years and I've never once been disrespectful to her. Why would I start now?"

"Like I said, I see how you look at her and I can guess your thoughts. Keep your hands to yourself and we won't have any problems." With those words, Able walked away to rejoin Hunter and Glory's conversation.

Zane stayed at the window, trying to get his racing heart under control. He wanted to tell Able that it wasn't like that, but it would be a lie. He wanted to bed her just as badly as any of those other men. As he stood there, seething from Able's rebuke, he was having a hard time figuring out what exactly separated him from those other men. He couldn't have anything with her aside from a quick tumble in bed.

He was an outlaw. While the gang would likely disperse because they'd found the enemy who'd brought them all together to start with and Castillo and Hunter were both recently married, it didn't change the fact that Zane was still a wanted man. While it was unlikely he'd be tracked down all the way to Helena, it was always possible. He had nothing to offer her.

Aside from that, loving Christine had taught him a harsh lesson that he would never forget. There wasn't enough love in the world to keep a person from betraying another. Eventually love ran out, or something more important came along. He didn't want any sort of relationship that involved anything more than physical pleasure. Once had been enough. It wasn't worth the eventual pain.

So no, he couldn't offer her more than any of those men planned to offer her. But he *could* respect her. None of those gentlemen would give her that. It wasn't much, but it was enough of a distinction that he felt a little better. He would keep his hands to himself, but only if she wanted him to. It would always be her choice, and if she chose to spend a night or two with him, then Able would have to accept that.

Chapter Five

Glory didn't know how it had happened, but she'd somehow reverted to the role of thirteen-year-old schoolgirl. Zane stood across the room, leaning against the window molding as he watched her. Hunter and Able had just left, so they were very much alone. Butterflies fluttered in her belly, and her hand went to her stomach to calm the wild beatings of their wings. He wasn't moving, wasn't talking, wasn't doing anything but looking at her, and she couldn't seem to keep hold of the thoughts wandering around her head.

Gripping the solid edges of her desk, she tried to keep her hold on reality. This was still her home and she was still in charge. "Thank you for staying," she said, doing her best not to look directly at him. Her hands as flighty as her thoughts, she shuffled some papers around on her desk until they were all precisely lined up.

Zane took his time walking back over to the chair across from her. The man moved as if he wasn't well over two hundred pounds. He was all sinew and strength, but without the lumbering that sometimes came with that muscle. "Can I see the letter for my-self?" he asked when he'd taken a seat in the wingback chair across from her.

She nodded and handed it over without touching him. If he thought her behavior odd, he didn't mention it as his gaze skimmed over the letter. She couldn't help but watch him as he did so. He wasn't classically hand-some like Hunter, but his ruggedness and quiet inten-sity, combined with his even features, somehow made him even more attractive. At least to her. She'd never cared for the look of a polished gentleman. She'd had that before and knew the treachery often hidden in the perfect package.

Zane was real. Her gaze touched the high arch of his cheekbones, the tiny lines around his eyes, and the strong line of his jaw. For the first time she wondered how old he was. He didn't have the deeper lines that came with age, but his eyes seemed intelligent in a way that made her think he'd seen a lot in his life. She re-spected that. Most of the men who came into Victoria House had struck it rich because they'd gotten lucky with a claim to a mine. They thought luck and money somehow translated to being clever and knowledgeable.

Zane was different. Something told her that he'd lived more than almost all of them. He glanced up from the letter, and she wasn't able to look away before he caught her watching him. She offered him a slight smile in the hopes that he thought her interest was only ca-sual. But when he spoke, she couldn't stop herself from watching his full lips shape each word. "You're sure that no one here knows who you are?"

She shook her head. "I've never told anyone. Only Able knows."

"What about Clara? Would he have told her?"

She realized now why he'd waited for Able to leave to begin this line of questioning. "No, Able knows how important it is to keep our secret. He wouldn't tell her."

Zane raised a brow, looking doubtful. "She's his wife. Don't you think she'd want to know about his past?"

It wasn't an illogical question, but Zane didn't know why they'd run or what was at stake. If he did, he'd understand that *no one* could know. Able stood to lose just as much as she did. "I trust Able. Besides, he doesn't want our secrets to get out any more than I do. The consequences are...too much."

His jaw clenched and she wasn't certain if it was because he was angry at her or the situation. She didn't know him well enough to say, a detail that was as fortunate as it was regrettable. Some long-buried part of her wanted to know him. To *really* know who he was as a person, as someone she could trust...as a man. That last thought made her belly flutter again, forcing her to look away. He was so astute, she had no doubt he would know what she was feeling.

"You don't think Able would—"

"No!" Despite herself, she met his gaze fully, determined to extinguish any suspicion against Able. "He wouldn't betray me."

"I wouldn't think so, but we have to consider all options."

She shook her head more firmly. "He wouldn't do this. He'd have no motive anyway."

"Five thousand dollars is a lot of motive."

She scoffed. "Trust me, Able doesn't need the money."

"No? He's married now and has a baby on the way. He might not have needed the money but things change." He paused, adding in a softer voice, "Love has a way of changing people."

He looked so resolute when he said that, that she wondered from what sort of experience he was speaking. He had a quiet, almost dangerous appeal that would attract many women, but she couldn't imagine the hard man across from her being tender enough to have ever experienced an emotion as sentimental as love. She'd seen his loyalty to Hunter and Castillo and conceded that *it* was a type of love. A brotherhood. But it wasn't romantic love and she couldn't see him ever allowing himself to experience that.

"I suppose it can, but in this instance it hasn't."

"How do you know?" he asked.

"Because Able has all the money he could want," she explained.

Zane sat back as he mulled over her words. "He does have fine clothes. Satin waistcoats. Wool suits. I always thought it was part of the uniform required to work here. I didn't realize that he was so well compensated."

"It is a requirement of the position, but you've got it all wrong. He doesn't simply work here. He's part owner of Victoria House." Correctly reading the shocked expression on his face, she said, "You're surprised."

"A little."

"It's understandable. Everyone assumes I'm the sole owner and we let them think that because it's easier. When we first arrived here... Well, let's just say that I wouldn't be here if it wasn't for Able." That was an understatement. She'd be dead by now if not for Able. It was because of him that she'd left South Carolina and ended up in Helena, though the Helena part had been serendipity. "Able and I worked hard together to make Victoria House what it is today. When the madam retired she left it to us both."

While Glory kept up the running of the business side of things, Able took care of the house itself. He knew everyone in it and where they were at any given time. He made sure there was never any trouble with the patrons. The letter must be a particular sore spot for him since it had appeared on his watch.

Zane studied her for a minute. There was no doubt that he was merely trying to read her expression, but she couldn't help but wonder what he thought when he looked at her. She stilled for his visual perusal but felt her cheeks go warm. Finally he took pity on her and glanced back down at the letter. She had to stop herself from letting out an audible breath of relief.

"The sender mentioned knowing your real name." Zane paused, but she didn't say a word. If he wanted to ask her about her real name, she wouldn't make it easy for him. Not that she'd tell him. The corner of his mouth ticked up as if he realized what she was doing. "Does Able also have a real name?" he asked, apparently deciding not to rise to her challenge.

She nearly laughed to herself, starting to enjoy this

play between the two of them. "He does. We never really intended to stay in Helena. The stagecoach we were traveling on had a broken axle. We managed to make it as far as the station, but there'd been another silver strike, so the driver ran off to make his fortune. Apparently so had every other man in town, because the madam came down to the station asking for any able-bodied men to help repair her leaky roof."

She did smile then, remembering how afraid she'd been that they had nowhere to go and their funds had been dwindling. They'd come a long way since then. "Able stood up and declared himself, well, *able*. So Able he became. She took us in after that. Thank God she did. We had nowhere else to go."

"And you became Glory?" He gestured toward her hair.

She inclined her head. The madam had taken one look at her dark red hair and called it her crowning glory. Many of the patrons had started referring to it that way as well, so the name Glory had stuck.

"And no one else knows your real name except Able?" he concluded.

"Able didn't leave this letter."

Zane gave a hesitant nod, as if not quite willing to give up that line of questioning, but realizing it wouldn't get him anywhere at the moment. She nearly smiled again. Let him stew. The one thing she knew with certainty in this whole mess was that Able wasn't responsible for the letter. Extortion wasn't in his character.

"Do you think it could be someone else from Victoria House?" he asked.

"I hate to think so. We're like a family here. My ladies are loyal."

"And you're certain none of them know who you are?"

"None of them know," she said quietly. "Only Able."

"Well, I suppose that's it then. We'll see what we can find out from the staff tomorrow." He clapped his hands to his knees and made to stand.

"What happens now?" she asked. If they were done with questions, she needed to go back downstairs to finish work for the night. The singer she'd hired for the evening should be almost ready to go on. "I have work to do, but you're welcome to go collect your things and move them to my suite."

He gave a shake of his head and a slow smile lifted the corners of his mouth. "I go where you go."

"What?" Her eyes widened. She knew what she *thought* he meant, but surely he didn't actually *mean* that.

"I don't trust whoever left this not to try to get to you. Able or I need to be with you at all times."

His words nearly knocked the wind out of her. "At all times? Even in my own house?"

His smile widened as if he was enjoying this. "Get used to me, Glory. I'm going to be around. A lot."

Sweet Lord above, she was in trouble.

The main lounge was the largest room in the house. It had been intended as a ballroom with a large chandelier gracing the ceiling in the center of the sizable space, flanked by two smaller ones on either side. They were the only original feature of the house left behind when the owner had sold it to the previous madam. The slivers of faceted glass, not crystal, flickered in the light of hundreds of candles, making it look like crystal. When the town had changed over to electricity several years earlier, Glory had opted not to change the chandelier. She loved the antique feel. Sometimes she closed her eyes and imagined she was in a grand London ballroom and a handsome gentleman would sweep her up into a waltz. But then she'd open her eyes to realize she was in Helena, where the gentlemen were in short supply. They might say all the right words, but they were all only interested in things that sparkled—gold, silver and copper—and she couldn't afford to forget that. Maybe that's how all men became once they reached a certain level of wealth. She couldn't honestly say for sure. She'd lived in her cocoon at Victoria House since she was sixteen.

The one thing she did know for sure was that even if a proper gentleman from London were to walk in, he'd have little interest in a brothel madam. Well, little interest beyond the physical. Not that it mattered to her. She'd had her chance at marriage and it hadn't worked out. Now she knew that it wasn't something that interested her. She liked her independence too much to ever give it up. It meant a lot of lonely nights, but the payoff was worth it.

The song ended, bringing Glory back to the present as the room broke out into polite applause. She smiled as she took to the dais to thank Sally and address the crowd. "I'd like to extend my thanks once again to Mrs.

Sally Roarke for gracing our little corner of the world with her beautiful voice."

The older lady inclined her head, and the men applauded again coupled with a few suggestive whistles. Sally was a favorite at Victoria House and made the trip about twice a year from St. Louis where she lived. None of the men seemed to realize she was the same Mary Walker who had worked here years before Glory had taken over.

When Sally had given a curtsy and waved her way out, Glory addressed the room again. "That's all the entertainment for the night, gentlemen. The house will be closing soon, so please make your final drink selections."

There were ten women working upstairs tonight. Most of them seemed to have already found patrons for the evening, but a couple were talking to men in the lounge. When Glory had taken over she'd brought in plush sofas and divans worthy of her previous life on a plantation. She'd also scattered tables throughout to encourage conversation, which encouraged drink sales.

"What if my final selection includes you?" A disembodied male voice called from a table of men in the far corner.

Glory didn't pay him any attention as she left the small stage. It wasn't unusual for the random man here or there to try to buy her time, though it was common knowledge that she wasn't for sale. Instead of replying, she focused on speaking to the few regulars in the audience. It was her ritual. She'd thank them for coming out, make conversation and move on to the next table, working the room before she retired for the evening.

She had never been as aware of another person as she was aware of Zane lurking in the background as she worked. He hadn't imposed or even really made his presence known. He'd taken a seat out of the way to blend in with the other customers, and he'd been a fixture in the house all week so no one even noticed him, but she could *feel* him. His gaze was like the lightest of weights pressing into her skin, massaging over her and leaving her warm and tingly in ways that were equally as disturbing as they were pleasurable. She didn't know what to do with the sensation, so she settled on ignoring it in the hopes that it would go away.

It never really did though, and as she made her way upstairs to retire for the night, she knew without looking that he'd followed her out the door. His large presence followed her up the stairs and down the hallway. She felt him pause behind her as she unlocked her door. Her eyes drifted shut as she took in his scent, a mix of leather and man. She couldn't describe it other than that. He smelled rugged and dangerous and it was all appealing in a very confusing way.

Pushing her door open, she stepped inside and held it for him. She managed to give him a small smile that she hoped was welcoming. It was so odd to have a man in her private suite. Able was the only man in recent memory she could remember ever being inside.

"Do you really think this is necessary?" she asked when she'd closed the door behind him and locked it. He was already across the room, checking the bathing chamber and her bedroom for the anonymous letter writer.

"Yes," was all he said.

Finished prowling for strangers lurking in the shadows of her bedroom, he walked back over to her. His brow was furrowed and his shoulders seemed stiff. "Do men always talk to you that way?" he asked.

"What do you mean?"

"That ass who wanted to…" His jaw clenched as if he couldn't bring himself to say the words.

"You mean the man who wanted to take me upstairs." Some small part of her warmed at the thought of him being upset about the question. It was an unreasonable way to feel. She and Zane meant nothing to each other, so he had no reason to feel upset about it. But still, it was nice to have his concern. "It's part of the job." She shrugged.

The muscle in his jaw worked as he looked away. It was clear that he didn't like that part of the job.

Deciding it was best to change the subject, she followed his gaze to the sofa. "I'm sorry that I'm not really set up for guests." She gestured to the small parlor that was equipped with a sofa and a couple of chairs. A dining table and a small kitchen area with an icebox took up the far corner of the space. "If you're hungry, I can offer you bread and jam." She shrugged in apology at her meager offerings. She usually took her meals down in the kitchen.

"I've already eaten supper." He voice was strong and calm. The fact that he seemed a little less lost than her in this arrangement somehow set her at ease. "You seem anxious," he said, raising a brow at her.

She nodded. Having a giant of a man, especially

one that she was so attracted to, standing in her private space would do that. "It's strange for me to have someone else here."

"Go about your evening as if I'm not here. You don't have to wait on me."

Easier said than done. Often she ended her nights with a long hot soak in the tub, but she didn't see that in her future tonight. It felt strange to be naked with him in the next room. She couldn't even think of doing that without blushing.

Instead of commenting on that, she said, "I'm sorry I don't have a cot for you. You can take the sofa. Tomorrow I can have a bed moved in."

He was shaking his head before she'd finished. "No, we don't want to rouse suspicion. Hopefully it'll be just a night or two and we can get the matter settled without anyone realizing I'm here."

Gossip traveled like wildfire through the house, so Glory very much doubted they'd be able to accomplish this arrangement without someone finding out, but she kept that opinion to herself. They'd deal with whatever problems arose when they had to. "Right. I'll get you some blankets."

She escaped to the safety of her room and opened the chest at the end of the bed. Pulling out the extra quilt that she used in winter to double up her blankets, she grabbed the second pillow from her bed and headed back to the main room. She had to force herself to let go of the breath she'd been holding when she saw Zane taking off his coat. His button-down shirt was stretched tight across his broad shoulders, and the muscles in his arms flexed as he moved, straining against the fabric.

This man was all physical power. She usually found that unappealing, preferring the efficient slimness required to properly wear a suit on the male form, but with Zane… She sucked in a deep breath and forced herself not to think about the tingling warmth spreading across her skin. It was best to keep her mind solely on the problem at hand. In this case his powerful form was the problem, because she had no idea how he was going to fit on her sofa. It wasn't dainty by any means, and she'd fallen asleep on it often enough reading to know that it was comfortable, but he was just so *big*.

"Sorry again." She dropped the quilt and pillow onto the sofa, casting a long look at the piece of furniture. "I'm not certain you'll fit."

To her surprise he gave her a smile—a real smile that lit up his whole face—as he draped his coat over the rolled arm of the sofa and sat down. His arms were spread across the back, taking up nearly the entire length of the piece of furniture. "I'll make it work, pretty lady."

His smile, coupled with the intensity of his gaze on her face, made her wonder if he was making a double entendre. She should've been outraged or at least affronted, but she found herself having to bite the inside of her cheek to keep from smiling. He'd always teased her, not put off by her confidence or the fact that she was in charge, and, most important, he never made her feel like he was insulting her or disrespecting her. Perhaps that was why she liked his teasing comments and the few times he'd used that nickname for her. They made her feel earthy and real, not the porcelain queen this place sometimes made her out to be because of the role she played.

Before she could respond, a slim leather-bound book slipped out of his coat pocket to land with a thud on her rug. She recognized it as his sketchbook, as it landed on its spine and fell open. The page was upside down, but it looked to be a drawing of a woman with a very revealing slit in her dress that exposed nearly her entire leg.

She'd seen him a few times at the bar writing or drawing in it—she'd never been able to get close enough to take a look—but then last week she'd searched his room. She'd been looking for an answer to why he was hiding out at Victoria House, in case the reason put her staff in danger, but instead she'd found that book. Flipping through it, she'd expected to find secret plans about God only knew what, but instead she'd found his drawings. Most of them were of places she assumed he'd been: buildings, farmhouses, desert and mountain landscapes; but some of them had been of women. Very *nude* women.

An unreasonable surge of jealousy crept over her as she stared at the woman in the drawing. She wasn't jealous because he'd obviously been with those women. She was jealous because she could never *be* one of them. It wasn't even a question of emotional attachment or her running a brothel and him being an outlaw.

It was because she was broken. Irrevocably. Her skin prickled hot and then cold at the unwanted reminder of why she could never be with him the way a normal woman could.

They seemed to come to their senses at the same time and both bent down to retrieve the book. She touched it first, but his larger hand covered hers. Surprised, she looked up and his face was only inches away. She'd never been this close to him. She could count his short black eyelashes and smell the pleasingly faint hint of whiskey on his breath. They were so close she could *feel* how solid he was just from their proximity.

"Sorry," she managed to whisper, drawing her arm back and rising. She meant to make a joke about the drawing, to say something about obscenities not being allowed in her suite, but she couldn't say anything. When she opened her mouth, absolutely nothing came out except another breath she'd been holding. Deciding to retreat while her dignity was still intact, she inclined her head. "Good night, Mr. Pierce."

Whirling away, she left him for the comfort and familiarity of her bedchamber. After she locked her door, she pressed her back against the cool wood. How was she ever going to get through the next few days with Zane being so close? Hopefully Hunter would find the person responsible for the letter very soon.

Chapter Six

Zane watched Hunter make his way down the boardwalk across the road. He waited until he'd reached the cobblestones that fronted Victoria House before he crossed to dodge the mud. Like many of the roads in town that weren't main thoroughfares, it hadn't been paved and was frequently at risk of becoming impassable due to rain. At some point Glory and Able had addressed the issue and had added cobblestones on the area of the street directly fronting their establishment so that mud wouldn't have much effect on business. Despite the recent rain and the fact that it was hardly past midday when the house opened for luncheon, men were making their way inside. He'd never realized how busy the place was or what exactly that success meant for Glory. She could be a target of far worse than the person who'd left that letter on her desk.

He thought of Harvey and the men who'd tried to forcibly take her business from her a couple of years ago, the first time he'd met her. She'd sent Hunter word that she needed help. Fortunately, all it had taken to make the businessmen realize she wasn't as vulnerable as they'd hoped was their gang showing up to a meeting alongside Glory with their guns on their hips. The men had gotten the point and left town. Something in his gut told him it wouldn't be so easy this time. This time it wasn't her business that was at stake. It was Glory herself, because some monster from her past seemed to want her. He'd tried his damnedest to pull information from her staff that morning, but no one seemed to know anything about her life before Victoria House. The staff turned over every few years as women moved on to other lives. He hadn't found one who was here when she'd arrived.

"What have you found out?" Zane pushed away from the wall when Hunter stepped up onto the boardwalk. They'd moved Cas to Hunter's town house at daybreak, and Hunter had spent the rest of the morning at the bank.

Glancing around to see if anyone was nearby to overhear, Hunter led him around the corner. "Nothing yet." Hunter grimaced, clearly exasperated. "The account was just opened last week and belongs to some company based in St. Louis. I've done some checking but haven't been able to find a person attached to the company yet. The address for the company is a post office letter box. I telegrammed for more information, but it could be a few days before we know."

"A few days?" The skin on the back of Zane's neck tightened. "We may not have a few days. It could take even longer to find this person once we have a name."

Hunter nodded in agreement. "I know. It's not great news, but it's all we've got right now."

Zane ran a hand across his brow, feeling a headache start to pound behind his temples. "You put any stock in what that letter said? You think the person really knows who she is? Where she came from?"

The grim look on Hunter's face confirmed his feelings. "I've been thinking about that and it seems credible. Why go through the trouble otherwise? Anyone here knows that Glory has her own men for protection." Aside from Able, the house employed two gunmen to keep the peace. They were always visible at the front doors and occasionally making the rounds of the parlors and lounges. "After what happened a couple of years ago, they know that she can call us in for help. It's not worth the risk."

"I've spent the morning talking to her staff." Zane sighed. "They all speak highly of her. Most of them had nowhere to go when she took them in. Others sought out Victoria House because they knew they'd be treated better here than any other brothel in the territory."

"You're thinking it's not someone on her staff?" Hunter asked.

"Doesn't seem to be. There *was* a singer who performed last night. When Glory introduced her she said that she was from St. Louis. I'll look into her, but if it's not her then…" Zane let out a frustrated breath and kicked at the dirt with his boot. "Then I don't know."

The lines between Hunter's eyes deepened. "You're worried, aren't you?"

"Aren't you?"

Hunter shrugged. "Glory has the money to pay this person. I hope we find who it is, but if not she'll be fine."

Zane shook his head in disbelief at Hunter's cavalier attitude. "She can pay, but what's to say this person doesn't report back to his boss that he found her?"

"I think that's unlikely." Hunter's gaze narrowed, his eyes becoming slits as he studied Zane. "What has you so upset?"

Maybe the fact that he was suddenly sharing tight quarters with the woman who'd kept him tied in knots. Or maybe it was because he'd barely slept last night because the pillow she'd given him had been covered in her scent. He'd recognized it as one from her bed, which meant she'd laid her head on it the previous night…or maybe even hugged it against her body as she'd slept. The thought of all the places on her body that pillow could've touched had kept him awake far into the morning. As a result he was tired and irritable today.

"I don't want anything to happen to her on my watch." His words came out forced and flat, a sure sign that they were only the partial truth. He didn't want anything to happen to her on his watch, but that's not what had kept him tossing and turning all night. That had been compliments of a near constant erection. It wasn't a surprise that Hunter picked up on the partial truth. They'd spent enough time together in their hunt for Derringer that they could read each other well.

"You realize Glory never entertains men, right?"

Zane gritted his teeth. "That's what I've heard. What are you saying?" In addition to learning that no one knew where she'd come from, Zane had learned precious little about the woman who fascinated him so much. But the fact that she never entertained clients was one of them. He'd been unsure if she occasionally might or had retired from that some time ago. No. He'd learned that she never slept with men, and she never seemed to take a fancy to any man. None ever appeared to call on her. He wasn't sure what to do with that information or why it mattered so much to him. Instead of analyzing it, he tucked it away to bring out later on.

"Nothing. Just making sure you know," Hunter said.

"I'm not interested in having her entertain me," Zane shot back, stepping away to walk back to the front of Victoria House.

"Hmmm. *Interesting.*" Hunter said the word as if Zane had just given him a fresh nugget of information.

Zane shook his head. This was a conversation he wasn't ready to have. The truth was he didn't know what he wanted from Glory. He couldn't offer her a future because he didn't want that. It appeared that she didn't indulge in casual affairs, so he didn't know where to go from here. Right now all he wanted was to tuck her against him to shelter her from the world, but he knew that she'd bristle. She wanted his help in tracking down the person out to extort her, and she might even take his protection in the form of a hired gun, but nothing more. She valued her independence and knew how to take care of herself. In fact, she was one of the strongest people he'd ever known. He'd watched her put grown men in their place with only the flash of her eyes. God help the poor fool who dared to go up against her, she'd verbally flay them alive or have Able toss them on their ass in the street. No, Glory didn't need him, at least not in that way. Maybe that's why she was so interesting to him.

"You want to talk about it?" Hunter asked.

Zane bristled. "About what? Glory?" He waited on the front stoop for Hunter to catch up to him.

Hunter shook his head, a half smile on his face. "Look, brother, I don't think it's any secret how you feel about Glory. I've seen the way you look at her. We've all seen it."

"We're doing this?" Zane took in the people going in and out of the general store down the street, ready to do almost anything to avoid this conversation.

Hunter sighed. "Glory isn't like Christine. She's cut from a different cloth."

Zane winced at the sound of *her* name and clenched his jaw so hard his scar throbbed. No one had mentioned Christine to him in years. After what had happened, it's almost as if they'd come to some silent resolution that no one would talk about her. Hunter was right. Christine had been the opposite of Glory. She'd needed his help to do everything from saddling her horse to accompanying her on rides around the Reyes hacienda because she hadn't wanted to ride alone. Those rides had given them plenty of time to talk which had led to kissing and so much more.

Christine had been a virgin when he'd taken her. Even now, though he loathed himself for it, he could hear her soft whisper as she found him in his bunk and told him that she loved him. That she wanted a life with him. He'd believed her then, and he still believed her. She *had* loved him, and yet, when it had mattered, she'd turned her back when her brother had beaten him to within inches of his life.

"I know that she's not the same, but it doesn't change what happened. It doesn't change the fact that love doesn't mean anything."

Hunter shook his head. "I understand why you'd feel that way. You have every right to. But it's not always that way."

Zane was glad that Hunter had found Emmy and things seemed to be working out for them. No way in hell was Zane going to open himself up to that hurt again. The pain of the whip splitting open his face had nothing on the agony of watching Christine turning away from him as her brother hit him over and over again.

Derringer and his men had blown through the ranch that night to demand that Castillo's grandfather give up trying to get his money back from them. One minute Zane had been in the barn brushing down a horse, and the next he'd heard shouting and the whole place had swarmed with men on horseback wielding rifles. He'd run for his gun but Bennett, Derringer's son, had come out of the darkness, riding his horse and blocking Zane's path.

Christine had told him about their affair and he was out for blood. Not only was Zane's skin the wrong color for Bennett's sister, but he didn't have nearly the social standing required to touch her. The whip had come from nowhere, lashing the side of his face before he'd had a chance to react. When Zane had run, Bennett had jumped off his horse and lashed him across the back several times, bringing Zane to his knees. Bennett hadn't even stopped when Christine had ridden out of the darkness pleading with him to spare Zane.

After her token protest that Bennett stop, she'd watched in silence. She could've handed Zane his gun, but Bennett had told her to stand down. He'd sweetened the deal and ensured her compliance when he'd promised her she'd lose her cut of the money they'd stolen if she helped Zane. She'd turned and left. It was the last time he'd ever seen her.

Some might say that it was a sure sign that she hadn't ever loved him. Zane knew that she had. He'd seen that look in her eyes, the same one that Caroline and Emmy gave their husbands. Christine had loved him as much as Zane had loved her. But it hadn't been nearly enough.

He wasn't going to let himself get pulled into that emotion again. He also wasn't about to open himself up to Hunter on the street in front of the brothel. "I appreciate your concern, but right now we need to focus on helping Glory." Hunter gave a reluctant nod, and Zane continued, "I'm going to talk to Sally Roarke, the singer from last night. I'll let you know what she says. It's suspicious she showed up here around the same time as that note."

"And I'll keep you updated when I hear something," said Hunter. "I'm hoping for a telegram soon from my contact in Chicago."

"Let me know as soon as you've heard."

"Will do." Hunter tilted the brim of his hat.

They parted ways and Zane made his way to the second floor, where Mrs. Roarke had been given a small suite. He'd tried to talk to her earlier in the morning but was told by her maid that she slept in after performances. He hoped like hell that she'd have something to do with that note. He hated the idea of someone out there being after Glory. If it were someone she knew, someone they had access to, someone simply looking for a few extra thousand dollars, well, that would make their lives a hell of a lot easier.

The hallway here was as elaborate as the downstairs: plush carpet lined the hall, bronze wall sconces, intricately carved wooden doors led to each suite, which he'd heard had an attached bathing chamber, an expense that made it rival the mansion out on the Jameson's estate. It was no wonder Victoria House managed to attract only the most exclusive clientele.

The floor was quiet at this time of day. The women didn't start seeing patrons until nightfall. When he paused in front of Mrs. Roarke's door, his knock seemed to echo up and down the still hallway.

The door opened and a maid peeked out. He didn't recognize her as someone who worked at the house. She was a small woman, smaller than Glory, with dark, beady eyes that darted up and down the hallway as if she'd expected someone else to be lurking. When they finally settled on him, she gave him a disapproving look from the top of his head all the way to his battered boots. Finally, she said, "She's awake now."

When the maid showed no interest in actually inviting him in, Zane said, "Then I'd like to talk to her now."

"Oh, let him in, Sue." That voice filled the room and

spilled out into the hallway, seeming somehow musical and exuberant even though she wasn't singing.

He felt a tiny surge of victory when the maid gave him a frown but opened the door and stepped back so that he could enter. Inclining his head to her, the corner of his mouth ticked up in a grin as he walked into the room. It was just as he'd expected. A large, four-poster bed sat in the back corner complete with gauzy bed curtains and plush blankets. Brass wall sconces filled the room with light, and the walls were done in a cream-and-rose wallpaper that managed to appear elegant rather than gaudy. He couldn't help but note the discrepancy between this and Glory's own modest bed-chamber. Why would she scrimp when it came to her own comfort? Was it because she didn't care about the lavish trimmings, or was she simply that conscious of the cost? There was so much he didn't know about the woman, and it was eating at him.

"Come join me, Mr. Pierce." The woman occupied a chair in the seating area and indicated that he should take the wingback chair across from her. She seemed quite at home in the room and not bothered at all to be welcoming him in her silk dressing gown. "Would you care for a cup of tea?" She reached forward and picked up the handle of a porcelain teapot, poised to pour him a cup.

He inclined his head as he sat down. "Thank you." He didn't give a damn about tea, but he wanted to be polite and court her favor.

The older woman gave him a smile as she poured him a cup and then refilled her own. "Cream or sugar?"

"No, thank you."

She nodded and proceeded to pour a generous amount of cream in her own cup. He studied her as she did. Even though she'd obviously only just risen, her dark hair was curled, falling around her shoulders as she leaned forward. Through a layer of artfully applied cosmetics, her face was just starting to show deep grooves around her mouth and eyes. She was very pretty when she leered at him, her painted red lips curving into a perfect bow as she reached for something under the table. "A splash of brandy?"

He did relax then, something about her putting him at ease, and held out his cup. He'd never cared for the American version of tea. He'd grown up with root tea on the reservation and his father, a white trader, had picked up a taste for it, so in his later childhood when he'd lived with the man, it was all he'd known of tea. His first taste of *this* particular type of tea had been on the Jameson ranch. Hunter had cut it with brandy then so it'd be palatable.

The maid hovered around in the background, clearly having nowhere to go except for the bathing chamber to give them privacy. The woman seemed to notice her and said, "Sue, go down to the kitchens and bring us a tray. Have you eaten yet?" She directed the question at Zane.

He nodded. "A little while ago."

"Just a plate for me then." The maid bobbed an awkward curtsy before she hurried out of the room.

"You'll have to excuse her. She came to me highly recommended, but I confess she sets me on edge. She's never calm, just flits around from one thing to the next.

It's not good for my nerves." She took a sip of her tea and Zane followed suit, content to let her talk to see what she'd say. The tea went down easy, warming his belly. The woman closed her eyes and leaned back in her chair. "That's good brandy, but then Glory always has the best."

"You know very much about Glory?"

She grinned again, revealing teeth that were slightly crooked but well taken care of, and opened her eyes. "Is that why you're here? You want to know more about Glory? Sue said you'd come by once already this morning."

Zane shrugged, unwilling to give too much away. Some of the other women had either sensed his interest in her, or had concluded from his questions that he must be asking because he was interested. He figured there'd be talk soon anyway. They could keep him staying in her suite a secret for a night or two, but if this went much longer than that, they'd all be wondering why he was spending his nights with her. He hadn't talked it over with Glory yet, so he didn't answer their questions, but he thought it might be best if everyone thought the two of them were lovers. The alternative was to tell the truth and Glory seemed adverse to anyone knowing about the letter or her past.

Mrs. Roarke looked him over, much like her maid had done earlier, but her gaze was slow and thorough. *Very thorough.* He shuffled uncomfortably in his seat when her gaze lingered on his crotch and again when she took in the breadth of his shoulders before moving on to his face. "You're not her normal type, I'm afraid.

I'm not sure you can expect to get very far with her if that's your hope," she said, shaking her head.

He frowned, wondering what the hell she meant by that. "Glory doesn't have a type. I'm told she…" He paused, loathe to use the words Hunter had used. "She…doesn't spend time with men." A fist of anxiety tightened in his belly as he wondered if they were both wrong about that. Of course, she had every right to spend time with whoever she wanted, but he didn't have to like it.

The woman laughed and shook her head. "Just because she doesn't spend time with men doesn't mean she doesn't *look* at men, that she doesn't have the same desires as any other woman."

It made sense, so he decided to probe a bit deeper. "And you know the type of men she prefers to *look* at?"

The woman nodded, raising a brow as she took another sip of tea. Zane was beginning to think that she knew more about Glory than he'd originally thought, that she was more than a singer who passed through a couple of times a year.

She waved a hand at him as she lowered her teacup back to its saucer. "You're far too big. Not only your height, which would be enough on its own, but your arms, your thighs, your shoulders. Everything is so thick, so muscular. Glory prefers slighter men. Men who are fit, but not to excess, who are of a normal stature." He must've been scowling because she laughed again. "I didn't say anything was wrong with how you look. Many women, myself included—" here she gave him another once-over; he crossed his legs and began to wonder if he'd make it out of her room unscathed "—prefer men such as yourself. Robust, healthy…" Her gaze made another pass of his person. "Big." She gave him another appreciative smile. "There is a danger about you, Mr. Pierce. Not only do you attract it, but you bring danger with you. It's appealing."

He didn't understand what kind of person was attracted to danger. Didn't she realize that danger wasn't some passing amusement? It had been a part of his life for so long that it was second nature to him, but not because he wanted it. Deciding that her likes and dislikes were not any of his business anyway, he steered the conversation back to Glory.

"How long have you known Glory?"

She gave him a knowing look, but to his surprise she answered the question. "Since she came here when she was a girl. I think she was around sixteen years old."

A cold sensation prickled down his spine, tightening his skin at this unexpected knowledge of her. He took in a deep breath through his nose. "What was she like when she arrived?" He knew he was treading dangerous ground. Glory didn't want him to know about her past. He reasoned that he needed to know to help her, but deep down he knew he would've asked anyway. He felt like a traitor, but it didn't stop him from leaning forward so he wouldn't miss anything.

"Hardly recognizable. She was thin." Mrs. Roarke shook her head. "She was so thin you could see her ribs. She was pale and she looked like she hadn't slept for years. She was clearly running from something. They both were."

"But you don't know what." He hardly had to ask to know what the answer would be. Glory had said that she'd never told a soul and he believed her.

She shook her head. "No, but I have my guess. You've seen the women in that house of hers out back?"

Over the past week he'd seen a woman and two young children in the back courtyard playing with chalk on the cobblestones. Another woman kept to herself, but he'd caught a glimpse of her as she ducked inside one day when he'd walked over to check on Cas. They'd looked different, one tall, and one plump and short, but their eyes had been the same. Hollow and bleak. He'd started to think of them as the ghost women. Shells of themselves, because their spirits had run away from whatever had harmed them.

"She was like them?" The words came out harsh and rough. He tried to imagine the vibrant and attractive woman he knew as one of those creatures and it hurt his heart to think of her that way.

The woman nodded. "Worse because it had taken her a long time to get away, I think."

"To get away from…"

Her brow rose again as if he should know. Zane thought he did know, but he didn't want to believe the sick twist of his stomach.

"She never said, but only one type of monster can put that look in a woman's eyes." She took another sip of tea, staring out the window as if lost in thought.

"A man." He didn't need to hear her confirmation to know that he was right. He needed to say it out loud to make it somehow real. To acknowledge that some man from her past had hurt her in ways he didn't want to think about, but he couldn't *not* think about them. She was small, *petite* was the word he'd heard someone say to describe her. The thought of some man hurting her made him physically sick.

Setting his cup and saucer on the delicate table between them, he leaned back, rubbing his palms down the coarse fabric of his pants. Impotent anger raged through him with no outlet in sight. He wanted to find this nameless person and make him feel some semblance of what she must've felt, but he couldn't. He had no idea where to even look.

The woman seemed to shake off her thoughts, looking back over at him to say, "Glory begged Madam Marin to open the house up to other women, but she refused. I'm not surprised, because she didn't even want Glory to stay at first. Said she'd scare off the customers. Able convinced her and soon Glory won her over. They were close." She gestured to the room. "Well, close enough that she left her all of this."

Zane narrowed his gaze at her, wondering if that was jealousy hiding in her words. "That must've been hard for you."

"How so?" She cocked her head to the side, sending a wave of curls flowing over one shoulder.

"Well, you'd been here longer. I think it's only natural that you'd assume she'd leave something to you."

The woman laughed again, tossing her head back. "Oh, no, I could never run this place. And besides, I was gone by then. A theater owner had heard me sing and offered me a position in Colorado. It turned out not to be that great, but from there I went to San Francisco and then I met my husband who was from St. Louis. I settled down a little, but he died only three years after we were married."

"I'm sorry to hear that," he said.

She waved off his concern. "I love singing, love traveling. I have enough bookings over the course of a few months to get me through the year. I'd never want to be chained to a place like this."

"You wouldn't prefer, say a few thousand dollars, to retire? To not worry about money anymore?"

She gave him a peculiar look as if just now realizing his questions weren't strictly about learning more about Glory. "I am retired, Mr. Pierce. I get to do what I love and I don't have to do it on my back anymore." She gave him a coy smile. "Not that I don't occasionally indulge myself." When he didn't seem inclined to take her up on what might have been an offer, she straightened. "Now what is this really about? I thought you wanted to know more about Glory."

"I do want to know more about Glory."

Her gaze narrowed in suspicion. "I believe that you do, but there's more. Tell me."

"I can't tell you. But I did come to find out if you mean her any harm, because let me warn you…I won't let anyone harm her. Not you. Not anyone."

To his surprise, she grinned and leaned back again with her elbows on the arms of the chair. "Well, now, looka here. Glory has her very own protector. I love it. She hasn't even slept with you yet to get you all—"

she swished a hand in his direction "—knight in shining armor."

Zane swiped a hand over the back of his neck, feeling that somehow he'd lost control of the conversation and he hadn't even seen it happen. "We aren't sleeping together. She's asked me for my help."

"Why does she need your help? Has someone threatened her?"

She looked alarmed enough that he was pretty certain her surprise was genuine. Shrugging, he said, "I can't explain the details, but she's had reason for concern."

The woman raised her brow again as if she knew something he didn't, and a slow smile curved her lips. "All right, Mr. Pierce, I can assure you that I have no intention of ever bringing harm to Glory."

"Can you think of anyone who would want to harm her? Someone who lived here at the House when you both lived here?"

She gave a nonchalant shrug of a shoulder. "No and yes. No one that I know has any reason to want her harmed, but who can tell with people? There may have been an odd girl here or there resentful of her and Able inheriting the House."

That thought had occurred to him, but it'd take a hell of a lot longer than a week for him to track down every woman who'd once lived here. And that was assuming most of them hadn't simply disappeared. People had a way of becoming other people out here.

He gave her a nod. "Thank you for talking to me." Standing, he said goodbye and let himself out, unsure if he'd actually done what he came there to do or not. He did have more information about Glory though, and he was reasonably certain that Mrs. Roarke wasn't responsible for the letter, so he'd consider it a win.

Chapter Seven

The room was quiet but for the steady sound of Glory's voice as she read a bedtime story to her charges. Most nights she was able to escape the business of Victoria House to put the children who resided in the nursery of the boardinghouse to bed. It was her favorite time of day. She loved spending time with them and came over quite often, but the evenings were particularly sweet. Victoria House could be bustling with greed and lust, but she only had to escape to this room for a few minutes to be reminded that there was so much more to life. The children's innocence and enthusiasm gave her hope.

"'Rapunzel, Rapunzel, let down your hair,'" she read, but after a moment a sound in the hallway outside caught her attention. The heavy scuff of boots on the hardwood floor when the boardinghouse so rarely saw men enter its doors. Her heart skipped a beat as she recognized the distinct cadence of Zane's steps. Funny how she had already memorized it in so short a time. But she'd listened to it last night and again this morning from her bedroom as he'd walked around her parlor.

She stuttered over the next line and five pairs of eyes stared up at her, eagerly anticipating finding out how Rapunzel would escape from the evil enchantress. Smiling at them, she stared down at the book in her hands and continued reading. It didn't matter that she couldn't see Zane. She could feel the weight of his stare when he looked around the partially open door, and she could sense his presence as he took up his self-imposed sentry post outside the room.

When the story was finished, she closed the book of fairy tales and sat it on the table next to her rocking chair. The children were spread out on the rug staring up at her.

"That's all for tonight. Time for bed."

There was a chorus of groans and complaints, but she and Charlotte managed to get them to the bunks that lined one wall. Charlotte took the newcomers; the two boys who'd arrived with their mother a couple of weeks ago, escaping an abusive home. Glory took the other three. They were children who'd been raised at Victoria House. Though she encouraged her ladies to take steps to prevent pregnancy, it sometimes happened. Particularly when the woman had a regular customer who charmed her with gifts and sweet talk. That was the case for Emily and Edward, whose father had come into town around five years ago. He'd spent all his nights with their mother and had eventually left, leaving her brokenhearted and pregnant with the twins.

They'd grown up here, along with Sarah who was nearly eight, whose mother had arrived when she'd been a baby and had chosen to stay and worked most evenings at Victoria House. Though Charlotte was Glory's assistant, a large part of her job was caring for the children. Glory spent some time every morning and evening with the children overseeing their studies and playing with them.

"Miss Glory, do we have to go to bed so early?" Sarah complained. "The sun's still out."

Glory smiled and pulled the thin sheet up to Sarah's chin. "Yes, you have to go to bed now." They had the same discussion almost every night in summer when the sun didn't set until well after nine o'clock at night. "You have a busy day tomorrow. Charlotte says you have two exams."

Sarah pulled a face, and Glory hid her laugh as she walked to the window to pull the curtains closed. "Good night, little ones." Glory gave them each a kiss on the forehead, even the two newcomers who still stared at her with big owl eyes, unsure of their world now that it had been upended.

Her heart ached for them. Their mother spent most of her time in her room, withdrawn from everyone. Glory knew from experience that it would take time to recover from whatever had brought her here. When she was ready, Glory would help her find a position in another town as a shop girl or maid or whatever lent itself to the skills she had, then she'd send the family off with enough money to get them by until they could get on their feet. It wasn't a lot. In the future she envisioned a school where she could train them for professions far more lucrative and dependable than shop girl that would keep them self-sufficient for the rest of their lives. But for now she took comfort in the fact that she'd helped many women find, hopefully, better lives in the years since she'd opened her boardinghouse.

"Do you want me to stay with them and make sure they go to sleep?" Charlotte asked when they stepped into the hallway. Zane was there, but Glory wasn't ready to acknowledge him yet. She still didn't know how she felt about this arrangement.

"Give them a few minutes, and then go on up to your room. You've earned a well-deserved evening off." Thanks to the faro tournament across the road, business was exceptionally slow tonight. She expected last night and Sally's second performance tomorrow night to more than make up for it.

Charlotte pushed a strand of dark hair back from her face, looking younger than her twenty years. She'd shown up at Victoria House four years ago, a new bride escaping an abusive husband. Sometime after she'd arrived, Glory had discovered she had excellent penmanship—far better than Glory's own hasty scrawl—so she'd made her an assistant. She also had a gentle way with the children and doubled as a teacher for them. Glory had yet to find a trained schoolteacher who'd take the job here, so they made do with what they had.

"I have a few letters to finish that need to post in the morning. I'll go back to my desk and finish those first," said Charlotte.

Glory waved her off. She *did* deserve an evening off, but more than that, Glory didn't want her questioning why Zane was in her suite. So far that day he'd been a silent fixture in Victoria House, and if anyone found his constant presence odd, no one had asked because it wasn't *that* noticeable. If he was known to be in her suite, however, that would be noteworthy.

"Besides, *you're* still working," Charlotte teased.

Glory put on her best hostess smile to cover her unease. "I'm *always* working. We have a rare night off, go enjoy it. Go have fun with the other ladies. I hear there's a high-stakes dice game going on in the courtyard again tonight."

Charlotte gave a hesitant smile and nodded. "You're right. We don't get many nights like this."

Glory swallowed her sigh of relief. "Have fun." Then she turned to Zane, reading the displeasure in his eyes. She raised an eyebrow and subtly gestured to Charlotte, indicating that he should keep quiet until they were alone.

He waited until they were outside in the courtyard. "What the hell was that, Glory?" He kept his voice low, but the undercurrent of anger was there.

"What are you talking about, Mr. Pierce?" She knew exactly what had him so upset, but she found she delighted in taunting him.

"You left the house without letting me know. We agreed that either Able or I would be with you at all times."

Plastering a smile on her face because they were approaching the women playing dice, she waved to them as a few called out a greeting and asked her to join them. "I hardly call crossing the courtyard leaving the house. I declare, you're behaving as if I took a jaunt across town."

Tension rolled off him as he waited for her to politely decline the women's invitation. As soon as they were past the group, he let out a huff of breath through his nose. "Whatever you call it, it was wrong and potentially dangerous."

Glory couldn't help but notice how several pairs of eyes lingered on them as they passed. Rumors would be flying soon if they weren't already. At least no one knew that he'd spent the night in her room last night. Hopefully they'd find the perpetrator quickly and this would be over. "Well, as you can see, the children aren't really that dangerous. I'm fine."

He narrowed his eyes at her, letting her know that her attempt at levity had been a failure. "It's not the children I'm worried about. It's you. You are my only concern right now and I can't keep you safe if I don't know where you are. Whoever got into your office, could be there waiting for you, knowing that's where you'd least expect it."

She frowned. She supposed it made sense if she looked at it from his point of view; however, she also believed that he was making a huge jump from finding a letter attempting to extort thousands of dollars from her to her safety being imminently at risk. "No one is going to be waiting in a dark corner to jump out at me. I appreciate your concern and dedication, but right now we should be more concerned with keeping my past in the dark. I really don't think my life is at risk. Yet." She added that last part because she *did* believe that her life would be at risk if her past ever caught up to her.

He was silent as he followed her up the back stairs

to her suite. The frustration pouring off him was nearly palpable. It warmed its way up her spine and wrapped around her in a way that wasn't unpleasant. It meant that he cared, that he planned to do everything in his power to keep her safe, and while she might take issue with his methods, she appreciated that she could depend on him.

Stopping at the door that took her directly to her suite, she chanced a quick glance over her shoulder at him as she dug the key out of her pocket. His jaw was clenched and he was too busy looking at each door as if the person who'd left the letter might be hiding behind one to notice her. She let herself indulge for a moment in the secret thrill she got every time she looked at him. In profile, his strong features appeared even more chiseled. She lingered on the braid near his ear, half hidden by his hair which flowed free to his shoulders. He was so different from her, yet she felt this strange kinship with him and didn't understand it. Exploring it would be pointless, nothing could come of them, but knowing that didn't stop her curiosity about him.

He looked down at her abruptly as if he'd felt her scrutiny, so she gave him what she hoped was a casual smile and pushed her key into the lock. Her heart nearly beat itself out of her chest when he put his hand on hers to stop her from going inside. The tingle of warmth that shot up her arm made her pull her hand back as quickly as she could. His brow rose, but he didn't comment. Instead he pushed the door open and stepped in front of her. She realized that he only meant to make certain that no one lurked inside.

"Come on in," he said a moment later.

She shook her head at his unnecessary attention to detail and followed him inside. He stood in the center of the room, seeming to almost fill the whole place up with the breadth of him. When he shrugged out of his coat as if he meant to stay for a while, she sighed and closed the door behind her. Apparently they needed to make this arrangement work for at least one more night. "I take it Hunter wasn't able to find out any information."

He shook his head and relayed the information he had from Hunter, which wasn't a lot. It was too early to be disappointed though. Hunter had only started his search this morning. They still had days to find the person. "And you've made no headway in finding out how the letter made its way to my desk?"

"I have my suspicions." He eyed her as he hung his coat on the rack beside the door.

"Which are?" she prompted.

He shook his head. "You'll find out when I know for sure."

"At least tell me the top suspects."

He merely shook his head again and the corner of his mouth ticked up. "You're too loyal. If I tell you, you'll give me a list of reasons the people I need to question further couldn't possibly be involved and it won't get us anywhere."

She frowned. "Well, none of the people who work with me would be in cahoots with this person, so I suppose you're right."

"And yet no one else had access to your study."

He tossed the words out there so casually. She knew that he had to be right, but at the same time she couldn't fathom someone conspiring with this secret person. When she realized he was simply standing there, she gestured toward the sofa. "Please have a seat." Exchanging verbal barbs with Zane wouldn't get this problem fixed, so she planned to drop the subject.

He didn't move right away. Instead he stared down at her as if trying to solve a puzzle. "I never realized how close you were with the children in the boardinghouse."

She shrugged. She'd tried not to get too close to anyone there. Most of the people she helped stayed at the boardinghouse for only a few weeks or months. It seemed pointless to form attachments. But she hadn't been able to figure out a way to keep herself from the children, especially those who lived here full-time. She'd seen them grow up from babies.

Before she could answer, someone knocked on the door. Zane made to answer it, but she got there first. This was still her home. He gave her a look of dismay but allowed her to open it. To her surprise, Beth, one of the kitchen staff, stood there holding an oversize tray.

"You ordered a plate to be sent up for supper?" the girl asked when Glory simply stared at her.

"Of course." She'd nearly forgotten that she'd stopped by that morning to give the order, preparing to spend most of the evening in her room reading since business would be slow. She'd hoped, perhaps naively, that Zane would be gone by now and the mystery solved. What surprised her now, however, was that there were clearly two plates on the tray.

Catching her eye going to the second one, Beth gave

a shy smile and said, "I thought your gentleman might be hungry too."

Glory's face flamed as she realized that rumors had already spread to the staff. Instead of commenting on it, she stepped back and Beth walked into the room to set both plates on the table. If Beth thought that he'd want a plate, did she also know that he'd spent the night here last night? It seemed a silly thing to worry about. She *was* a brothel owner, they *were* in a brothel, but the idea of everyone thinking that she and Zane had slept together twisted her up inside.

After Beth had unloaded the plates laden with food, the bread basket, a pitcher of water and two glasses, she turned back to them and seemed to read the awkwardness in the room. "Did I misunderstand? Is he not eating here?" When no one answered immediately, she pushed a strand of hair behind her ear and turned back to the table. "I'm sorry. I'll take the extra plate away."

Finally gathering her senses, Glory rushed forward. Zane was apparently allowing her to take the lead in how to handle this with the staff. She needed to act casually so as not to stir up unneeded drama. In the end, it really didn't matter if anyone thought they were seeing each other in a way that wasn't business-related or not. The only one who seemed torn up about it was her. "No, it's fine and very thoughtful of you, Beth. Thank you."

The girl paused but glanced over her shoulder as if to ask if she was certain. Glory gave her a nod and an encouraging smile. "Thank you," she said again. "I'm sure Mr. Pierce is hungry."

They both looked to him for confirmation, but he

was staring at Glory with a strange expression on his face. Amusement mixed with something she couldn't name. Something that had her breath catching as her stomach tilted.

"If you're sure…" Beth said.

Glory assured her again that she was and showed her out. When she turned around, Zane had made his way to the table, eyeing the beefsteak on his plate as if he were famished. She found that she was a little jealous to have lost his focus and immediately admonished herself. She kept going back and forth with what she wanted from him, which was driving her mad. She was always in control of herself and what she wanted. This was an entirely new situation for her and she was disappointed that she wasn't handling it very well. She wanted him, yes, but she couldn't have him. It was simple.

Pulling in a deep, fortifying breath, she took her seat at the table, noting how he waited until she was seated comfortably to take his own. Her stomach rumbled as she took in the bounty of food before her. Beefsteak, creamed peas, roasted potatoes and a steaming basket of bread. Fresh baked bread slathered in butter was her absolute favorite, so she picked up one of the small loafs and took a bite.

He hesitated before picking up his knife and fork. "Are you certain you don't mind me eating here?"

Why was everyone questioning her certainty so much lately? Deep down she knew it was because of him. Or more appropriately her reaction to him. Because she couldn't keep her head straight with him around. "Of course."

She must've torn off a piece of her bread rather savagely, because his eyebrow rose and his lips twitched before he finally cut into his steak and brought the bite to his mouth. She couldn't help but watch how his full lips closed around the fork, and the way his eyes half closed as the flavor hit his tongue. She'd never been so jealous of an eating utensil in her life. His tongue came out to swipe over his bottom lip and she couldn't help but imagine that tongue tasting her own lips, tasting other parts of her. Would he be as focused on her as he was on his meal? The question did outlandish things to her belly.

How did he do this to her? He was simply a man like any other man. And he'd be gone soon, a tiny voice inside her said, so she'd better look while she had the chance.

Catching her watching him, he said, "The food's as excellent as always."

The dryness of her mouth made it impossible to stay anything, so she nodded a little too vehemently and grabbed her water glass. As she drank she resolved not to look at him anymore.

They ate in silence for a while. Finally, when he'd finished his steak and she was halfway through hers, he said, "Tell me more about the children."

"There's not much to tell." She did her best to focus on the food on her plate as she spoke. "Sarah has grown up here as have Emily and Edward."

"You seem partial to the twins."

Had he watched her from the hallway? "Their mother recently left to marry a man in Chicago. He was a customer here and they kept up a correspondence after he returned home. One thing led to another and…well, you know how things go." Glory was genuinely happy for their mother, but at the same time she had a terrible feeling about it all. "The twins have been sad since she left, so I try to give them extra attention." Lord knows how bereft she'd felt when her own mother had abandoned her, and Glory had been fourteen at the time. She couldn't imagine how a child of four must feel. Alone, scared, heartbroken.

"He's not the children's father?"

She shook her head. "No, their father is long gone. We haven't seen nor heard from him since before they were born."

He seemed pensive as he took a drink of water. When he swallowed he asked, "Why didn't she take them with her?"

Glory sat down her fork, attempting to swallow down the sudden lump in her throat. She'd been concerned ever since their mother had asked if they could stay for a while, until she got settled in Chicago. A part of her had wondered then if the time would ever come when she'd send for them or if her new husband would disapprove of having them around. "She wanted to get settled before sending for them, but it's been months now and though she's sent letters, she's not mentioned having them join her."

"You think she's going to abandon them." It wasn't a question. Anyone with a working brain could tell what was happening.

"I hope that's not the case, but I fear that it is."

"What will you do?" Lines formed between his handsome brows as he asked that—how could anyone's brows be handsome? She was annoyed at herself, which was quickly followed by frustration. Frustration with herself. Frustration with the twins' mother. Frustration with him for being so nosy. She wanted to ask him what business was it of his, but at the same time she wanted to tell him everything—every fear and worry that she had.

Staring into his dark brown eyes she had the feeling that he would welcome that, which immediately soothed her pique. "I'll keep them, of course. Or perhaps I'll send them away to a boarding school. Maybe they'll have a better chance at life that way without the taint of a brothel soiling them." Lord knew that everyone in Helena would never let them forget they were brothel children if they stayed here.

"You want them to stay though?" he asked, correctly reading what she didn't want to say.

"They're very clever children. I'd like them to stay, but that wouldn't be in their best interest I'm afraid." She took a bite of creamed peas before she could say anything more. She'd come to realize a long time ago that the people she encountered in this life were transient. Victoria House wasn't a place where anyone came to stay forever. Everyone left eventually, except Able, and now that Clara was going to have a baby soon, Glory had started to wonder when they'd leave. This was her home and she loved it, but even she could admit this wasn't a place to raise children.

Not that children would ever be in her future. *He* had made sure of that. And it seemed her current profession precluded even the option of adopting children. She'd yet to become accustomed to all the ways life could be unfair. Her independence came at a heavy price. When she realized that her hand was absently rubbing the scar hidden beneath her gown on her belly, she discreetly put it back on the table.

If he'd noticed, he didn't say anything and simply stared at her. When it became apparent that he wasn't going to stop, she met his gaze, but she couldn't speak immediately. There was that look again, the one that saw everything. Her heart skipped a beat in her chest. "Wh-why are you looking at me like that?"

"Like what?" he said, his voice low and intimate.

"Like you see things in me." It was an odd way to say it, but it was the truth. He looked at her as if he could see everything that she was.

If he thought her wording was strange, he didn't comment on it. Instead, he simply said, "Perhaps because I do."

Chapter Eight

Zane couldn't learn enough about the woman across the table to sate his curiosity about her. The more he learned about her, the more he wanted to know. She'd surprised him at nearly every turn.

Every day she dressed impeccably in gowns straight out of Paris. Her hair was always styled with not one strand out of place. She spoke in a way that was careful and articulate, her accent softening the edges of her words. She wore cosmetics in a way that enhanced her natural beauty. She was someone who seemed ageless. The knowledge in her eyes could've been that of someone twice her age, but her face was youthful. As a result, he'd had no idea how old she was or what sort of life she'd had. To Zane, someone who prided himself on his ability to read people, she'd been a mystery.

Today he'd learned that she'd been little more than a child when she'd landed on the front stoop of Victoria House, and somehow she and Able had made this place what it was today. She'd arrived here with nothing and was now legitimately one of the wealthiest landowners in town and she wasn't even thirty years old. He couldn't pretend to know what she'd been through in her life, but he could appreciate the strength it had taken to get to where she was.

His own life was much different than what he'd thought it would be as a child. He didn't believe that she'd ever imagined ending up here. In that way they were the same. Transplanted by life, they'd both had to adapt to things they'd have never thought to face. Yet in some ways they were worlds apart. Her stable life here was nothing like his life spent out under the stars, chased by other outlaws, by the law, by people who hated him because he was marked with the look of his mother's people.

He didn't know what life had in store for their future, but he was a believer in counting your blessings while you had them. He preferred to live in the present. And right now he sat across from the most fascinating woman he'd ever met. Life and the Creator had brought them together. He didn't want to question how or why or what the future might bring. He only wanted to appreciate now, visions of doom be damned.

"You can't possibly see anything in me that I haven't told you." She glanced down at her plate as if she didn't entirely believe that.

He blinked, having already forgotten what they'd been talking about. But it came back to him as he searched her features for some sign that she might want more than this arrangement they had. "You tell me more than you think you do," he replied.

She glanced up at him, her eyes worried and somehow relieved at the same time. This woman was a contradiction. "I don't," she whispered.

"You tell me that you're compassionate, caring, bold and intelligent. You're feisty when you need to be, but mild when you don't. You take care of everyone around you." When he paused, she blinked and looked down at her plate again, absently toying with what was left of her food with her fork. "But no one takes care of you."

Her shoulders went rigid, but she didn't argue with him.

"I don't know what you want though. What do you want in life?" It really wasn't any of his business, and she had every right to tell him to go to hell, but he couldn't help but push her a little.

"You don't know that?" She smiled at him, her carefully crafted mask back in place. He'd seen that mask every night downstairs. It slid into place so easily he hadn't even recognized it for what it was at first. Now he saw that it was armor. Maybe she thought that a smile could cover up her vulnerability, that it was something she could hide behind, hiding who she really was.

Somehow over the past week he'd been able to see behind it, and the woman he saw was even more beautiful. Giving her a grin, he said, "I know that you like to fight injustice when you see it. That disadvantaged women are of particular concern to you."

She shrugged and relief flashed in her eyes. "There you have it. I guess you were right, I do tell you quite a bit. It's my hope that one day women will have an equal place in this world. That they won't be stuck in unfortunate situations because they have to rely on someone else."

She was intentionally leading the conversation back to safer territory, making it about the women she helped instead of herself. He thought of what Mrs. Roarke had said to him earlier, and he had to know if it was true. It had been eating at him all day. "Because you were once in that situation? Did you have no one to help you when someone was hurting you?"

She froze, but the truth was written on her face before she could disguise it. After a moment, she swallowed, the muscles of her long, graceful neck moving slowly. Finally, she nodded, and the relief that coursed through him was so strong he nearly sagged in his seat. He couldn't believe that she was finally opening up to him. "It was a long time ago, but it's how I came to be here. It's why I'm afraid now."

He knew that he should take that little nugget and be thankful, but he was greedy for more. He told himself that he needed to know as much as he could to better protect her. It was true, but he wanted to know for himself. "Was it a man, Glory? Did a man hurt you?"

To his surprise a spark of anger flashed across her features. Her eyes hardened and she said, "I never want to see him again. The way I left…"

Her voice trailed off and Zane realized that his hands were clasped into fists on the table. He forced himself to relax them, but inside he was seething that someone had dared to hurt her.

Visibly trying to calm herself, she took a deep breath. "I'm certain that he's very angry with me and would love to find me."

"It's been many years. Surely he's moved on." Despite his best intentions, his voice came out harsh and rough.

She shook her head. "I'm certain he's moved on, but he hasn't forgotten. He'll want to be vindicated."

He clenched his jaw to stop himself from asking her for details. That was a line he wouldn't cross for fear of pushing her away. His scar ached as if to remind him that they all had things in their pasts they'd rather not talk about. He wouldn't ask for details, but that didn't mean he didn't need to know the identity of this person to help her.

Taking in a deep breath, he let it out slowly, hoping it would calm the anger raging inside him, but it only seemed to stoke the flame. "What's his name?"

"No." She shook her head. "I'm not telling you any more."

"You don't have to tell me what happened." He held up his hands as if to say he'd surrendered. "But I do need to know who he is. If I know, then I have a better chance at finding whoever wrote that letter."

"We don't know if that letter is anything but a shot in the dark attempt at extortion." She reminded him.

"We don't," he agreed. "But *if* it is, then we need to know now rather than later. I can backtrack, try to find a link between whoever opened that account and the man who hurt you."

She was already shaking her head before he'd finished talking. "I'll take my chances. If it's nothing but an empty threat, then it'll go away. If it turns out to be more than that, then we'll face that when the time comes."

"Dammit, Glory." Zane rose to his feet and began

pacing, trying to work out the excess energy of his frustration. "You're so damn stubborn."

She stood, her cheeks pink with her own anger and frustration. "This has nothing to do with me being stubborn. It's just good sense. If I tell you who he is and you start making inquiries, then he could find me from those inquiries. He's not a stupid man, Mr. Pierce, and he has means."

"If he's so smart and has the money to search for you, then he *will* find you. There's no if. I need to know who he is so that I can head him off." He already regretted raising his voice, so he tried to keep his voice even.

Her brow furrowed as she seemed to consider his words, but then she shook her head and walked away from him, her thoughts turned inward. "I'll take the chance that this is an empty threat. Haven't you ever heard the idiom 'let sleeping dogs lie'?"

Of course he'd heard it, he simply didn't think it was particularly applicable to this situation. He'd rather be prepared than wait for this unknown snake to strike. "You take that chance and you're prey. Let me know who he is and I can find him."

She gave a soft, humorless laugh. "You'll find him? Find him and what then?" she asked, turning back to face him.

"I'll find him and put an end to this." He came to a stop in front of her, aching to touch her but keeping his hands firmly in his pockets so that he wouldn't.

"I don't need you to fight my battles for me, Mr. Pierce." She tilted her head up to meet his gaze and he noticed the tiny little sprinkle of freckles across the bridge of her nose. They were hidden under the layer of powder she wore. He'd never been close enough to notice them, but seeing them now immediately made him wonder if she had freckles anywhere else.

"Hey, you asked me for help. I'm trying to help you, but I need you to cooperate."

"You're right. I hired you to help find the person who sent the letter, and to make sure that I'm safe in my home. That's all."

"So you're fine with the fact that he could show up here any day and catch you by surprise?" He knew it was a low blow, but he needed her to understand how dangerous her situation was.

"Fine? Am I fine with it? No, it's a fear that I live with every day, but so far it hasn't happened. I won't have you going all the way to South Carolina to find him, when it's entirely possible that he has no idea where I am." Her voice finally rose on that sentence, breaking the reins she'd held on her control. Even in her anger, she was beautiful. Fiery and strong. Breathtaking.

He realized that they were standing nearly toe-to-toe, so he took a step back, trying to control his emotions. "I know that you do."

Still angry, she pulled herself up to her full height which wouldn't have reached his shoulders had her hair not been pulled up on her head. "Why do you care so much? This isn't what I hired you for."

"I don't want you hurt. I don't like the idea of him out there…waiting to hurt you again."

The rest of his anger drained away when her eyes widened in shock. She only just now seemed to realize that he was asking her these questions because he cared about her. "Why?" He watched her soft lips form the word, but he barely heard the sound.

"Isn't it obvious?" He swallowed, suddenly prepared to be more honest with her than he had ever been before. "I care about you, Glory. I want to know you're safe." He didn't want to care about her, but he did. Christine's image flashed in his mind, a reminder of what had happened the last time he'd let his guard down. This was different, he wouldn't let it go so far as it had with Christine. He could care for Glory without falling in love with her, but that didn't explain why his heart was pounding against his ribs.

She sucked in a breath and his gaze met hers. Her hazel eyes were darker now, swirling with emotion and heat. To his surprise, her pupils were dilated, nearly obliterating any sign of green.

"And I think you care about me," he whispered, knowing that he shouldn't be so honest with her. Her rose scent tickled his nostrils, making his stomach churn with equal parts need and premonition.

She gasped. The sound of her breath scraped pleasantly over him, causing him to imagine her making that sound because he was inside her. One night wouldn't change things. He could have her and still keep his distance. The thought of having her beneath him made his gut clench pleasurably.

"And I think you want to kiss me as much as I want to kiss you," he whispered. Her soft lips parted and her eyes widened. Her pink tongue darted out to stroke her bottom lip, making it moist for him. The need to taste her was a magnet, drawing him in, making his lips tingle in anticipation. He bent his head down, moving closer inch by inch, giving her time to move away, but she stayed, her breath coming faster, fanning across his lips. Sensing her hesitance, he paused an inch away, allowing her time to pull back or to tell him to stop.

She didn't. She let out a ragged breath and fisted the skirt of her dress, but she didn't back away. His palms itched to touch her, but he sensed that it would be a step too far. The heated air between them was thick with tension. "Say yes to me," he whispered, hoping that she would but prepared for her to push him away. He sensed that she'd have to take the lead in whatever happened between, but that didn't mean he wouldn't nudge her along.

For a moment, the only sound in the room was their breathing mixed with the ticking of the clock on the mantel. "Yes." The soft whisper burrowed inside him, grabbing something deep within him and pulling him to her.

His lips touched hers. The longing of countless days and night coalesced into that perfect moment when her soft lips parted beneath his. She moved slow but certain in her movements as she set their pace. Testing her, he brushed his tongue against her bottom lip. She surprised him by returning the featherlight touch, stroking his tongue with her own. He groaned and gently pushed forward, delving into her wet heat. She moaned deep in her throat and her hands came up to smooth over his chest, settling over the beat of his heart. Her fingers clenched in his shirt.

Blood roared in his ears, urging him to take more,

but he didn't want to push too far too fast. Instead, he pulled back, breaking the kiss to stare down into her eyes. His chest squeezed tight as if he'd just run a mile. Fear and excitement mingled together in her eyes, and he again hated the bastard who had put the fear there. Before he could say a word, the fear won out. She firmly pushed him away and whispered, "I'm sorry. I can't," and then she ran to her bedroom and slammed the door.

Zane leaned against the wall, his heart threatening to pound its way out of his chest. If one kiss had done this to him, how would it feel after he'd spent himself inside her? A tingling sensation moved down his spine, tightening his groin as all the blood in his body redirected to that general area.

He cursed himself for pushing her so far. He should've stopped before he kissed her or broken the kiss much sooner. She'd opened so sweetly for him, and now he knew exactly how she tasted. He wanted more. He was walking a dangerous line with her. One night with her shouldn't be enough to make him lose his heart, but he'd be lying if he said he wasn't concerned that he wasn't halfway lost as it was. Because almost as great as the need to have her was the need to hold her and let her know that she was safe, to drive the fear from her eyes.

Closing his eyes, he forced himself to relive the night when Christine had turned her back on him. He needed the reminder that love wasn't worth the risk.

Chapter Nine

The next morning Glory sat at her dressing table, her lips still tingling from the kiss from the night before. She'd tossed and turned for a while last night before finally settling into a deep dreamless sleep, but the moment she awoke she'd remembered it all over again. She ran a fingertip over her bottom lip, remembering the soft heat of his mouth and how his tongue had felt against hers. A dart of electricity sparked down to her belly, settling there with a slow burn. A blush stained her cheeks in the mirror and she couldn't stop the ridiculous smile that curved her lips.

Zane Pierce was a much better kisser than she'd assumed he would be. His size suggested brute strength and a lack of finesse, but he'd been surprisingly gentle and attentive. Over the years she'd had men steal kisses from her before. It was like a strange badge of honor with some of them, and she knew about that ridiculous wager in that betting book across town. Since that had come up a year or so ago, the men had progressed from stolen kisses to flirting conversation meant to somehow sweep her off her feet. None of them ever swept her off her feet.

Not one in the entire twelve years she'd been here. But last night Zane had made her knees go weak. Had she not been pressed against the wall, she was certain that she would've fallen. The thing was, he'd made her weak in the knees before he'd even kissed her. It had started when he'd given her that heavy-lidded look of his that meant he was thinking naughty things. The final blow had come, however, when he'd asked for her permission.

None of the men had ever asked permission. Not one. Despite the fact that she wasn't selling herself every night, they walked into the house as if she owed them whatever they demanded. More than once Able had been forced to show a man out because he wasn't happy she wouldn't take him upstairs. Zane had looked as if he expected her to turn him down. She knew that she probably shouldn't have, but when he'd allowed her to take the lead, she'd been unable to refuse them what they both wanted. How much harm could one little kiss cause anyway?

A crinkling of paper and a flash of white caught her attention. A folded piece of paper slid nearly soundlessly across the hardwood floor of her bedchamber. The distinct thump of Zane's boots moving away from the door had her heart beating in her throat. On quiet feet because she wanted to keep the moment of discovery to herself, she walked over and picked up the paper before returning to her stool. She expected to open it to find a note and listened for the front door of her suite, imagining that he was simply telling her he was leaving for the morning. But when she opened it, she got a surprise.

A beautiful rose in full bloom stared back at her. Each petal was artfully sketched in dramatic detail. It was breathtaking. She ran her fingertips over the graphite lines, picturing him sitting out on her sofa drawing them for her. His fingertips must have traced over the lines as hers were doing now. Had he realized how she loved roses? Had he hoped to make her smile? Or perhaps the drawing had been a casual amusement. Did it mean anything to him or had it simply been a pleasant way to pass the time?

Tucking the corners of the drawing into the frame of her mirror, she smiled again at her reflection. The woman smiling back at her was almost unrecognizable. It was the same face with the same red hair that stared back at her every morning. The same smile that she'd learned long ago to keep plastered on her face was there, but this morning something was different. The eyes were different. They were smiling in a way she hadn't seen in a long time. It was silly to think that it was all because of Zane, but it had to be him. He was the only thing that had changed. He was reminding her of what it meant to enjoy the little things.

A smile, a drawing…a kiss.

Butterflies swarmed in her belly as she remembered that kiss all over again. If she closed her eyes, she could still feel the soft pressure of his lips on hers. She'd never enjoyed a kiss before, albeit she'd never been kissed by someone she *wanted* to kiss. Would it be possible for her to enjoy *more* with him?

She shook her head, but the idea of more swirled around in there anyway, seeming like it could be a possibility. Maybe, though almost definitely not. It was an insane idea. They were too different. She was too damaged. He was a rambling type of man who would never be happy here for long. She knew all the reasons it wouldn't work, but those reasons did nothing to stop the flare of ridiculous hope that flickered to life inside her.

Suddenly anxious to see him again, she rushed through the rest of her morning ablutions. Her stomach tilted and whirled as she imagined what she might say to him or what he might say to her. The kiss didn't have to change anything, but she knew that it had because every time she looked at him now she'd remember that it had happened. She'd remember how good it felt to be the center of his world for those few slow-moving seconds. She'd remember how she'd liked it. She'd know how very much she wanted to repeat it.

She chose to forget the feeling of panic that had bubbled up inside her and made her run from him. It wasn't his fault she was so anxious with men. In fact, she rather thought that had he been her first, the experience would be nothing but delicious fun.

Smoothing a hand over her belly to calm the nerves that had started up at the prospect of seeing him, she opened her door and stepped out into the parlor of her suite. He'd been sitting on the sofa but stood when he saw her. He watched her with an expectant look on his face as if he'd been just as anxious to see her as she'd been to see him. For a moment, they simply stood watching each other.

"Thank you for the rose," she said, breaking the charged silence.

His shoulders seemed to relax as he took a cautious step toward her, followed by another, but his expression was neutral. He wore the same clothes from last night, and she realized how much of his own comfort he was sacrificing to stay with her every night.

"I'm glad you like it." He took in a breath, his jaw tightening. "I wanted to apologize."

Her breath caught in her throat. He'd no doubt seen her fear when she'd run, but she didn't want him to apologize for kissing her. Not when he'd asked her and she'd said yes. Not when she'd kissed him back and for one brief moment it had been perfect. If he apologized, then it could take it all away. It would mean he was sorry that it had happened and she didn't want that. She wanted to be normal. She wasn't, but she *wanted* to be, and she didn't need one more reminder that she wasn't. And she shouldn't expect him to understand that. She knew that she was being incredibly unfair to him, but her hands tightened into tense fists at her sides and she prayed that everything she was feeling wasn't reflected on her face.

Realizing that she was ranting in her own mind, she made her face very still and asked, "For what?"

"Because we argued." He tipped his head down to look at her as he came to a stop in front of her. "And because I called you stubborn."

The relief that swept through her nearly leveled her. She wanted to ask him what he'd thought of the kiss, but she wasn't brave enough to bring it up. She'd faced down men trying to force her to sell her business to them without flinching, but she couldn't bring up a kiss to Zane. Instead, she grinned and said, "It's fine." Making a show of looking around to check that no one overheard, she added in a near whisper, "Besides, I am a *little* stubborn."

The corner of his mouth tipped up in a smirk. His eyes somehow deepened, becoming so dark they were nearly black. When his gaze flicked to her mouth, she knew that he was reliving the kiss. "Then I don't need to apologize for...?" He allowed the question to trail off into the heavy but not uncomfortable silence between them.

She shook her head and that acknowledgment made the fire that had been temporarily banked flare to life. His heated gaze met hers and she swallowed past the need to touch him, to feel his solid presence beneath her palms, to touch her mouth to his and relive the wonderful magic he'd stoked to life within her.

"You ran away." It wasn't a question, but an open statement. He wanted her to fill in the blanks, and she found herself doing that before she'd even realized it.

"I did." She nodded, chewing her bottom lip because she was unreasonably nervous. "I feel quite ashamed about that if you want to know the truth."

"Don't feel ashamed." He reached out as if he might hold her hand, but he stopped at the last second. Instead of holding it, he ran his knuckles over the back of her hand, an almost touch that seemed far more poignant than it should. Tiny prickles of pleasure coursed over her hand, warming her palm.

Her eyes glued to that point of contact, she said, "There are things that have happened..." No, she wouldn't go into the past now. It would only tarnish what she knew would live in her memory as a glorious moment. His eyes were warm and soft when she met his gaze. "Please just know that my running had nothing to do with you. What we did was lovely."

He took in a long steady breath, his beautiful lips parting. A sprinkling of stubble had grown in overnight on his chin and upper lip. "Yes, it was."

The flames from his gaze licked up her neck in a nearly tangible touch. Her skin prickled, tightening with the need for more of his touch. She gave a slow nod, words somehow escaping her beneath the weight of his interest. "Yes, but I'm not certain I'm capable of going further."

"No further." He took a step closer and her heart leaped eagerly into her throat, prompting her to step back. "But more of the same?"

God yes. She wanted to kiss him again. She wanted to spend the entire day kissing him, but she wouldn't. *Couldn't*. Her entire life since her escape had depended on her being calm and in control. It was faintly disturbing how she wanted to give in to him now, which is partially why she made herself abstain. She needed to get her head on straight before trying that kiss again. It wouldn't do for her to go making more of it than she already had.

"I have things to do this morning before we open for the day."

He clenched his jaw and disappointment flashed in

his eyes as understanding dawned across his face. When he would've said something, she shook her head, dropping her hand to her side. "I'm needed to go over the menu for the evening. Why don't you go to your room to freshen up?"

Predictably, he shook his head. "We've been over this, Glory. Where you go, I go."

She couldn't help but roll her eyes at his needless protection. "Fine, but let's get you to your room first so you can freshen up and change your clothes. We're going to have to move you in if this goes on much longer."

Zane followed her silently as she led the way to the second-floor servants' quarters. He'd tossed and turned all night thinking about that kiss and wondering if he'd pushed too hard. He raked a hand through his hair, pondering why he'd even bothered pushing. She was clearly not interested in an affair; he was not interested in a relationship. There was no reason they should continue and yet he found that he couldn't stop pursuing her.

In the early morning hours, once he'd realized that he'd never get back to sleep, he'd turned on the lamp and started sketching a rose. With Glory's rose scent surrounding him, the premonition his aunt had shared with him as a child refused to leave him alone. He'd hoped the sketch would work as a reminder—one more reason he couldn't have Glory—but it had somehow come to represent her as he'd drawn. Each petal had become another layer of the woman who haunted him. Another way for him to caress the curves that had been denied him.

She had very good reason for keeping him away. She

was obviously frightened of men. Last night she'd told him that someone had hurt her—that *a man* had hurt her—and he had a very good hunch that it was the man from whom she'd run. The man who was now hovering at the edges of her hard-won security and threatening it. Zane had never despised anyone he hadn't met as much as he despised *him*. He needed to focus on finding that man and setting things to rights for her, instead of dreaming about her naked.

When he'd been around ten years old, Zane had helped his father track down a man who had been smuggling guns to his mother's people. His mother had been dead for a few years by then and it was from the bullet of a gun that man had smuggled to them. Zane had never met the smuggler, but he'd hated him. At night, he'd lie awake staring up into the stars, planning all the many ways he wanted the man to die. He'd hated him with all the venom in his ten-year-old heart.

This eclipsed that. Even as a child, Zane had known deep down that his hatred had been misplaced. His mother had died because the rifle had malfunctioned. It had been an accident, nothing more sinister, but Zane's life had changed forever. Not only had he lost his mother, but he'd been sent to live with the father he barely knew. All that anger had been funneled into hatred for the man who'd supplied the guns, but the gunrunner hadn't really been responsible for her death.

This man, however, had purposely harmed Glory, and his specter hung over her constantly, promising more harm. Whatever he'd done to her, it had been compounded over the years by the fear of discovery.

The man deserved what was coming to him when Zane caught him.

His gaze narrowed on the woman who walked in front of him. Today she was wearing a stylishly cut, bourbon-colored gown that emphasized her narrow waist and the flare of her hips. Her small frame made her seem tiny and fragile compared to him. He imagined that if he held her waist his fingers would easily meet. What sort of bastard would harm her? The thought of it caused him to clench his jaw so hard that the sound of his teeth gritting caught her attention and she gave him a glance over her shoulder. He vowed to find the sender of that damned letter. And then, whether she agreed or not, he'd find the bastard that had her living in fear.

The hall in the servants' area was neatly kept but without the extravagance of the front of the house. The floors were covered in simple rugs and the walls in pale yellow wallpaper. It was homey and cheerful here, without the heaviness of formality. They turned the corner and a glance confirmed there was already a wait for the bathing chamber shared with the tenants at this end of the hall. Some of the servants lived in town, but many preferred to stay on the property. Zane had been given a small, well-appointed room on this end of the second floor.

Digging the key from his pocket, he stepped around her and unlocked the door to his room. When she would've waited for him in the hall, he grabbed her arm and tugged her inside the room.

"Surely you don't think I'll be accosted in the hall-way?"

Zane didn't know what he thought, but he wasn't taking chances with what he'd learned about her past. The bastard could have paid any one of the servants for information about her. What was to stop him from paying them to bring her to him? His movements were jerky with suppressed anger as he grabbed extra clothes from the bureau opposite the foot of the bed. Anger was his only refuge from the desire pounding through him. If he could think about finding that man, then he wouldn't think of how good she'd feel under him.

"You'll be safer with me," was the only explanation he offered her.

She sighed dramatically, but he wasn't interested in arguing with her again today. "Are you really planning to shadow my every movement?" Her voice came from right over his shoulder so he turned to face her.

"Unless you're with Able, if that's what it takes to keep you safe."

She gave him a quick once-over. "Then we really need to get you some new clothes."

He looked down at his clothes. Thanks to his years with the Reyes Brothers, he was able to afford quality clothing. His breeches and shirts were custom-made, not the ranch hand quality clothing that could be purchased ready-made on the shelves of a general store. "What's wrong with my clothes?"

"Nothing." She gave a shrug of her delicate shoulder. "But we have standards at Victoria House. You need a waistcoat and matching coat at the very least." She looked back down again. "And you need proper shoes, not boots."

"These are quality leather," he said, rolling his foot from one side to the other to show off his boots. They were the single most expensive item of clothing he'd ever purchased, but they'd been worth it. Rain or snow, they'd held up well and kept his feet dry.

"It's not the quality but the style. If you're going to be seen at Victoria House lurking behind me, then you need to be dressed like a gentleman not a…a…"

"A gunslinger?" He smirked, filling in the blank.

"Exactly." The smile she gave him was so bright that he blinked, momentarily stunned by how beautiful she was. He was always aware of her beauty, but sometimes it would catch him by surprise all over again.

"I doubt I'll be here long enough to warrant a brand-new wardrobe."

"Of course not, but I'll set up an appointment with Able's tailor for this afternoon. He must have a suit that he's been working on for Able that he could alter for you."

Zane shook his head. "No, thank you. I don't need another reason to have Able dislike me."

She laughed, seeming strangely lighthearted when compared to how grumpy he felt after his sleepless night. "I'm sure he'll understand, but I agree. He *really* doesn't like you. What did you ever do to anger him anyway?"

After his brief discussion with Able two nights ago, he realized now that it was Able simply being overly protective of her. Even a fool could sense Zane's interest in her, and since Able knew her past, he knew they wouldn't suit. In some ways, Zane had begun to understand Able's position and he could appreciate his protective instinct. After the way she'd run last night, Zane knew that he should listen to him, but he also knew that he couldn't stop this attraction between them. Instead of answering, he shrugged.

"And don't worry about the cost. You're working for me so I'll pay for it."

"I can pay for it." He frowned, disliking the fact that she thought he couldn't. True, he didn't have the sort of wealth that would afford a mansion like this, but his work with the Jamesons had been lucrative. He'd be set up for a few years.

She didn't seem to be paying attention as something about the sparse room had caught her attention. Aside from the bureau and the bed, it held a single bedside table and a washstand. "I just realized how much you must be sacrificing to stay on here for a while longer."

"What do you mean?"

"Only that you must be looking forward to getting home soon. This room leaves a little to be desired when it comes to the comforts of home." She met his gaze again and he realized how little they knew of the other's life.

"I don't…" He cleared his throat, uncertain why the admission was so difficult. "I don't have anywhere to get home to."

"Oh?" Her expression was so stunned he felt the need to explain.

"I was working at the Reyes hacienda when it was burned down. When Cas decided on revenge, well, let's just say I had my own reasons for wanting revenge too."

She glanced at his scar and he gave a curt nod, unwilling to go into the story. He didn't see a reason to bring Christine's name up between them. "We've been sleeping in boardinghouses and under the stars ever since." Not counting the few brief times they'd sought refuge at the Jameson Ranch outside Helena. He had his own room there, but it had never been his home. Hunter had mentioned him staying on there now that their hunt for Derringer was over, and Zane supposed it had been assumed that he would. Though he'd never made the conscious decision.

Now that he thought about it, he wasn't entirely certain where his life would go from here. Before he'd landed at the hacienda, he'd been wandering from job to job. Before that he'd spent a childhood traveling with his father, a trader, from reservation to reservation. Sometimes he'd spend the summer with his mother's people, but he wouldn't go back to the reservation permanently. It didn't feel like home.

"Then you must be looking forward to starting your life again." She gave him a smile that was incredibly understanding, and he didn't quite know what to do with it. The woman had every right to judge him. Here he was, a humble suitor with nothing to offer a woman like her, who had every physical comfort she could want.

"I'm looking forward to not having Derringer at my back."

She grinned at that. "Unfortunately, I know just what you mean." She was teasing him. Her own shadow of menace still lurked and she could tease him with it.

The woman was amazing. They were far more similar than they were different. While he couldn't offer her physical things, he could offer her protection. He could put a stop to that lingering danger hanging over her. "I'll get rid of him, Glory. Tell me who he is and I'll make certain that he never harms you."

"I wouldn't take my danger and make it yours." Her smile fell, but she held his gaze. Her hazel eyes were wide and solemn.

"It's not your choice. I'm staying until this is over." He meant it. In that moment he resolved that this wouldn't stop with finding the sender of the letter. He couldn't leave her until he knew that her past was well and truly in the past.

Shaking her head, she said, "This is only about the letter. I won't have you in danger because of me."

"I do what I want." Maybe this was his new calling. He'd right the injustice done to her, whatever it had been.

The warmth of her palm pressing against his chest surprised him. He found himself wanting to lean into it, craving more of her touch.

"Please don't, Zane. I want you to stay safe."

Her touch didn't surprise him nearly as much as the sound of his name coming from her lips. He immediately wanted to hear it again. He wanted her to whisper it in his ear as he pushed inside her. He clenched his fist against the urge to hold her against him. It wasn't what she needed from him right now. "I know how to take care of myself."

"Glory? You about ready for our meeting?" Able's voice came from the open doorway.

She jerked away as if she'd been unaware of how closely they'd been standing. "I'm ready." She smiled at Able.

Able gave him a surly look, but didn't say anything more. Zane knew that they met every morning to go over plans for the day. Able then stayed with her until his duties called him to man the front door in the early evening.

She surprised Zane again when she turned back to him, this time holding out the key to her apartment. "Feel free to use my bathing chamber. It looks like the one down the hall is a little busy."

He took it. The heat from her body had warmed the metal, so he savored that warmth in his palm. At least he'd earned her trust. "I'll need to interview your staff again today, in case I missed something."

"Between the two of us, we've covered them all," Able said. Disapproval turned the corners of his mouth down.

"I plan to keep talking to them until we have something to go on." He couldn't accept that no one knew anything. Turning his attention back to Glory, he added, "Especially Charlotte. I'd like to start with her."

She nodded in resignation. "I'll let her know to expect you."

Chapter Ten

Not only had Zane spent the previous night thinking about Glory and the future they couldn't have, he'd spent it going over all the information he had about the letter. He replayed every conversation he'd had with her staff the day before, looking for anything he'd missed and coming up with a plan for following up today. Because he wasn't allowed to reveal the reason for his questions—that Glory had received a threatening letter—he'd felt the interrogations had been less than thorough. Despite how Glory felt about revealing that vital piece of information, Zane knew that it was necessary.

Today he needed to focus on Charlotte and what she knew about that letter.

The third floor wasn't a main area where patrons were allowed, but there were enough women coming and going to their rooms at various times during the day that it would be unlikely someone would have the time to pick the lock without being seen. Of course it wasn't impossible for a professional. By all accounts, no one had seen or heard anything coming from her study during the window of time the letter had been left. Also, the study window looked out over the street, so no one could have come in through that way without being seen. Either the person who'd left it had been a clever thief with experience picking locks or Charlotte knew something about it. She was the only person with intimate knowledge of Glory's activity. It was possible she'd somehow gained access to Glory's study.

Locking the door to Glory's suite after his quick bath, he stopped at the entrance to Charlotte's office. He'd heard her arrive a few minutes ago and he paused to study the girl. She couldn't be more than twenty with an almost skittish demeanor. She seemed harmless and loyal to Glory, but he'd learned early on to never underestimate anyone.

Rapping his knuckles against the open door to announce himself, he said, "Mind if I speak with you again?" They'd spoken briefly the day before, but he hadn't had enough information then to ask the right questions.

She glanced at the empty hallway at his back. "All right. I believe Glory has already gone downstairs."

"I know. I wanted to talk to you."

She nodded, straightening some papers on her desk and smoothing a strand of dark hair back in place.

He couldn't understand if her nerves were because of her guilt or because of his size. Both could be likely. To put her at ease, he moved slowly and deliberately, folding himself into the single chair opposite her desk.

"I know we spoke yesterday, but I thought of a few more questions."

She gave him a tremulous smile. "Of course. I'm happy to help in any way I can."

"Good, I know we both want what's best for Glory." He took his time, studying her, not getting to the point, in an effort to see what she'd say in the meantime. Sometimes waiting was all it took to get necessary information.

"Wh-what's happened? I know you said yesterday that you couldn't go into detail, but if something has happened I'd like to know. Is Glory in danger?"

He thought the concern on her face was genuine, so he gave a brief nod, giving her bread crumbs. "We think it's possible."

Visibly upset, she ran her hand down her face. He sat forward, watching her closely. "Have you thought of anything else since yesterday?"

She shook her head. "No, nothing. It's like I told you. That day was like any other. I didn't see anyone up here who didn't belong here. There was nothing out of place in my desk. Nothing was disturbed."

"And no one else has a key to this room?"

"No, no one." She shook her head emphatically, her brow furrowed as if to convince him. "Can you at least tell me why you need to know? What's happened?"

Zane took a breath, knowing that what he was about to do was against Glory's wishes, but it couldn't be helped. He needed to reveal the letter if they wanted answers. "There was a letter—" Before he could say more, her face crumpled.

"Oh, my God!" She dropped her face into her hands and her shoulders started to shake. "I knew it. I knew I should have done it. I thought it was odd, but he seemed harmless enough." Her eyes were reddened and bright with unshed tears when she raised her head. "Please believe me. I didn't know there'd be any harm."

Zane stayed very still, keeping his expression neutral until he could get to the bottom of what she was saying. "What should you have done?"

She shook her head. "I thought he was an admirer. She gets those sometimes. Men like to send her gifts or notes. Usually they deliver them to the house and Able gets them first and sends them up. But this man—God, I don't even know his name—he found me downstairs. I suppose he'd seen me talking to her. I'm not certain why he singled me out. He tried to give me a letter and asked me to deliver it to her in private. I knew that she'd be busy for the rest of the night, and I wouldn't have a chance to see her so I told him no." She covered her face again. "Was the letter important? Should I have taken it?"

Zane believed that she wasn't in league with whoever this stranger was. She probably *had* thought that it was a simple note of admiration that at its worst was attempting to arrange a meeting with Glory. "And this happened the day before yesterday?"

"Yes." She nodded eagerly. "Early evening, I suppose. There was an early dinner rush because Mrs. Roarke was performing later and there were more men in town who'd arrived early for the faro tournament. We were so busy. Please tell me I was correct in not taking it. Was it important? Was it from her family?"

Relatively certain that she was telling the truth, he tried to soothe her concern. "It was important but he found another way to get the letter to her. We're trying to figure out who the man was so we can find him," he said, taking out his sketchbook from his coat pocket to make notes.

She hung her head. "I should've asked him who he was. I should've asked him what he wanted with her."

"It's okay, Charlotte. Let's go over your meeting with him again. Tell me everything, every detail you can remember, even if it seems unimportant."

She nodded her agreement and calmed down enough to tell him what time the man had spoken to her, the details of their brief conversation, and to give a physical description. The description could've matched any number of men in Helena, a town known for attracting all types. He was a slight, well-dressed, well-spoken man probably in his fifties with a receding hairline and gray hair. There was absolutely nothing that would make the man stand out. She was certain that she hadn't seen him before and she wasn't even certain she could recognize him again if she saw him. Their entire encounter had lasted for perhaps two minutes. Not enough time to commit the stranger to memory, but Zane suspected he'd orchestrated it that way so that he'd blend in.

If Charlotte hadn't had a hand in delivering the letter to her mistress's desk, then Zane had to believe the man was a professional. If he was very experienced, he'd have found a way to slip upstairs undetected and pick the lock. All of this combined to convince Zane that the man was true in what he'd written in his letter. He was a private investigator hired by the man in Glory's past to find her. Zane also suspected that it wouldn't stop at the five thousand dollars the man wanted. He'd take the money and report back to the person who'd hired him. The man in Glory's past had probably paid him well to find her. What was to stop the investigator from taking the payment from Glory and turning her information over to him anyway? He'd double his fee with very little effort on his part.

Cold certainty washed over Zane. This wouldn't end until the man from her past was found.

"I swear to you that I had no idea what was in the letter." Charlotte had finished up recounting the meeting. "I don't even know who he is." She paused, winding and unwinding a length of her hair around her index finger in a nervous gesture that made her seem very young. "You believe me, don't you?"

"I believe you."

Relief made her shoulders visibly sag as some of the tension drained from her body, but she was still worried. Her brow furrowed again as she asked, "What was in the letter? Is Glory in trouble? Is she in danger?"

Zane hesitated, unwilling to reveal too much. Rumors in this place could spread like wildfire and get out of control. On the other hand, Glory was in danger and he needed everyone to be on the lookout for a possible threat. He decided to stick as close to the truth as possible. "Can I trust you?"

She nodded. "Yes, I promise nothing leaves this room."

"She's not in danger yet. It's possible that someone from her past might be looking for her. I need you to keep everything we've said in this room secret, but if you hear of someone looking for her, let me know immediately."

"Of course. I swear to you I won't say a word about this to anyone."

The girl seemed sincere, but even if that much got out into the rest of the house, it wouldn't be so bad. They could use the extra eyes and ears, and it was hardly a secret that everyone here seemed to be hiding from something.

"Thanks for your time." He stood, intending to make his way downstairs. Glory had probably finished up her meeting with Able. Zane would need to stay with her while Able readied himself for the evening's work.

"Glory said for you to meet her and Able at Sainsbury's after our meeting. I think she wants to buy you a suit." She gave him a shy smile. "I guess you'll be working here for a while."

He'd been afraid that Glory had been serious about the new clothes. He didn't mind protecting her. He *wanted* to protect her. But he didn't like the idea of her dressing him up.

"There you are. I was beginning to wonder if you'd show." Glory couldn't help the way the corners of her lips tugged upward the moment Zane stepped into J. Sainsbury's shop. He was so broad and tall that he seemed to take up the whole storefront. His gaze slid over the store as if he was expecting something to attack from one of the shelves. She had to bite the inside of her lip to keep from laughing.

One side of the narrow shop was lined with shelves full of ready-made shirts and pants, with a couple of wooden mannequins dressed in coats and waistcoats to display Mr. Sainsbury's skill. The other side displayed bolts of fabrics in various textures and colors. Broadcloth in shades of blue, gray and black, soft colored linens and lawn, somber seersucker, along with silks in every color of the rainbow. Even some plaids for trousers.

"Don't worry, we can avoid the plaid if you prefer," she said.

His narrowed gaze finally landed on her as he took off his hat, and ran his palm over his head as if he were smoothing his hair down. She smothered another laugh at how discontented he seemed. She'd seen him backing up Hunter when they'd forced their way into Victoria House a couple of months ago looking for Emmy, their runaway hostage; she'd seen him roughing up that man who'd been stalking Castillo; she'd seen him when he'd carried his half-dead friend in when Cas had been shot. He'd handled that all with confidence and calmness. She'd never once seen him look as uncomfortable as he looked now.

"Oh, we'll avoid the plaid." One of the mannequins had on a deep red silk waistcoat shot through with black thread. It was a showpiece to draw attention from window-shoppers on the street. Not that Sainsbury needed the business. It had taken begging on her part and a 20 percent premium to get him to agree to see them today because he was overbooked. Every man in town who cared about his standing in Helena was on the wait list to have a Sainsbury suit.

"We'll avoid red silk too," said Zane, eyeing the mannequin with a look she could only equate to suspicion.

She couldn't help but giggle. "Consider it done."

"Ah, Mr. Pierce." Sainsbury's assistant hurried in through the curtains that separated the fitting areas in the back of the store from the main room. Pins of various sizes stuck out of a gingham cloth swung over his shoulder and a length of measuring tape hung down from his neck. "We've been waiting for you." The older man was slight in build, barely taller than Glory in her low-heeled shoes. Zane towered over them both. "Come on to the back and we'll take your measurements."

Zane followed, holding the curtain open for her so that she could precede him to the back. Zane had to duck to walk through the curtained archway.

"Remove your coat and boots." The man led them past several curtained alcoves and pointed to a coatrack in the corner. "Stand on the dais and I'll be with you shortly." After giving the instruction he disappeared into another room where the clothing was stored.

Zane hung up his coat, and put his gun belt on the peg beside it, then he leaned down to unlace his boots before kicking them off. As he took his place on the dais, Glory allowed herself a moment to look at his clothes. The length of his pants was perfect, and they pulled in just tight enough at the waist. She couldn't quite pull her eyes from the way the fabric clung to the muscles underneath, cupping his form perfectly. The fabric didn't sag there like it did for some men, and while she was certain it was due in large part to the fact that he was fitter than most men, she could also recognize the work of a skilled tailor when she saw it. He wasn't the usual gunman who traveled through town looking for work. Apparently the outlaw business paid well.

As she settled herself in a chair, she studied him a little longer than was strictly necessary. She didn't want to imagine it, but she couldn't stop thinking of what he might look like beneath his clothes. The very notion of that was so foreign to her that she probably let it go too far before stopping herself. He'd be wide and broad, his muscles defined. Would his chest be as bronze as his forearms? She shifted, realizing it was stifling in the small space. The silk of her gown seemed to be sticking to her skin so she tugged at the neckline.

"I hope you haven't been waiting long." His voice made her look away, catching his knowing gaze in the mirror. He didn't appear upset that she'd been looking him over. He even seemed to be holding back a smile.

She shook her head and tried to appear as if she hadn't been gawking at him. Gesturing to him, she said, "You've clearly seen a tailor before. Why do you seem so uncomfortable?"

"Can't get accustomed to strangers making my clothes."

She stared at him for a moment in silence, unable to believe how her heart was beginning to pound. She wanted to know what he meant. What had his life been like up until now? What would it be like after he left? Before she could stop herself, she heard herself asking, "What do you mean? Did someone you know make those?" She gestured to what he was wearing.

He took in a breath through his nose and she could almost see him turning over the question in his mind. "No, these were made in Denver. The Jamesons and I spent a winter there a couple of years back." He paused, making her think that's all he planned to tell her. Her heart sank a little, but perked back up when he continued. "I spent most of my childhood with my mother's people. We didn't have tailors or seamstresses. People we love make our clothes. It still seems odd the way you do it here. Impersonal and detached."

She'd never thought of it that way. "I suppose you're right. When I was a child, my mother made all of our clothes, though most of mine were altered versions of my older sister's."

"You had an older sister. Any brothers?"

"Why do I feel like you're always trying to get information out of me?" She wasn't really annoyed. Mainly she was covering because of how much she wanted to tell him. So much of her life had been spent not talking about her past, but talking to him was easy. She *wanted* to tell him things, to make a connection with him, because he might be someone who could understand. It was probably silly to think so, and she didn't really understand why she did.

Instead of answering her question, he offered up some information of his own. "I had two older sisters."

"Had?" An unexpected pain tugged at her heart.

He shrugged. "I think they're still living. We had the same mother, but my father was white. A trader who traveled through our village from time to time. After my mother died, I went to live with him and we lost touch. I heard they married and moved north to Canada years ago when the tribe was moved to a reservation in Oklahoma."

"I'm sorry."

"For what?" He turned to look at her fully.

The response had been automatic. What was she sorry for? Him losing touch with his sisters? His mother's death? "For the pain on your face when you told me that."

His expression didn't change but something in his eyes did. She'd surprised him. She didn't know why but that made her happy. Able's deep voice rumbled out from one of the curtained alcoves where he was being fitted by Sainsbury himself. Sainsbury's assistant came bustling in a moment later, effectively breaking up whatever moment had been happening between them.

"You're in luck. We have a shirt that we can alter to fit." The man came to a stop next to the dais and set a few waistcoats in various shades of gray and black on a rack next to it. "Take off your shirt, Mr. Pierce, so that I can note the adjustments we need to make."

Zane's hands went to the buttons of his shirt, and Glory couldn't keep her eyes from the bronze skin he revealed in the mirror as he unbuttoned each one. She nearly leaned forward until she caught herself when he revealed the indentation between the well-formed muscles of his chest. The line went all the way down to his stomach, where she could just make out ridges of muscle. His thick fingers pulled the tail of his shirt from his breeches, and she silently gaped at the bare expanse of skin revealed to her.

Her fingers curled into the arms of her chair and her heart threatened to pound out of her chest. It wasn't from fear this time. No one could harm her, and this was in no way sexual. Maybe that was the very reason she actually experienced arousal instead of apprehension. Well, that, coupled with the memory of that kiss and being pressed against him. He was shrugging out of the garment before she came to her senses enough to realize that she had no business watching such an intimate scene.

"I—I'm sorry. I should leave you to your privacy."

She pushed out of the chair, but his voice froze her in place. "Stay."

That one word filled the room, echoing in her mind. Her gaze found his in the mirror again, but she couldn't tell what he meant by that word. Nevertheless, she found herself sinking back into the soft cushion of the chair. Only when she was settled, did he continue. One shoulder, hardened and sculpted with muscle, shrugged out of the shirt, followed by the second. His muscles rippled and bunched under his smooth skin as he moved. Scars crisscrossed his right shoulder in a pattern of pink and white. She couldn't tell what had made them, but the wounds must have been painful. Her heart ached that he'd had to endure whatever it was that had happened. They were too wide to be healed cuts from a knife, but they had a similar slashing pattern. There were more scars along his rib cage, an accumulation of nicks and cuts from his rough lifestyle, she supposed.

He paused with the shirt drooped at his waist as he unfastened it at his wrists before handing the shirt off to the assistant. As the man draped it over the rack, Zane stood tall in front of her. His back and chest were so defined she imagined that an artist would have an easy time sculpting him from stone. Her gaze transferred to the mirror so that she could see his front. One of the scars from his shoulder blade curled around his shoulder. Closing her hands into fists, she imagined what it would feel like to run her palms over him. A light patch of dark hair started at his lower belly, and she imagined it abrading her skin as she traced it. It led downward, disappearing into his pants.

The assistant came back over, breaking her line of sight. Thankfully. She hadn't realized she was basically panting and took a moment to collect herself as he helped Zane into the shirt. He pinned and prodded, adjusting the fabric, before holding up a selection of waistcoats.

"Whichever one she prefers," she heard Zane say a moment before the assistant brought the samples over for her.

She managed to get herself together enough to select the charcoal silk shot through with dark gray piping. She was starting to think that she might be able to make it through the rest of the fitting as Zane shrugged into the waistcoat. He turned to face her, holding out his arms so that she could get a good look.

"What do you think?" he asked.

"It'll do."

He smirked, his eyes catching hers and holding on. Apparently it was no secret how he affected her. However, she actually managed to smile back. This flirting between them was starting to be fun. She knew now— after that kiss—that he wouldn't push it too far, and as a result, she could feel herself relaxing around him. Maybe they had no future, but they could have flirting.

"Happy to meet your high standards, pretty lady."

She laughed. He did look good. Better than good. Sainsbury's assistant had pinned in the waist, showing off Zane's powerful but lean frame. God, she'd have to keep some of her more forward ladies off him when he showed up tonight like that. They all knew the rule against liaisons among staff, but it might be worth repeating it before the night was over.

"I think we may have less luck with the pants, but we'll see what we can do." The assistant's voice interrupted her musing as he picked up a stack of breeches and held one up to Zane's long legs. "Why don't you take those off and try this pair? I'll see what I can do to alter them."

The second Zane's hands made to go for the fastening on his pants, she fled the room. There was no way she could make it through seeing *that* part of him. As she came to a stop at the counter in the front room, she fanned herself to calm down, but she couldn't wipe the smile from her face. She kept imagining what was hidden in those breeches and giggling like a schoolgirl.

It felt good to giggle. It had been years since she

could remember laughing so much in the span of an hour, and never had it been over a man. At fourteen she'd been robbed of her adolescence, and couldn't ever remember feeling such ridiculous infatuation over a man. Her hand went to her stomach, marveling at the butterflies that fluttered around as she tried to imagine Zane naked.

She wondered if this is what her sister had felt when she'd gone all soft and weak every time the boy who brought them fish came to the yard. She'd had a sweet spot for him, always making sure that she was on the porch when he came by. Only this was no mere fish boy. Zane was a man, fully formed and powerful. A ripple of pleasure coursed through her belly. It was a foolish feeling and she knew it, but she allowed herself to indulge in the novelty for a little longer. After all, he'd be gone soon and she'd only have these moments to remember.

"Hello, Miss Winters. I've never seen you looking so radiant."

Glory gasped as she turned toward the sound of the low, slightly menacing voice to see a man standing in the shadows.

Chapter Eleven

William Harvey stood inside the shop's doorway. If the little bell on the front door had rung when he'd entered, Glory had been too preoccupied to notice. She couldn't quite understand why her heart was racing now. He'd alarmed her, but it was only Harvey, not someone worse. Not *him*.

Her eyes drifted closed in relief. Clearly she was letting this mysterious letter get the better of her. Or maybe Zane's overzealous vigilance was getting to her. He was making her overly suspicious that every shadowed figure that moved was her past coming to get her.

"I've startled you." Harvey looked pointedly at the hand covering her heart before looking up at her face. She could've sworn his gaze left a layer of grime as it roved over her bosom on the way up.

"I didn't hear you come in." She held her hands clasped before her in an attempt to appear calm.

"I'm surprised to see you here too, my dear. I didn't realize you offered tailor services to your customers."

Harvey had a way of always trying to remind her of

her place in the world. She tightened her mouth in annoyance, but tried not to show any emotion. Emotion was weakness to men like him. To all men really. She hadn't met one who hadn't tried to use it against her.

"I'm here with Able," she corrected him.

"Ah." He walked farther into the room, closer to her. He wasn't nearly as large as Zane, but he had a way of making the narrow space feel even smaller. "I wasn't aware that Sainsbury saw men like him."

"What do you mean?" She stiffened her spine, prepared to verbally flay him. Able was closer to her than her own brother ever had been. When her brother had turned his back to her pleas for help, Able had taken her far away from South Carolina.

"He's the help." Harvey shrugged.

"We're in Helena, Mr. Harvey. There is no 'help' here. Only those who haven't made their fortunes yet. As I recall, your own father lived in the work camp when he arrived here."

He grinned, unperturbed by her bringing up his own humble roots. "Touché, Miss Winters." He shuffled a little closer, coming to a stop a mere foot away from her. "I always have liked your spirit. Have you given any further thought to my proposition?"

She stiffened when he ran the fingertip of his index finger up her arm. In the summer heat of the small shop, she'd taken off her thin pelisse and gloves soon after arriving. She found herself missing the layers of cloth that would separate his skin from hers. "Your proposition?" She shifted backward on her heels, trying to stall him. There was no way in hell she planned to take their friendship further, but she preferred not to completely alienate a man who could be very powerful, very soon. If he were elected, he could wield the power to shut her down.

"Come now, Miss Winters, playing coy doesn't become you." His prominent brow furrowed and he leaned forward. "You know what I want."

She could smell the tobacco on his breath, and her stomach roiled in protest as the scent brought back memories she'd rather see dead and buried. She was starting to feel restrained even though he hadn't touched her again and she could feel the solid presence of the velvet curtains behind her. All she had to do was run through them. The thought calmed her pulse a little. "I think you're getting a little ahead of yourself. The vote doesn't take place for months. You're a strong contender, but the ballots haven't been counted."

He held the grin, scraping his teeth along his bottom lip as he eyed the cleavage exposed by her gown. It was a fairly modest frock, more for shopping and going out about town than for flirting in the lounges of Victoria House. Nevertheless, his eyes were fastened to the slight mound of her breasts.

"The vote may not be official until the autumn but I assure you the ballots have been counted and I've come out on top."

Dammit. Had he paid someone off or was he simply feeding her talk in the hopes that she'd believe him?

"There's a council meeting at the end of the week. I've seen the agenda and Victoria House is on it. Should

I put in a good word for you, Glory, or would you rather I side with the good people of Helena?"

She opened her mouth to tell him to go to hell, but she couldn't force the words out past the lump in her throat. She employed many people, and most of those were women with nowhere else to go. That wasn't even counting the women who had passed through the boardinghouse. How many women were on their way to the house even now from some remote part of the territory? Every other week it seemed like another one showed up needing help.

"I would be grateful if you'd put in a good word." She kept her voice low and measured, hoping he didn't hear the disdain she felt for him.

He inclined his head. "I'm certain you would, but I can't do something for nothing. Can't have people around here thinking I'm weak once I'm an elected official." She gasped when his fingertip came back, only this time it traced the edges of her bodice instead of her arm.

Despite her best intentions, she reacted on instinct and slapped his hand away. She knew from hard-learned experience that fighting back was never the way to go in situations like these. She was inevitably smaller than her tormentor. A slap might work on normal men, but not men like Harvey. Not men like *him*. They both thrived on terrifying those who were smaller than they were.

Harvey reacted true to form. He grabbed her arms and pulled her against him, backing her up so that her back pressed against the bolts of fabric lining the wall, giving her no quarter and no way to move away from him. Shoving his face into her face, he said, "That was stupid."

She heard Harvey. She smelled the cigars on his breath. In her mind, she saw *him*, and she was back in that bedchamber from so many years ago. Hard hands pushed and pulled, positioning her how they wanted. Holding her down when all she wanted was to leave that place forever. Nausea rolled in her stomach as he laughed, his breath in her face, his body over hers.

A wet mouth touched her neck and she couldn't decide if it was Harvey or *him*, if it was real or imagined. She only knew that she needed to get away. She couldn't breathe and dark spots flashed behind her eyes as gray played at the edges of her vision.

Somewhere through her panic, she heard the most wonderful sound in the world. The metallic click of the hammer being pulled back on a revolver.

"Get your goddamn hands off her."

Zane stared at the place where his gun pressed into Harvey's temple. Part of him wanted Harvey to refuse and give him a reason to pull the trigger. The other part of him thought he should've already pulled the trigger. As the two sides fought it out, Harvey relented. He dropped his hand from Glory's breast, and Zane clenched his jaw at the sight of the rumpled fabric. The son of a bitch had no right to touch her.

When he'd stepped away from her completely, Zane put himself between the two of them but he didn't holster his gun.

"How do you know she didn't want it?" Harvey smirked.

For one split second Zane realized the bastard was right. He'd walked in from the back room because he'd heard muffled voices, and he'd wanted to make sure Glory was safe. When he'd seen Harvey crowding her against the wall, all he'd seen was a man's hands on her. He hadn't even bothered to notice who the man was. At the time he'd reacted on instinct, wanting to pull the ass off of her. Zane had to admit that he'd have reacted that way no matter who the man was who'd touched her. It had been instinct because he couldn't tolerate the thought of another man touching her. Somehow in this mess, he'd started to think of Glory as his when he knew he had no right to think that. She belonged to no man and had made that clear to him.

Zane's hand clenched tighter around the grip, aching to grab Harvey and pound him for daring to touch her. None of that really mattered right now. Whether she'd wanted it or not, she clearly didn't now because she wasn't intervening on Harvey's behalf.

"No one wants you here, Harvey. Go home."

"I have an appointment." Harvey pulled himself up to his full height.

"Get the hell out of here." Zane bit out each word slowly and succinctly so there'd be no mistaking what he said. "She wants nothing to do with you. If you ever touch her again, I'll kill you. If you ever come to Victoria House again, I'll kill you."

"That's big talk for some—"

"Go!" Glory surprised them both by interrupting

him. Zane glanced over his shoulder to see her step around him, her finger pointed toward the door. "Zane works for me now."

Harvey looked between the two of them as if trying to figure out if she was Zane's employer or lover. Zane had to resist the urge to growl.

"That explains the suit," Harvey said, taking in the clothes Zane wore.

Out of patience, Zane stepped forward, spurring Harvey into action toward the door. "You're going to regret you made an enemy of me. Both of you." With those words Harvey slammed the door behind him.

Zane holstered his gun and let out the breath he'd been holding, relieved that the violence hadn't escalated. Harvey was wealthy, but he was small potatoes compared to the clout the Jamesons held in this town. No matter what Harvey tried, Zane was confident that his own association with the Jameson name would help him.

Glory had wilted at his side. She was shaking, her eyes closed as she breathed in and out as if that simple act was taking all of her concentration. He shouldn't have let her out of his sight. It had been a bad idea to flirt with her in the dressing room, but she'd been so damn adorable with her flushed cheeks that he hadn't been able to stop. He'd been glad when she'd run out of there because it was going to be damn hard to change his pants with an erection and that's exactly what would've happened had she stayed a second longer. But had he kept his head and not flirted, she'd have had no reason to go flying out of the room and into the front of the shop. He'd put her at risk.

What if he hadn't come to check on her? How far would Harvey have gone?

"You okay, Glory?"

The question only seemed to make her trembling worse. He stood there feeling as inept as a fawn on an icy lake. One wrong move could send him crashing to the ground, but he couldn't *not* move. He couldn't not do anything. Every fiber of his being was telling him to pull her against him, but he knew she didn't want that from him. She'd made it clear how she valued her independence.

A muffled sob broke out of her, causing her shoulders to shake. Aw, hell. As gently as if she were made of the thinnest glass and could break into a million pieces if handled the wrong way, he put his arms around her. Much to his surprise, she didn't resist. In fact, he'd only barely moved toward her before she threw herself against his chest. It was the strangest feeling in the world. Strange, but good.

He tightened his arms around her, feeling her heart beat against him, breathing in her heady rose scent. She felt warm and solid in his arms, not as fragile as he'd first imagined. And to his surprise, that warm, solid strength somehow worked its way inside him, settling somewhere deep in his chest, making it hard to breath for a minute. When he could finally take a deep breath, he filled his lungs with Glory. She was all around him.

"Thank you," she whispered.

He nodded, unable to speak past the lump in his throat.

Able pushed his way through the velvet curtains, still

tugging his clothes into place from his fitting, probably summoned by Zane's and Harvey's angry voices. He paused abruptly when he saw them. His dark gaze going from Zane to Glory and back again.

"It was Harvey, but he's gone now," Zane said. The fact that his voice was so low and steady surprised him.

The large man took a breath and nodded. His gaze lingered on Glory for a minute before something seemed to change on his face. Anger gave way to some sort of acceptance and he met Zane's gaze again. With a nod, he ducked back into the dressing area. As bizarre as it sounded, Zane felt as if he'd given them his blessing.

Zane tightened his grip on Glory, unwilling to let her go just yet. He knew something had changed between them. Whether they liked it or not, they seemed to be on a runaway train headed for whatever was waiting for them. Only he didn't know what that was.

"I want to go home." Her small hand rested on his chest but not in a manner that was meant to push him away. It simply rested there above his heart. The heat of all five of her fingers and palm warmed his skin through the shirt and waistcoat he wore. His heart pounded beneath them.

"Give me a minute to change clothes, and I'll take you."

She nodded, but didn't step back right away. His hands clung to her small waist, reluctant to let her go. Her eyes were soft and open when they met his. The vivid green swirled around the brown, giving them depth. She took in a breath and her bottom lip trembled slightly. He wanted to touch it with his own, to kiss her and tell her that he'd make everything better. But he knew it was a lie. At best he'd make things manageable for her. He'd find the phantom from her past and put him to rest once and for all, but then he'd leave her.

Chapter Twelve

The inevitable sadness of leaving her colored Zane's every thought of Glory. It was like the sweetness of going home to his mother's people. Seeing their faces brought back so many memories of his childhood that the initial arrival felt good. It made him feel warm and whole for a time, but the feeling didn't last. Deep down he knew he didn't belong there and soon those feelings overshadowed the good ones. Then he'd leave.

Looking at Glory and holding her was like that. The initial feeling was amazing, but he knew it'd change eventually. He didn't belong in her world any more than she belonged in his. His scar tingled with the reminder of what had happened last time he'd forgotten that.

He dropped his hands from her waist and forced himself to step back. She was wearing one of those decorative hats ladies sometimes wore. The kind that was somehow attached to the hair piled high on her head with a little black veil that didn't even come down enough to cover her forehead. It sat more slanted than usual, so he reached out and pushed it back into place.

He recognized it as an excuse to touch her again, but didn't check the impulse. Life was too short not to do the things that felt good; the trick was to keep his heart out of it. He had a feeling it was going to be damned tough to do with her.

"Oh." She dipped her head and reached up, pulling at pins and rearranging them to settle her hat. When she walked over to the mirror in the corner, he slipped into the back room to quickly change back into his own clothes.

She was ready to go when he returned to the front of the shop, and she looked as poised and confident as she ever had, with her chin titled the slightest bit upward and a smile on her face as she bid goodbye to the assistant and called out to Sainsbury, who was still hidden in one of the alcoves in back.

"They'll have your suit altered and sent over by evening. I'd appreciate it if you'd wear it tonight when you join us downstairs." They stepped out onto the boardwalk and she hailed her carriage, which was tucked inside an alley off the larger street. This part of Helena was just off the main street, Last Chance Gulch. It was more fashionable here and had progressed from the years of mining to a more cosmopolitan atmosphere. She looked like she belonged. Hell, she could walk down the Champs-Elysées in Paris and fit right in.

"What?" She'd caught him staring and looked up at him, a slight smile on her face.

"I've never had anyone buy me a suit before."

She gave a soft laugh. "No? Then maybe you need to find better friends."

He grinned at her, enjoying the teasing. "Is that what we are? Friends?"

She nodded. "I'd like to think so."

"Then why don't you call me Zane and stop it with the formal Mr. Pierce?" He knew he had her when her face blanked. She tugged on her bottom lip with her perfect white teeth and dipped her head. When she looked back up a moment later, she was smiling again.

"Well played, Mr....Zane." Pink colored her cheeks. It was a good color on her.

His smile widened, and he realized that he'd smiled more in the past couple of days with her than he had in the whole of the past two years. Somehow over the course of the afternoon they'd broken down a wall that had been between them. Now, here they stood on the boardwalk, grinning at each other like a couple of love struck idiots.

The thought sobered him. Not love struck. They were simply a couple of people who'd only just begun to realize how very much they liked each other. *Liked*, not loved. It was an important distinction. He immediately changed the subject. "Should we wait for Able?"

Her carriage rolled to a stop in front of them, and the driver jumped down to open the door. It was by far one of the fancier contraptions on the street. Since Helena was made up of all types of people, the streets were full of open wagons, hansom cabs and simple buckboards. Hers was one of the few carriages with glass windows and the plush, dark blue interior he saw when the driver opened the door.

"He has a few errands to run. I'll send the carriage

back around for him once we arrive home," she said over her shoulder as she allowed the driver to help her in.

The man gave Zane a quick once-over. Like most men in town, the driver was a little grizzled and without the polish of a proper manservant like the ones he'd seen on his one trip back East. He was probably a workman who'd come too late to see any real luck in the mines, and had found work at the brothel. He didn't say a word as he waited for Zane to enter and then closed the door behind him.

"What do you know about the driver?" he asked in a low voice when he'd settled in the seat across from her. The carriage swayed a little when the driver pulled himself up into his seat in the front.

"Harold?" She laughed. "You really do see danger in everything don't you?"

He shrugged. "I like to be thorough."

"Harold's an old man who came out here to live with his adult daughter and her new husband. He buried them both a few years ago when the influenza swept through town. He keeps the carriage in good order and takes care of the horses."

"You don't think he'd enjoy a few thousand dollars?"

"He might." She gave an elegant shrug of her shoulder. Something about the gesture managed to be completely feminine, and completely Glory. He'd miss it when he was gone. "But he wouldn't know anything more about me than anyone else does."

Zane frowned, acknowledging that she was right. Anyone could be a suspect with the amount of clues revealed in that letter. The only way to find the person was by narrowing down the timeline. He sighed as he sat back, enjoying the soft upholstered bench. He'd never ridden in a carriage so nice. Never ridden in a carriage at all aside from the cab he and Cas had hired to convey them from the train station to their hotel in Boston. Even when he'd stayed with the Jamesons out at the ranch, Zane hadn't taken the opportunity to ride their carriage into town, always preferring his horse instead. A man could get used to this, he decided as he stretched his legs out in front of him.

She sat across from him but over to the side and smiled as she arranged her skirts out of his way. "You've never ridden in a carriage like this before?"

He shrugged. "I've never ridden in a carriage."

She tried, but she couldn't quite hide her surprise and only just managed to stop herself from gaping. "Surely you jest."

Shaking his head, he said, "No. Never had any carriages on the reservation. We used packhorses and the occasional buckboard."

"And after you left?"

"I travel light." He grinned.

She nodded her understanding, but he was sure she didn't. A woman like her had to be accustomed to just about any luxury she could want. She had running water, electric lights, an actual telephone. All of them more things that separated them. He scraped his hand over the back of his neck, messaging the tension there. He was making himself dizzy with his back and forth over her.

He changed the subject instead of thinking about it. "Do I need to do something about Harvey? What does he want anyway?"

She gave a bitter laugh and stared out the window. "The same thing they all want. Power and money. He thinks he can scare me into giving him control of Victoria House."

He thought she gave herself too little credit. Even without Victoria House she was prize enough for many men, especially men like Harvey who needed trophies and accolades to guard against his insecurity. "You're not worried about him then."

She shook her head. "No, not really. I'm more concerned about the upcoming vote and what it'll mean for Victoria House. It's no secret that Helena is becoming more civilized. There's less tolerance of saloons and other houses of vice. I very much doubt Harvey will have the means to save it though."

"What do you plan to do? Would you close?"

"Able and I have taken steps over the years to guard against this. We've expanded the dining and gambling business to help stay afloat once the inevitable happens. Though I can't say it won't hurt if we have to close the brothel. The brothel funds 100 percent of the boardinghouse and relocation expenses of the women and children we help."

He frowned as he wondered what changes the next year would bring for her and Able. Would she be able to dodge her past without the safety of Victoria House to protect her? She'd created her own little kingdom there.

"I haven't had a chance to tell you about my conversation with Charlotte this morning."

"Oh?" A worried crease appeared between her eyes and her hands tightened to fists in her lap as if she were bracing herself for whatever he had to say.

"She claims to have had a conversation with a man who asked her to deliver a letter to you." He quickly relayed the story of Charlotte talking to the man downstairs. "She thought it was a love note."

Glory frowned as she studied the beaded reticule in her lap, anxiously plucking at a tassel. "You believe her?"

"I do. Does the timeline sound right to you?"

After a moment she nodded. "We were busy that night. You remember."

He inclined his head and breathed a sigh of relief that the story seemed to check out. It would be better for Glory if the conspirator were a stranger and not in any way associated with someone she knew. It'd be painful otherwise. "Do you believe Charlotte?"

She nodded again. "Yes. I only wish I remember seeing the man she described. I don't remember talking to him. Does she know who the man was? Did she get a name?"

He told her the description of the man, but he'd come directly from his talk with Charlotte so hadn't been able to search. "I'll make a sketch tonight with Charlotte's help and go to the hotels. Maybe someone will remember him."

"Let's start with The Baroness. Martin Hines, he's the manager there. He runs that place with an iron fist.

Show him the drawing and he can tell you if the man stayed there. I'll ring him when we get home and he'll come right over. How long do you think you'll need for the drawing?"

Zane tried not to show it, but a flare of jealousy sprang to life inside him at how casually she spoke of Hines and how confident she was that he'd do her bidding. Zane saw her every night downstairs at Victoria House charming the customers. She knew Sainsbury, Harvey and probably every man they drove past. It was her job, and the jealousy wasn't fair but it was there nonetheless. "That's a good plan. Shouldn't take me longer than an hour, depending on how much Charlotte remembers." Which didn't seem like much from what she'd told him earlier.

His words must have come out stiffly because Glory frowned, cocking her head to the side as if she was trying to figure him out. Then she gave him a knowing smile. "My employees are very conscientious."

He frowned, wondering what the hell that had to do with their conversation.

"Martin Hines. He's an employee. That's why he'll come right over when I ring him."

He heard what she was saying but he didn't know how her words fit in their conversation. How was Martin Hines of The Baroness Hotel her employee?

"I *own* The Baroness, Zane," she said, putting him out of his misery.

He couldn't react, he could only stare at the woman across from him. She'd amazed him yet again.

She shrugged in response to his unspoken question. "I bought it early last year when the talk of statehood picked up. I created a company with which to purchase it, that's why it's not common knowledge that I'm the owner. Seemed to be a good investment at the time."

"You *own* The Baroness?" He couldn't seem to wrap his mind around it. It was one of the best hotels in town. In a town filled with mining riches, that was saying something.

"And a few buildings over on State and over on Sixth. I lease them out." She sighed. "So you see, losing Victoria House will hurt if it comes to it, but I'll hardly be destitute. My main concern is for all those who depend on the House. I'm afraid I won't be able to keep up the boardinghouse without it. With my funds tied up in real estate, they're not very liquid."

By all accounts she'd arrived here with nothing. In scarcely more than a decade she'd been able to do what so many others wouldn't have been able to accomplish. "You really are something."

She blushed again and shrugged. "You say that, but you also saw what happened back there with Harvey."

"I did. I saw how brave you were."

"Not brave. I couldn't move. God knows what would've happened had you not been there. I couldn't have stopped him." She gave a bitter shake of her head and looked out the window.

He moved quickly before he could think better of it and sat on the seat beside her. "Glory, I can't pretend to know what you've been through. Since you won't tell me I can only guess and I pray that my guesses are a hundred times worse than reality. But on the off chance that they're not…" He tipped her chin up so that she'd look at him. He waited for her eyes to meet his, a thrill of pleasure tingling down his spine at the heady contact. "You're the bravest person I've ever met, and what you've been able to do with your life… I can hardly fathom it. Even queens need knights to protect them sometimes."

Her full bottom lip trembled before curving into a soft smile. "Is that you…you're my knight?"

He stared at her mouth, wanting to take it beneath his. Needing to dip his tongue into her heat and taste her again. The two sides of him were at war again with one side urging him to indulge while he could and the other warning him away from the horrible pain he'd experienced with Christine. She wasn't Christine. She knew her own mind and wouldn't let her family stand in the way. But the truth was that nothing good ever lasted, he'd learned that lesson long ago.

She was Glory, and for the moment that lesson didn't matter. She was good and kind and fiery. She was everything. Her fingers clutched the fabric of his shirt, drawing him closer. He leaned down, her breath was hot and sweet on his lips. The tiny gasp she made curled down into his belly, tightening and pulling him even closer to her. The second his lips touched hers the carriage came to a jarring halt. The heavy tread of boots on the cobblestones outside the carriage had them jerking apart just as the door opened. Victoria House loomed above them.

Her eyes were wide in shock but he couldn't tell if

it was discomfort that he'd tried to kiss her or surprise that they'd nearly been caught. Whichever it was, he allowed her to flee and sat in the carriage for a moment, trying to catch his breath.

Chapter Thirteen

Glory sat at the bar in the large dining room waiting for Sally to join her for a chat before the evening rush began. It was very early in the evening yet and other than a few men playing cards in one of the gaming rooms and a private meeting in one of the salons, the house was quiet. Sally was set to perform again later tonight, so Glory expected the rush to come closer to the performance time. Since many men had undoubtedly left town after the faro tournament the day before, it'd likely be a less hectic night.

For that, she was grateful. Gone were the days she and Able were anxious about a few slow nights. Madam Marin had left them with some debt and had cleaned out the bank account before leaving for her retirement in San Francisco. That first year had been agonizing and full of constant worry about paying back the loan while keeping the staff in food and clothing. Glory was grateful they'd made it through.

Now she could sit in peace and chat with an old friend. It really was the little things in life for which she'd learned to be grateful. Sally planned to leave in the morning and Glory felt as if she'd barely been able to see her friend with the shadow of uncertainty looming over her this week. Taking a deep breath, Glory resolved not to think of that letter for the next few minutes. Instead she closed her eyes and listened to the peaceful notes of the piano coming from the ballroom. Janie sometimes liked to practice in the early evenings before they got too busy.

"He's rather partial to you, you know."

Glory turned from her seat at the bar to see Sally walking across the room toward her. If the woman had spoken any louder, the entire room would've heard her. The entire room consisting of Penelope behind the bar, Zane sketching as he spoke to Charlotte near the cold fireplace and a customer eating a solitary meal across the room. He glanced up at Sally but went back to eating and reading the book opened on the table next to his plate. Penelope gave Glory a knowing smile, but, thankfully, Zane and Charlotte seemed undisturbed by the proclamation. With any luck, he hadn't heard Sally.

Waiting until her longtime friend had made her way through the maze of empty tables to find a seat beside her, Glory said, "I suppose I don't need to ask about whom you're referring."

The woman gave an unladylike snort and threw her head back. "Penelope, be a dear and get us a couple of brandies." Getting herself settled on the well-padded seat of the stool, she said, "I think you know very well that I mean tall, dark and handsome across the room there, doll."

Glory followed her gaze to Zane. His brow was furrowed in concentration, his lips forming a nearly straight line as he focused on the sketch. The graphite pencil held between his surprisingly long and graceful fingers moved skillfully across the page.

"Do you think he's so focused in bed?" Sally's whiskey voice interrupted her study of him.

"Sally!" Glory felt her cheeks flame.

"What?" The woman managed to look perfectly innocent until she smirked, her gaze drifting over to him again. "Can't you imagine all of that intensity focused on you?" She gave a shimmy of delight that made Glory laugh. The sound drew Zane's attention. Frowning, he looked up to see what the ruckus was all about, and Glory turned back to her friend, feeling very much like a schoolgirl caught watching him.

She could very much imagine what Sally had said. She could imagine it so well that she didn't need any help from Sally. "That's inappropriate." Her scolding lacked any heat though, especially when she couldn't stop herself from glancing back at him.

"Come now." Sally gently shoved her shoulder against Glory's. "It's not *that* inappropriate."

"He's an employee." The shop had sent over the suit earlier, so he was wearing it in preparation for the evening. The coat was spread tight across his shoulders, and the waistcoat emphasized his narrow waist. It looked good on him. More than good. He looked like he'd been born to the suit, while somehow retaining that untamed sense of danger that was such a part of who he was. Maybe it was the scar on his face, hinting at the wild things he was capable of.

"Bah. He's not going to be here for long, is he?"

"No, I suppose not." The words came out a little more forlorn than she'd have liked.

Penelope set down their brandies and leaned forward. "I have to agree with Sally. He's smitten."

Was their attraction that transparent? Even if it was, she had a hard time attributing such a tame word to him. *Smitten* didn't suit him at all. Zane simply wasn't a man to become smitten with anyone. He might like her. He might want to sleep with her, but he'd never be smitten. Those were two very different beasts. Lust was lust. Smitten implied something more and she wasn't ready to believe someone like him could feel that way about someone like her.

They were different. He was the wind, traveling the world wild and free; she was a tree…she frowned at the analogy. Maybe not a tree. A flower then. A *rosebush* with her roots firmly in the ground. Their paths might cross from time to time when he rustled her petals, but it wasn't something that could last. He might be all tender and gentle with her now, but the truth of the matter was that he wouldn't be around long. He wouldn't have the patience for dealing with her and her particular issues. Even if he did, what would be the point? He'd be leaving. She didn't want something frivolous and fleeting. She was surrounded by that every day.

He'd made it clear he wanted more, at least physically. They'd kissed. That didn't mean he was smitten, but she couldn't help but wonder what the others saw.

Picking up her brandy, she took a small sip, telling herself that it didn't matter. The liquid warmed her as it went down to settle in her belly. She hardly ever drank the stuff, but tonight was special since Sally would be leaving tomorrow. She meant to talk more about her friend, but when she opened her mouth that's not what came out.

"What makes you say that?"

"I asked him back to my room a few days ago and he turned me down." Penelope shrugged. "Said it was because you told him to keep his hands to himself while he's here, but I saw the way he watched you." She gave Glory a good-natured smile. "He'd have turned me down anyway."

Glory couldn't stop the smile that curved her lips, so she took another sip of brandy to hide it. She told herself it was because she was glad he'd followed her rule of not fraternizing with her staff, but deep down she knew it was because she didn't want to think of him with another woman. "It's nothing. Obviously, he's handsome. I think he does find me attractive, but we're not schoolchildren. We know that it's not meant to be."

Penelope raised an eyebrow, but didn't comment as she turned back to finish stocking the bar for the evening rush.

Sally drank some of her brandy and shook her head, opened her mouth, and then closed it only to shake her head again.

"What do you want to say?" Glory prodded. The woman had never been known to keep a comment to herself.

"Only that some things never change, I guess."

"What does that mean?" Glory was afraid that she knew very well what that meant. Her celibacy, while no one's business, had seemed to become an interesting topic of conversation of late.

Sally grinned, turning her glass around and around on the polished mahogany of the bar top. "You try to keep yourself too safe, Glory. That's all I meant. Live a little. You like him, and it's no secret he likes you. See what happens."

"It's not quite as easy as that, believe me, if it was I might take your advice."

"Oh, really?" Sally raised a doubtful eyebrow. "How come it's not so easy? Have a little fun. You both clearly want to." She grinned and whispered, "In case no one has told you, you don't have to be married to explore your physical urges."

Glory rolled her eyes at the woman's crude snicker. Then she raised her shoulder in a defensive shrug and took another sip of brandy to keep from answering right away. The truth was that some demons were easier not to face. Did she like kissing him? Of course she did, but she didn't like the panic that had followed that kiss. She didn't like all the strange feelings she didn't know how to handle. The fear, the doubt, the nearly overwhelming certainty that all of that wasn't worth the passing pleasure of kissing him when he would be leaving her life anyway.

"I…I have issues with…" It was as close as she'd ever come to admitting the truth to another living soul.

"With men," Sally finished for her. Turns out everyone

had probably already figured that out as well. "I know. But you're missing out on something you clearly want, doll. Give it a try. See what happens. Do you trust him?"

Glory nodded without even having to think about the question. She did trust him.

Say yes to me. She could still hear his husky voice as he uttered that command. A shiver of longing worked its way through her body, and she glanced over at him again. He must have sensed her attention because he looked up from the sketch. The heat of his gaze warmed her cheeks like a tangible caress. How could he do that with only a look?

"Then you've got nothing to lose," Sally whispered over her shoulder.

His eyes went back to the drawing, releasing Glory from his hold. Sally was right. She didn't really have all that much to lose, the problem was she didn't know if she had the courage to reach out and take what she wanted. Despite what Zane thought, she knew that she wasn't all that brave. She'd merely been surviving, and she acknowledged that she was pretty good at that.

Living took real courage. She hadn't been doing a whole lot of living in the years she'd been here. She'd existed. She'd made the absolute best of her lot in life, but she'd been too busy hiding and hoping never to be found to actually live. Now that she realized that, she wondered if she'd been doing it all wrong.

Was it possible to reach out and take what Zane was offering and still be whole when he left? Or better yet, maybe she'd be a little bit better for the time they spent together? Was she brave enough to try?

"Drawing's all done."

It wasn't until Charlotte's happy voice interrupted her musings that Glory realized she'd been daydreaming. Penelope and Sally were deep in conversation about a vaudeville act Glory had been attempting to book for the ballroom with little luck. Charlotte stood before her, holding out the drawing as a child might do when seeking approval. She'd apologized all afternoon for not coming forward sooner and was doing her best to make things right. Not that there was anything to make right, as far as Glory was concerned. Charlotte hadn't known about the letter so she'd had no reason to come forward sooner.

"Wonderful." Glory forced a smile—it was so easy to smile without thinking about it after all her years of practice—and took the drawing. Zane had done a fabulous job capturing the man's features. A middle-aged man stared back at her. His salt-and-pepper hair was thinned and combed to the side. He was clean-shaven with fine features, and he looked remarkably unremarkable. He could've been any of a dozen men who came through the doors every night. Her heart sank. She hadn't realized how she'd hoped something might come from the drawing. That perhaps it'd jar her memory of seeing him that night.

"I don't recognize him," Glory said.

All three women looked over her shoulder. Penelope gave a shrug. "Neither do I."

"Go ring Martin and ask him to come over for a moment."

Charlotte went off to do that, and Zane stepped forward.

"Thank you for doing this," Glory said. "I hope it helps."

He inclined his head. "I hope so too."

Glory became aware of a particularly intense stare coming from the stool beside her. Sally gave her a pointed look and smiled at Zane. Rolling her eyes, Glory decided that if she was planning to pursue something with Zane, then she'd do it in her own time and with plenty of privacy. "I'm needed in the courtyard," she declared with a smile and pushed her unfinished glass of brandy toward Penelope. "Sally, you may come find me later if you wish to continue our talk."

The woman's laughter followed her from the room as well as the sound of Zane's boots. She didn't pay attention to him though, and he seemed content to linger on the periphery of the courtyard when they stepped outside. Emily and Edward were there playing with Mary, a young serving girl who cared for them a few afternoons every week when she wasn't serving drinks and meals inside. The courtyard held a single oak tree, and a couple of years ago, Able had hung a swing from one of the limbs with thick rope and a sawn-off board. Edward squealed and laughed as his sister did her best to push him on the swing. She nearly fell forward with the momentum.

Glory's heart twisted in both pleasure and pain as she watched them. They were so small and hopeful. Two little people just wanting to love and to be given love in return. She'd be able to shield them for a while yet, but determined then and there that it was time to stop waiting and to start living. She'd contact their mother and force the decision. Either she sent for them or Glory would take over their care. She'd keep them as her own.

Her heart started beating harder at the prospect of keeping them. After resigning herself to the idea of never having children, she realized now how much she wanted them. She'd have to tread carefully—no. No, she was done with being careful. Sally was right. Her life was right in front of her and she hadn't been living it. She'd allow herself to love them even knowing that their mother might come back and swoop them up. Until then and for long after, she'd love them.

"Glory!" Finally noticing her, they called out, "Come play!"

Glory rushed over to them, not caring that she'd already dressed in her evening attire. She'd go and change if it came to it. For the next while she indulged them, playing on the swing and building castles in the small sandbox. She'd had the bags of sand brought in special for them. It wasn't until Zane interrupted that she realized the shadows were longer in the courtyard. At least an hour had passed.

The twins stared up at him when he walked over, curious but not wary of the stranger in their midst. They'd probably seen him around. To her surprise, he smiled down at them and crouched. "I see you have a fine moat around your castle," he said to Emily.

She beamed up at him. "Mine's deeper than Edward's."

Edward understandably took offense to this and set

about digging his out a little more with all the intensity a four-year-old could muster. He clamped his tongue between his lips and his chubby arms worked harder with the miniature shovel.

"That it is," Zane agreed. "But Edward's is nice and wide. I'm told that is also a very important feature when it comes to moats."

For the next several minutes, the four of them made sure both castles were equipped with excellent moats. Satisfied with their progress, Zane retrieved two wooden boats from the bucket of toys off to the side. "I bet you'd both like a rowboat for crossing the water."

They agreed and set about sailing their boats in the imaginary water. When they were occupied, Zane leaned over to her and said, "Hines has seen the drawing. He recognizes the man."

Her heart nearly tripped over itself, but the solemn look in his eyes told her he spoke the truth. Nevertheless, she needed reassurance. "He's certain?"

Zane nodded. "He said the man spent the night at The Baroness. Said he was leaving on the last train out. It was the same night you found your letter. He gave a name, though I'm certain it's a fake, and a St. Louis address. Hunter has confirmed it's the same address he found."

It wasn't much really. The address led to the same information they already had about the sender of the letter. Hunter was already doing all he could to track down the owner of the letter box. No easy feat considering the address was around fifteen hundred miles away. However, it was the confirmation she needed to verify what she'd already known, that no one in her employment had left that letter. Her staff was loyal. It was a small thing, but she was grateful to have it confirmed.

Zane had turned his attention back to the twins. A slight smile curved his lips as he watched them playing, making her wonder if he'd ever thought of having children of his own. He'd surprised her with how effortlessly he'd been able to play with them. She nearly shook her head at the direction of her thoughts. Sally had made her see how pleasant indulging her curiosity with Zane could be in the short term, but there was no reason she should be thinking such long-term thoughts about him. It shouldn't matter to her in the slightest what his plans were for a family in the future. She wouldn't be a part of them.

"What name did he give?" She asked the question almost absently. It didn't matter since Zane already assumed that it was a fake name given to cover the man's true identity. It made sense that he wouldn't use his real name if he was trying to hide who he was. She asked it more because she thought she should than from having a genuine desire to know.

"Justin Dubose."

Her world tilted on its axis. It was the last name she ever wanted to hear. Her hard-won security, her independence, everything she'd ever worked for was gone with his utterance of that name. She took a deep gulp of air but it felt as if something squeezed around her chest, not allowing any of it in.

"Glory?" Zane kept his voice calm, probably so that he wouldn't alarm the children, but she could see the alarm in his eyes. He touched her back and shifted so that he was facing her.

The twins looked up at them, their little faces pinched with concern.

She finally managed to take a breath, but her heart was still racing. "It's *him*... It's *his* name."

The drawing wasn't Justin though. Justin's nose was more prominent and no one would call him fine-featured. He'd been handsome, though with a notably cruel twist to his mouth. The man in the drawing had been bland. No, the man hadn't been Justin, but he'd used Justin's name, which meant his letter wasn't a lie. He was telling the truth when he claimed to know who she was. There was no doubt in her mind that he'd tell Justin where to find her.

If he hadn't already.

The next few minutes passed in a blur. Thank God Zane was with her. While she was still dealing with the aftershocks of her world coming apart, he seemed to know just what to do. He gathered the children and her and took them all to the boardinghouse. Mary was there waiting to get them ready for bed, along with the other children, but Glory couldn't give them up just yet. Zane seemed to understand and didn't rush her.

Instead, he calmly helped her get them changed into their nightclothes and waited inside the door as she hugged them all good-night. She didn't notice at first, but at some point as he guided her back to Victoria House, his hand slipped from her elbow to her hand. His palm felt so warm, his fingers so strong and comforting around hers that she didn't even think to pull away. She squeezed tighter, holding on to him as the one solid thing in her world right now.

"Let's get you upstairs until we can figure out a plan," Zane said when they stepped inside the back door.

"I need Able."

Zane nodded, and they took a detour through the house. She caught the attention of a maid leaving one of the salons and asked her to have Able meet her upstairs. The girl nodded and hurried off to the front of the house, where Able had probably already taken up his post for the night. Zane tightened his grip, leading her toward the back stairwell, when Sally popped out of the lounge as if she'd heard Glory's voice.

"Glory! There you are. I thought we'd finish our chat before my performance." Her steps slowed as she approached them, and her brow crinkled. "You look like hell, doll. What's wrong?"

The sight of her old friend was enough to jar Glory back to life. She took in a breath, hiccuping over the lump in her throat. "Come with me upstairs." She needed something familiar with her, something that would help reassure her that her whole world wouldn't crumble simply because Justin had found her.

"Of course." Sally put her arm around her to walk beside her up the stairs.

Regrettably, this made Zane let go of her hand. She missed him instantly, but his heavy tread on the stairs behind them was reassuring.

Able was already at the door of her apartment when they arrived. "Is he here?" Able asked. Maybe he could read the answer on her face.

"Not yet," she replied.

Able's nostrils flared as he took in a breath and his jaw clenched. He was worried.

"Come in. I'll tell you," said Glory, and within moments they were inside and she sat on the sofa. She could smell the rose water she'd used that morning. She could hear the ticking of the clock. The world was slowly coming back into focus.

Zane crouched down in front of her, his hand on her knee. "I'll be back soon. I'm going to talk to Hunter."

"Why?" As she spoke, Sally's hand moved up and down her back in a soothing motion.

"Because we're going to find him and we're going to stop him." Zane didn't give her a chance to respond before he left.

Chapter Fourteen

"You!"

Zane was brought up short by the unexpected accusation as soon as he walked through the door of Glory's apartment. She stood across the parlor, staring at him, her eyes wide in both fear and anger. She wobbled a little as she stared him down, bringing his attention to the tumbler of whiskey in her hand.

"Yes, it's me." He proceeded cautiously, wondering what the hell had changed in the two hours since he'd left her to go talk to Hunter. It probably had something to do with that drink in her hand. As he shut the door behind him, Charlotte and Sally watched him from the sofa.

"I told you, I don't want you looking for *him*." Glory gave a snort and tossed back a swallow of the amber liquid, making a face as she did. A strand of red hair had come out from its pins to curl down over her shoulder. She peered into the glass, mumbling, "This isn't brandy." He'd never seen her so unpolished and undone. There was something appealing about it.

"It's whiskey, doll, you finished the brandy so I switched it for you," Sally answered helpfully.

"How much of that has she had?" he asked the woman.

"Notalot," answered Glory. She spoke so fast that the words ran together.

His lips twitched as he attempted to keep from smiling at the way she stood there swaying, trying her best not to look like she was drunk.

Sally shrugged innocently but somehow managed to look guilty as sin at the same time. "Not much. That's only her first glass."

He looked to Charlotte for confirmation. "It's only her first glass of *whiskey*," Charlotte clarified. "She and Sally finished off that fifth of brandy first." She nodded toward a side table which held the now empty bottle.

"Oh, posh." Sally waved her hand. "It was only *half* full when we started. Who gets drunk off that much? I drank much more than she did before I even got here."

Zane squeezed his temples. Two hours. He'd been gone for two hours and that's all it had taken for Sally to get Glory drunk and unsteady on her feet. He did believe there was some truth to Sally's protestations of innocence though. She didn't seem nearly as affected as Glory, meaning she'd probably had much more experience drinking than Glory. He hadn't seen Glory drink anything but a glass of wine the entire time he'd been staying at Victoria House. Charlotte confirmed it when she said, "It's because Glory rarely drinks. I'm sorry, Mr. Pierce. I only just arrived a few minutes ago."

"No need to apologize," said Zane. "Glory makes her own decisions."

Charlotte looked uncertain, but she nodded.

Sally sighed in dramatic fashion. "She was upset. I simply kept refilling her glass to get her to calm down." Charlotte gave her a critical eye, but didn't say anything.

"H-h-hey!" Glory waited until she had their attention. "I'm right here. Stop talking about me."

Zane bit down on the inside of his cheek to keep from smiling. Her fury lacked its usual heat. She was strong, kind, fiery and apparently adorable when drunk.

"Glory, doll, I have a half hour until my show. I have to go." Sally walked over and gave her a hug before turning back to Zane. "Take care of her," she mouthed as she let herself out.

He inclined his head in confirmation. That was a request he could follow.

"I'll be down when you go on," Glory called out.

The hell she would. Zane wasn't letting her downstairs in her condition. He came to a stop in front of her, and she blinked, apparently only just realizing he was so close to her. "Don't you think you've had enough to drink?" He held out his hand for the tumbler.

She scowled and held the glass behind her back. "Maybe."

If she thought it was out of his reach, she was sorely mistaken. He was nearly twice her size and could have easily reached around her, but he didn't. Instead he put his hands in his pockets and sighed. "Why are you so angry with me?"

"Because... I told you I don't want you to have one thing to do with him and you went and got yourself involved anyway."

"I hate to tell you this, pretty lady, but I was already involved. I've been involved since the night you came to me for help." Sooner than that if he was being honest with himself. He'd have helped her at the first sign of trouble, whether she'd asked him for help or not.

Her scowl only deepened. "You know what I mean. You were s'pose…" She frowned at the way the word had come out and tried again. "You were *supposed* to find out if the letter was real or not. I didn't want you all tangled up in…" She waved her hand, forgetting that she was holding a half-full tumbler of whiskey, so some of the golden liquid spilled out onto the rug.

He ran a hand over the back of his neck to keep from reaching out to take it from her. Charlotte hurried to the bathing chamber and came back with a towel to wipe up the spill.

"Now that we know it is real, what did you expect me to do? Did you think I'd sit here and do nothing? Or did you think I'd run off because my job is done?"

Glory frowned down at Charlotte, seeming to be confused about the mess she was cleaning up. Shaking his head, Zane took the glass and gently pried it from her fingers.

"Stop that!" she yelled and swatted at his wrist. "Hey! That's mine."

He stepped back with the glass and set it on the side table. "And it'll be right here waiting for you. You can have the rest tomorrow."

She crossed her arms over her chest and then stomped over to the window.

"Charlotte, can you leave us?" he asked.

Still on her knees, she looked at him and then over at Glory, clearly uncertain if she should leave him alone with her. "Glory?"

"'S fine, Charlotte. Thank you."

Glory didn't turn from the window, even after Charlotte shut the door behind her. Zane slowly walked over to her, giving her time to move away or to turn around and confront him. Finally, when he was close enough to reach out and touch her, he asked, "Why are you *really* so upset with me?"

Her shoulders lifted as she took a deep breath, but she let it out on a ragged sigh that was suspiciously like a sob. "I don't want anything to happen to you."

He was helpless against the warmth that seeped into his chest. It tugged him forward, and he was resistant to stop himself until he could feel the heat from her body against his front. He brought his hands up but stopped himself just short of pulling her back against him. Instead, he rested a cautious hand on her shoulder. She didn't pull away, so he left it there, letting his fingers gently squeeze her arm, absorbing her warmth through the silk of her dress.

"I'll be fine, Glory. I know what I'm doing."

She shook her head and her shoulders straightened as if she'd passed through the momentary weakness. "You men. You all think you know everything." The moment of tenderness was over when she swung around, dislodging his hand as she marched to the other side of the sofa. "But you don't know anything."

Apparently belligerent could be added to adorable to describe Glory drunk. He'd never seen this side of her.

She was always so controlled and reserved. He liked it. He liked it a lot.

"Are you…are you *smiling*?"

"Definitely not." Zane wiped away whatever smirk had been lurking around the vicinity of his mouth.

She glared at him suspiciously before uncrossing her arms to wave a hand at him. "You men with your knives, and your guns, and your…" Her gaze traveled down his body to narrow in on the general vicinity of his crotch. "Your male appendages." The word *appendages* was exaggerated and said very slowly so that she wouldn't stumble over it in her inebriated state.

He wisely brought his hand up to cover any smirk that was stupid enough to show on his face. He rather appreciated his male appendage and hoped to keep it intact.

"You all think you always know everything. This time you don't."

"I know that I want to keep you safe."

This only made her shake her head again. "But you don't know him. You don't know what he is, what he can do. What do you think? You can just walk up to him and it'll be over."

Ah! He hadn't included her. That's what had her hackles up. He'd been so anxious to have Justin Dubose investigated that he'd hurried over to Hunter's without talking to her about it first. "You're right," he said. Her eyebrows shot up in surprise. "I don't know him like you do. I should've had you come with me. We could've talked to Hunter together and come up with a plan."

Her brow furrowed and her lips pursed as she thought

over what he'd said. She seemed suspicious of his intentions, so he took a cautious step forward, wary of making her feel cornered. "I've asked Able to meet us in the morning and we can talk more about a plan then. Forgive me?"

She hesitated, but eventually gave him a jerky nod. When she did it was as if the air went out of her. Her shoulders slumped forward and she let out a ragged breath. She'd been using her anger as a buffer so that she wouldn't feel the fear and pain that was shining out from her eyes.

"You don't know him." She said it again but this time she stated it quietly.

He wasn't one to brag, but he'd been in plenty of tough situations before. There was the time they'd had a two-day shoot-out in that abandoned canyon outside Denver with men intent on turning Castillo in for the reward money. There was the man who Bennett Derringer had paid to kill him. That son of a bitch had been ruthless, tracking the gang for weeks and nearly getting the better of Zane outside a saloon in Texas. Then just last week he, Castillo, and Hunter had had the pleasure of facing Bennett down again. Zane's scar throbbed from the memory of staring him down for the last time. There'd been satisfaction in seeing the man who'd given the scar to him get his comeuppance. Just as there'd been satisfaction in killing Buck Derringer, the man responsible for the murder of Castillo's grandfather. A little bit of justice had been restored to his world.

He closed the distance between them, coming to a stop directly in front of her. Maybe he was too close, but he couldn't stop this need to feel her, to reassure them both that she was safe. He wanted to help restore justice to her world too. "I've faced down my own ghosts. I can damn well destroy yours too."

"He's not like other men… He's a monster." She didn't seem to mind the proximity. Her hazel eyes were wide and fearful as she stared up at him, but she didn't move away.

Zane frowned. Her expression was so vulnerable, he knew that she meant what she said. She was terrified, but he loved how she tilted her chin up and her eyes were fierce. There was strength and determination beneath all that fear. The backs of his fingers touched her jaw, and his thumb settled on her soft cheek to gently stroke over it. Her skin felt like satin. She didn't pull away. In fact, she subtly turned into his touch. Desire tightened in his belly, urging him to kiss her, needing to feel her against him, to reassure them both that they were safe. That they were together.

"He's flesh and blood. He can be stopped just like any other man." His voice held a rough edge.

The sudden weight of the conversation seemed to have sobered her a bit. Her eyes were clear, and though it was soft, her voice came out strong and distinct. "He's capable of so much worse than any other man. You can't even imagine. I saw it with my own eyes."

What had she seen? He wanted to ask, to try to see it for himself, but he couldn't ask her to dredge up those memories for him. It would be unfair.

"I'm sorry you saw that. I'm sorry you knew him."

Closing the distance between them, her palms came

to rest on his chest. Could she feel how hard his heart pounded? She turned into his palm and placed a soft kiss there. The contact sent heat lancing up his arm to settle low in his belly, where it burned bright and hot.

Her lips trembled when she took a breath. "The Dubose estate was a horrible place. We used to hear stories as children."

He barely breathed as he waited for her to continue, hungry for any scraps of her past that he could get.

"The people who worked for him…sometimes they'd disappear. He owned them as if they were slaves. The war had been over for years but that didn't mean anything there." Her eyes seemed unfocused, as if she was remembering.

Gently taking her by the arm, he led her to the sofa. She slowly dropped down onto it and he sank down beside her. As soon as he put his arm around her shoulders, she turned into him. He closed his eyes as he held her close, tucking her against him. Her rose scent mixed with the decadent aroma of brandy teased his nostrils, warning him of dark days to come if he gave in to her, but he was weak when it came to her. She turned her face into his chest as he ran a soothing hand up and down her back.

"Did Able work there?" He had trouble imagining the strong and proud man he knew working for anyone like that. At this very minute, Able was downstairs making certain things ran smoothly to give her time to calm down.

She nodded against his chest without lifting her head up. Something about that tore right through him. He held her tighter, his palm sliding up her back to rest on the back of her head. His fingers delved into her hair, touching that glorious silk for the first time. It was smooth and thick beneath his fingertips and, despite his best intentions, he couldn't help but wonder what it'd feel like wrapped around him. He wanted to make her feel better, to take away her fear for a little while and give her a reason to forget everything.

But that's not what she needed from him right now. He sensed that she wanted to talk more so he listened.

"Able went to work there a few years before I arrived. He hated it." Her voice was bitter. "But the only way to leave was in a pine box."

"How…" He squeezed his eyes shut, hating the thought of her being at that horrible place. The need to know was so strong that he couldn't stop himself from asking the question, though he dreaded the answer. "How did you come to be at that place?"

She sniffed and he dipped his head, burying his nose in her hair. "My family didn't have much. We had a big house, and it had been nice once, but it was falling down around us. Even before the war my family had been down on our luck. My parents sold off the land until we barely had enough left to farm."

A sick premonition churned in his stomach. He had a feeling he knew where this was headed, but he didn't say anything. She needed to talk, so he'd listen and she'd continue at her own pace. Finally, she said, "I don't know how it happened, but one day he was there at our home. The next week my parents took me to the Dubose estate and that's where I stayed."

The sound of Sally's voice belting out an indistinct song from down in the ballroom wafted through the silence of the suite. It was the only sound aside from the beating of his heart. In that moment, he hated her parents almost as much as he hated Dubose. How could they leave her with him knowing the horrible things he had done and what would happen to her?

"I was fourteen and I learned what it meant to belong to someone. The word *no* meant nothing. We all belonged to him, everyone on the estate did."

Goddamn. She'd only confirmed what he'd suspected, but somehow it was so much worse *knowing* rather than simply imagining that it might be true. Rage burned him alive from the inside out. Dubose was a coward and a monster, but he was also a man. Zane wanted to make him bleed for every pain he'd ever caused her.

She pulled back enough to look up at him. Her expression was wary, as if she didn't know what to expect. Did she think he'd think less of her? Her bottom lip trembled a little, but her eyes were still clear. There were no tears and he wondered if she'd cried herself out years ago. Tenderness swelled within him, momentarily tamping down the rage. He wanted to tell her he was sorry, but it seemed inadequate and useless in the face of what she'd been through. How did an apology convey the depth of his sorrow for her anyway?

Tipping her chin up, he slowly leaned down, giving her time to pull away. When she didn't, he gently closed his lips over hers. She sighed into his mouth and relaxed into him, moving her lips against his. After a minute he pulled back to take a breath and pressed his forehead against hers.

"How long before you escaped?" He had to know how long she'd been forced to endure that madman.

"Almost two years."

He squeezed his eyes closed so tight that he saw spots. To live in terror for so long was unthinkable to him. He couldn't even fathom the courage it had taken to face it.

"Able lost his wife and child in childbirth, and I think it pushed him over the edge. He decided to risk escape rather than stay there any longer. I found him and begged him to take me with him. Thank God he agreed."

He tightened the arm around her waist, pulling her as close as he could until there wasn't a breath of space between them. If he could have, he would've taken all her fear into himself. He couldn't even begin to imagine what horrors she'd both seen and experienced. He didn't even want to. Yet, he couldn't seem to stop. The images flashed through his mind anyway.

Tomorrow he'd thank Able himself for taking her away from that place. Somewhere at the edge of his consciousness were all the reasons he couldn't stay with her, but they didn't matter tonight. Tonight they were together and he wouldn't think of the future. Nothing mattered but Glory.

Her small hand moved up his chest to curl around the nape of his neck and draw him back down to her. This time her lips took his. It was a slow and tender kiss meant for comfort. He took his time with her, letting his lips learn the shape of hers. The tip of his tongue lightly traced along her bottom lip. She opened wider for him and he delved inside, tasting her sweetness. Much to his surprise, she deepened the kiss. Her tongue chased his and she was nearly in his lap.

His blood had thickened, like honey sliding through his veins to settle in the pit of his stomach and even lower. Every fiber of his being wanted her. He was as hard as a rock and nearly throbbing for her when they parted enough to gasp for breath.

She smiled up at him and kissed him again, a soft caress of her lips, as if she couldn't stay away. Desire urged him to go further, but he wouldn't. Not tonight. She was too vulnerable now and more than a little drunk.

"We should get some rest," he said, using up every last ounce of restraint that he had.

She grinned again. He couldn't understand how she could keep smiling after all that had happened. Rage and tenderness were at war inside him. She rose, still a little unsteady on her feet, and surprised him by holding out her hand. "Will you come with me?"

He stared at that hand, recognizing the moment for what it was. She was offering him a tiny opening into her life. This wasn't about the past, this was about moving forward. He took her hand before he could even think of what it might mean for them. Closing his fingers around hers, he followed her to her bedchamber.

She offered him her back. "Can you help me?"

His fingers were suddenly clumsy as he worked the fastenings, parting the rich blue silk to reveal her undergarments. When she shrugged out of the gown, he thought he should turn away but he was frozen where he was, unable to look away from her. He felt like he'd felt the first time he'd ever lain with a woman, even though he knew this night wasn't going to end up in sex. Yet, it seemed so much more intimate somehow. His palms were clammy.

The corset and some sort of underskirt followed the gown, tossed over the trunk at the foot of her bed. One by one the pins came out of her hair to be tossed onto the dresser. He swallowed hard as he watched the red waves cascade down to her waist. She looked shy and eager as she looked up at him. His hands moved with a mind of their own as he responded to her expectant gaze. He took off his coat and waistcoat and toed off his shoes before following her to the bed. She lay down on one side and he climbed into the bed beside her.

Her eyelids were heavy. He knew it'd be minutes before the brandy's effects put her to sleep for the night. "There's something else I want to tell you."

Rising up on his elbow to see her better, he said, "Anything." His curiosity about this woman was insatiable.

Taking in a shaky breath, she said, "I was there for over a year when I…I became pregnant with child."

Rage coursed its way through him, and his instinct was action. He wanted to go out into the night and pull Dubose from whatever hole he was hiding in. His heart pounded, urging him to go, but he fought the impulse. It wasn't what she needed from him and it wouldn't be wise. Not until they knew more about Dubose's plan.

Instead of saying anything, he put his hand on hers. She immediately turned it over so they were palm to palm.

"One night…" There were no tears in her eyes, but there was deep sadness on her face and in her voice. "He already had adult children and hadn't wanted any more. He pushed me down the stairs. I went into early labor and…I lost the baby."

"I'm so sorry." His eyelids sank closed as he tried to imagine her pain and confusion when that had happened. He couldn't do it. The torture she'd faced at the hands of that madman was unfathomable.

When he opened his eyes she was staring up at him. Her face open and solemn. "I'm sorry. Maybe I shouldn't have told you that. I didn't want to make you sad, I just wanted… I wanted to share it all with you."

"Don't be sorry. Please don't ever be sorry with me."

She smiled and touched his face before turning over on her side away from him. "You don't have to stay all night if you don't want to, but would you mind staying until I go to sleep?"

He nodded, too awestruck by the woman before him to find his voice. Realizing she couldn't see his nod, he moved slowly closer to her, wary of how small she felt next to him. He suddenly felt too large and clumsy, as if one wrong move could mar the perfect creature before him. She was a queen and he was a lowly subject that had somehow stumbled his way into being allowed to touch her.

He expected her to pull away, but the moment his arm went around her waist she snuggled back into him. He let out a breath he hadn't even realized he'd been holding. Her small frame fit perfectly against him. She was small where he was big, soft where he was hard. God, was he hard. He gritted his teeth against the sudden arousal that pulsed through him. She must have felt him, throbbing there against the most perfect backside he'd ever felt, but she didn't say anything or move away.

Finally, after a few minutes, the tension left his body and she relaxed into him even more. He'd never lain like this with another person. Not even Christine. Their meetings had always been quick and rushed. They'd never had the luxury of simply being together. The idea of it had never even occurred to him, but he liked it. Glory's presence soothed something in him that he hadn't even realized needed calming. Her hand found his resting on her stomach and she surprised him again by lacing her fingers with his. He gently tightened his hold and closed his eyes as he buried his face in her hair. He didn't know what tomorrow would bring, but for now he was with her and that was all that mattered.

He fell asleep almost immediately. The weight of all that he'd learned pulled him down into a dark sleep. The scent of roses filled his dreams. So decadent, yet so dangerous. Sights from his childhood flashed across his mind's eye one after the other until his dreams finally settled on the one that had been haunting him for the past several days.

His mother's sister stood before him, as she'd been after his mother's death. Her young face was already creased from the wind and weather. Worry had put a sadness in her eyes that he'd recognized even at such a young age.

"What have you seen, Aunt?"

She'd been anxious about what to do with him, afraid that the soldiers would come take him away if they found out his father was white and his mother had died; afraid that they wouldn't and he'd starve to death because there was no food.

When the warriors left the reservation to go find food there was always fighting. Everyone knew it was only a matter of time before there was another massacre or the tribe was moved again.

"I saw three deaths for you, little one. One came in the morning, when you were covered in my tears. Your father can take you away from here and we can avoid that one. One comes when the moon is low. A flower is to blame. The white men call it a rose. Avoid them and you avoid that death. The third one comes when the moon is high and full. When you are gray. That is the good one, little one. That is the one you should accept."

Zane jerked himself out of his sleep. Glory stirred beside him, rolling over onto her back, her breaths deep and even. He couldn't help but stare at her by the light of the moon and the streetlamp that came in through the window. She looked so peaceful lying there, as if untouched by the awful things she had experienced in her life.

Was there anything to what his aunt had said? At the time he hadn't questioned her. As soon as he realized that she really meant to send him away with his father, he'd wailed and resisted leaving the only home he'd ever known. He'd only met his father a handful of times when he'd drifted through camp with supplies. He didn't want to leave with him.

His own misery had made him not question the rest of her vision. He wasn't sure if he should believe it now, but the dream unsettled him. Gently tucking Glory's hair back off her forehead, he left the bed to get his sketchbook. It was the only thing that could calm him down on nights like this.

Chapter Fifteen

Glory awoke to soft morning light filtering in through her pale blue curtains, casting a soft glow over her bed. The first thing she noticed was that the space beside her was empty. She lay there for a while, wondering if the past night had been a dream. She could remember sitting with Sally in the parlor, but after that things became a little bit hazy. She'd been afraid for Zane and angry that he hadn't talked to her about finding Justin. They'd argued and she'd eventually told him about her past.

Well, most of it. There were some things she couldn't tell him, not yet anyway. Maybe not ever.

Then he'd lain down with her. She pressed a hand to her stomach, remembering the press of his palm there. Last night had been no dream. It had felt so good to have him at her back with his arms around her. For the first time in a long time she'd gone to sleep with a feeling of peace surrounding her.

Even this morning she carried that feeling with her, which was a surprise. Justin had found her and she knew that meant he was coming for her. But while she was concerned and even anxious about that, she felt lighter than she had in years. When she took a deep breath her chest didn't feel pinched with the weight of all that she'd carried with her since stepping foot on the Dubose estate so many years ago. It actually felt good that she'd talked to Zane.

A door shut in the other room, so she sat up quickly listening for any signs of Zane. How did he feel this morning? Had he left her as soon as she'd gone to sleep? Had he stayed? Had her confession changed things between them? His familiar step moved across the parlor, prompting her to get to her feet.

Grabbing her dressing gown from the armoire, she put it on over her chemise and sat down at her dressing table to run a brush through her hair. A piece of paper caught her eye as she reached for the brush and she paused, her heart skipping over itself as she recognized the paper as that from Zane's sketchbook. The bottom corners of the parchment were slightly worn and softened from months of being held in his hands and carried in his coat. The top edge was jagged from where he'd torn the page out of his sketchbook.

Her heart pounded as she turned it over, but nothing could have prepared her for what she saw. Her own image stared back at her, only it couldn't be her. Could it? The woman was stunning in her sleep. She lay with one arm in a graceful sprawl above her head and the other on her belly. Her hair fell around her in a riot of waves. She looked both peaceful and confident, innocent and mischievous. Glory recognized the chemise as her own, except the ribbon between her breasts hung free leaving the valley between them exposed.

She gasped as she noticed the chemise was see-through and even stupidly looked around on impulse to make sure no one was around her to see the drawing. A faint outline of her nipples and areolae could be seen through the material. Heat warmed her cheeks as she looked closer to make sure that's what she really saw. Yes, they were both there, the shading there was different than the rest of her chemise. Surely he hadn't *seen* her like that. Her own nipples grew hard beneath the linen of her chemise at the thought of him looking at her. She giggled and opened her dressing gown to look at herself in the mirror.

"Dear Lord," she whispered. The dark pink was just barely visible through the thin material and the ribbon had fallen untied. He'd seen them. He'd stayed awake after she slept and drawn her and he'd seen them through the fabric.

Her blush spread from her face to her chest. She couldn't seem to stop smiling as she realized how much she wanted him to see. She wanted to feel his hands on her skin and to know what it felt like to have his mouth on her. It felt as if she was waking up after a long sleep and she really liked the feeling.

Running the brush through her hair, she quickly braided it over her shoulder and tied off the end with a piece of ribbon. Deciding that Able might come up this morning, she hurried into the first gown she pulled from the armoire. It was a simple morning gown in white muslin and one of the few she had that she could wear without much assistance with the fastenings. She was nearly breathless as she rushed out the door. Zane looked up from where he stood at her dining table filling a glass with water.

"Good morning," she said, unable to read his expression. This was like their first morning together all over again. Her unsure of him but unable to stifle the inexplicable feeling of hope that wanted to take hold of her.

He smiled and the hope dug its roots in a little bit deeper. "Good morning. How do you feel?"

"Surprisingly good. I didn't mean to drink so much." Sally had kept filling her glass and the fiery liquid had helped, she had to admit. It had kept her terror at bay. Even now she could feel it starting to creep back in, but she wouldn't let it. She was stronger than she'd been the last time she'd seen Justin. This time would be different. This time she could fight back.

"Charlotte came by to check on you this morning, so I asked her to send up breakfast. I wasn't sure if you'd be up for going downstairs."

Well, that explained the plates of steaming food and coffeepot on the table. She was gratified to see that there were two plates. He meant to take his own breakfast with her.

"I feel good, but thank you." She really needed some water, but other than that and a light headache, she felt better than she should. "I'd rather have breakfast with you than go downstairs."

His expression changed in an instant. His eyes became hooded and deep and he gave her body a quick sweep as if remembering what she looked like beneath the clothes. Her nipples beaded again, sending a tight dart of pleasure rushing through her. His gaze warmed every place it touched her.

His smile broadened and he set the pitcher of water down and walked over to her. Coming to a stop only inches away from her, he tilted her chin up. He was so tall and broad he completely towered over her. At first she had found that unsettling, but now it made her feel protected and safe. He wouldn't use his strength to bring her harm.

She slid her palms up his chest and around the nape of his neck, feeling as if she had some right to touch him after all they'd shared. Lacing her fingers together, she pulled him down for a kiss. His mouth was hot and tender as it closed over hers. He also seemed more hesitant than he'd been last night, the kiss was slow and easy. When he pulled back, she stared up at him, searching for the reason why. But his smile was still in place and he kissed the tip of her nose.

"You're beautiful in your sleep."

Her face burned again. "Thank you for the drawing. It's beautiful, although I think you tend toward flattery."

He laughed, a soft, deep sound that moved through her in the most delicious way. "Is it still flattery if it's true?"

She couldn't answer that. She didn't think it was true, but she was glad that he saw her that way. "Thank you. You make me feel beautiful."

He opened his mouth to say something but he was interrupted by a knock at the door. She sat down at the table while he went to answer it. She'd become accustomed to not answering her own doors with him around. Able stepped in, mumbling a greeting to Zane, but his gaze found her. She was touched by the concern she saw there. Able's friendship had gotten her through so much, she couldn't imagine what would've happened without him.

"Morning." She forced a brighter smile, because now that those few precious moments with Zane were over, reality was starting to intrude. Justin was coming and they had a very big problem to deal with.

Able pulled up a chair and Zane took his seat across from her.

"Breakfast?" She offered him her plate. When Able shook his head, she asked, "How's Clara?"

"Good." His brow was furrowed as he said that. He was clearly upset.

"How are *you*?" She reached out and squeezed his hand.

He shook his head. "I never thought this day would come. I knew it was possible, but after the first few years I didn't think it was likely. Why would he still be looking after so long?"

Zane paused from cutting through a piece of sausage on his plate and looked up at her, as if he had wondered the same thing.

She shrugged. "Justin isn't like anyone I've ever met. He doesn't like it when things don't go his way. He *really* doesn't like it." In Justin's mind she belonged to him and he couldn't cope with the fact that she'd gotten away.

Able nodded along, likely remembering his own run-ins with him.

Zane frowned and put his fork and knife down. "I won't let him take you back, Glory. I promise you that."

Glory took a breath. She knew that he'd try and that he'd even likely succeed, but she didn't like the danger that she was putting everyone in. An idea that had been lurking in the back of her mind came to the forefront. "I've been thinking…" Both men looked at her expectantly. "I think it's me that he wants. He thinks he owns me and it must have been eating at him all these years that I escaped. If we split up, I could draw him away from you. I could leave."

Able shook his head immediately. "It's too late for that. He knows I'm here. He'll stop here anyway."

She nodded in agreement. If Justin was still on their trail after all these years, then that was likely true. "I think you have to go too. We simply go in separate directions. Chances are he'll follow me and you'll have a chance to get away once and for all."

Able squeezed her fingers. "Do you really think I'd let you face him alone?"

"No." It had been worth suggesting the option, but she'd known that Able wouldn't agree to it. "I want this to be over. I don't want to run anymore, but I don't like that I'm putting everyone in danger. If he comes here, the women, the staff, anyone who gets in his way becomes his prey."

"They'll all be in danger anyway. Justin Dubose is a madman. He won't care that you're not here anymore. They're connected to you now and he could use them to lure you back," said Able.

It was impossible to argue with his logic. Justin was the devil incarnate.

"He's right." Zane caught her gaze and held it. "If Dubose is half as bad as you both say he is, then we have no choice but to fight him. Our chances are better here on our own terms."

She nodded, torn with the reassurance of that statement and the fact that she wanted Zane as far away from Justin as possible. "We need to come up with a plan. How long do we think we have before he arrives?" There was no question that he was coming.

"Hunter sent out a telegram late last night," said Zane. "He'll have a solicitor from Charleston let us know if Dubose is still at his estate. With any luck we'll hear back by tonight, maybe tomorrow. If we know he's still there, or when he left, that should help us narrow down a time."

"That's good." If he hadn't left yet then they would likely be able to intercept him, but they'd have to cross that bridge when they had more information. She felt confident that they could handle this, so this time when she smiled it was a little more genuine. "In the meantime I think we need to start the process of closing the boardinghouse."

"What?" Able's surprise wasn't unexpected. She'd never have wanted to do that in a million years.

"I think we have to do it temporarily. If he shows up here, I don't put it past him to try to use the children or women there to get to us. We have to send them away for their own safety." The very thought of sending Emily and Edward away tore at her heart, but it would be so much worse if Justin got to them. He had no regard for human life. He'd proven that to her over and over again.

"It's the smart thing to do," Zane agreed.

"I already have a couple of positions in Seattle lined up for the two women staying there. I'd hoped to give them more time, but I think we need to put them on a train as soon as possible." She'd settle extra money on them to help them get situated in a room before having to start their new jobs in their new town.

"What about Emily and Edward?" Able asked. He knew what the twins had come to mean to her.

She swallowed thickly. "I'll have to telegram their mother and let her know to expect them." Pain welled in her chest and she had to blink past the prickling of tears. She didn't want to lose them, and especially not if their mother didn't want them. But what else could she do? She couldn't keep them here and submit them to facing down Justin with her.

Zane reached across the table and took her other hand. She nearly sobbed from the tenderness of that touch. "Do you know if she wants them?"

She shook her head. She hadn't had time to write to her.

He squeezed her hand. "I'll talk to Hunter and Emmaline. The kids would be safe out at the Jameson ranch. I'm sure they'd be happy to have them there for a little while."

Tears of gratitude filled her eyes, nearly spilling down her cheeks before she could blink them back. "Do you really think they'd agree to that?" Keeping them near—keeping them safe—while avoiding sending them to a mother and stepfather, who may very well not want them, would be the perfect solution.

"I do." He gave her a comforting smile.

Able cleared his throat. "Do you think they'd be willing to have Clara come along?"

Zane nodded, none of the previous ill will between them evident in the exchange. "I think they'd like that."

Able nodded and she squeezed his hand again. With Clara so close to giving birth, she could only imagine how it must hurt to send her away.

"Let's pay a call after breakfast. I'd rather ask Hunter and Emmy in person," she said. In that moment she realized exactly how lucky she was. Justin might be coming, but she had Able and now she had Zane. It was almost scary how quickly Zane had come to mean so much to her, but he had. What she felt for him was real and one day soon they were going to have to talk about what the future might have in store for them. But for right now, she was simply going to appreciate what she had while she still had it.

Chapter Sixteen

The carriage ride to the Jameson town home was mercifully quick, because it had been one of the stranger trips she'd ever taken. Able sat next to her, his brawn leaving her very little room in her corner. Zane sat across from her to give Able room to stretch out his long legs, which meant that Zane's long legs practically caged her in. There was one on either side of her two. That's not to say that she minded him caging her in, precisely. She rather liked that each jolt of the carriage had her legs bumping into him. It was just that it was so awkward with Able looking down on him like a disapproving older brother.

It reminded her that she needed to talk to him and figure out what his problem was with Zane. If things were going to go as she hoped, then she'd need Able's cooperation.

The carriage rolled to a stop and the driver came down to help her out. Zane dutifully moved his legs out of the way and she left him and Able to fight out which of them would follow first.

The house was a lavish affair, built within the last decade in the fashionable part of town. Glory had specified that they should use the back door, because she knew gossip would spread should she use the front door, and she was conscious of protecting the reputations of both Emmy and Caroline. Rumors were likely to spread anyway, but her carriage was inconspicuous and it was midmorning, hardly the usual time for people to be out calling. She hoped they'd get lucky and no one would notice them. Although she'd taken the precaution of dressing in black and had a long veil covering her face and hair.

The door was opened by an elderly woman as soon as she reached the stoop.

"Good morning, Miss Winters. You're expected in the parlor." The kindly woman waited for them all to come inside before leading them to the front of the house and opening a pair of tall French doors. The room was tastefully done in shades of rich brown and amber.

The two couples were already waiting inside. Castillo and Caroline were settled on a settee next to the window. His color had returned, and he looked much better than the last time she'd seen him. She couldn't see any hint of his bandage, but he sat awkwardly and seemed to favor his side. It was one of the clues that he was injured; the other being that Caroline kept her hand in his, as if even now she was afraid that he could be taken from her.

When he made to stand, Glory waved him back down. "Please don't stand on my account."

Caroline flashed her a grateful smile when he sank

back down. "He keeps trying to behave as if he doesn't have a hole in his side."

He grinned and pulled her hand to his mouth to place a kiss on the back. Glory wasn't quite prepared for the pang of jealousy that knifed through her at the scene of such domestic bliss. She stood there staggered with longing at the obvious affection between the two of them.

It wasn't that she coveted Castillo for herself, it was that she wanted that sort of relationship in her life, that easygoing affection, that absolute certainty that the other person was going to be there for the rest of their days. She had longed for that for a while now and had forced herself not to admit it, but the urge had been there needling her when she retired to her room alone at night with only her books for company. It was there when she woke up in the morning and drank her coffee alone at the window. The truth was that she had a very fulfilling life. She took care of a lot of people. She had a successful business. Not only the brothel and club, but she'd bought enough property over the past few years to be one of the wealthiest landowners in town. She had no reason to be discontented with her life.

Or she hadn't until Zane had come into her life. The past days had shown her how fulfilling it could be to have someone. Last night had shown her how fulfilling intimacy could be. Opening herself up to Zane and having him hold her while she'd slept had been so much more than she could've anticipated. It left her craving more.

"Welcome, Glory." Emmy had been standing next to

Hunter at the cold fireplace, but she hurried over and embraced her.

Glory smiled down at her, amazed at how she'd changed from the girl who'd grown up in Victoria House to the beautiful young woman she was today. No one would have guessed that she'd been in a salon in Victoria House mere months ago, auctioning off her virginity. Or that marriage to the man who'd placed the highest bid would come so soon. Glory had been uncertain given the unconventional way that Emmy and Hunter had met, but marriage seemed to agree with her. She was glowing like a woman in love and well taken care of.

"Thank you for agreeing to see us on such short notice." She squeezed Emmy's hand and addressed the room. She'd only rang them on the telephone a scarce half hour earlier and Hunter had urged them to come as soon as they could.

"Anytime, Glory," Hunter said.

"Come and have a seat." Emmy led her to the settee that sat across from Castillo and Caroline. Then she greeted Able and Zane. Once Able was seated in a high-backed chair facing the fireplace, and Emmy sat beside her, it was time to get to the reason they were there. Glory absolutely hated having to ask for help, yet here she was and it was the second time this week she'd had to come to them.

As if sensing her discomfort, Zane reached forward from where he stood behind her and placed a hand on her shoulder. He'd naturally seemed to gravitate toward her and she'd liked that a lot.

"I assume Zane told you all about my predicament?"

Castillo leaned forward, wincing. "He said that a man from your past had found both you and Able. That he's possibly on his way here."

"Yes, that's right. I've decided that if we're to be ready for him, I need to close the boardinghouse." She explained her plan and about Emily and Edward.

"Say no more." Emmy took her hand again. "We'll take them out to the ranch. They'll be safe there. Hunter has enough hands out there that this man won't know what hit him if he tries to follow them."

"Are you certain you can keep them safe?" Glory asked, looking from Emmy to Hunter.

"We'd be honored to have them," Hunter answered.

Emmy smiled. "We handled my stepfather and his gang of thieves, we can handle the mystery man from your past."

Before Glory could say more, Emmy said to Able, "You should consider sending Clara as well. She'll be safer out there."

"I'd be obliged to you," said Able.

"It's not an obligation. We're happy to help out. We've come to think of you and Glory as extended family." Hunter's wide smile lit up the parlor. It was no wonder every debutante in town had gone into fits when they'd heard he was engaged. Or at least that had been the rumor; Glory wasn't close with any debutantes.

"You should come too, Glory," Emmy said more quietly.

"I agree," Able added. "You go wait it out at the ranch and we'll take care of Dubose."

Glory didn't know whether to be offended that he

wouldn't want her included or grateful that she had people who cared about her. She decided to remain neutral. "I'm not running. It's time to end this."

Able gave her a firm nod and Emmy smiled. "When do you think we should go? Today? In the morning?" Emmy asked.

Glory's mind started swimming with all the things they needed to do within the next few days. Now that it was finally happening, she had too many things to do to be worried. She barely noticed when Hunter called for Zane and motioned that they should step into the other room.

Zane followed Hunter across the wide hallway that bisected the house into a room nearly identical to the parlor they'd left. The only difference was that this one was deep red and cream. He'd never understand why people needed so many rooms for socializing. He couldn't ever imagine wanting that many people in his space.

Hunter stopped near the window and pulled out a folded piece of yellow paper from inside his coat. It looked like a telegram. "I received this minutes before you arrived. It's from the Charleston solicitor I telegrammed last night."

"Already?"

Hunter sneered. "It must've been the outrageous sum I agreed to wire to his bank." His smile faded as he looked down at the paper. "It turns out Dubose is a wealthy landowner in the low country. He's fairly well-known in Charleston social circles."

All of that was to be expected. Glory wouldn't be so afraid if the man wasn't without some means to pose a serious threat to her. "Has he left yet?"

Hunter frowned and handed over the piece of paper before running a hand over his chin. "That's the strange part. He says that Dubose has been gone for weeks. To Europe. Something about a tour of France."

Zane scanned the telegram confirming that Dubose had left three weeks ago, which meant he'd be in France by now. "I don't believe it. He's on his way."

"Or already here."

At those ominous words, Zane looked up. Hunter looked concerned. "You don't think he's been here all along?"

Hunter shook his head. "Probably not. We don't know how long he's been looking for them. The investigator he hired only just made contact, so I think it's likely that he had no idea where she was before then. Maybe he's only now decided to find her and set off on his own to do that. Hell, I don't know." Hunter ran his fingers through his hair and paced the length of the window.

"It doesn't matter. We've already been vigilant." Zane folded up the paper and handed it back to Hunter. "We still have to get the children and Clara to safety. The men are still at the ranch, we need to bring some of them into town and have someone at the train station so we know if Dubose comes in that way. The rest we need outside Victoria House. We'll make sure no one gets in or out without us knowing." He was thankful the gang had decided to wait out Castillo's recovery at the ranch instead of going their separate ways.

"Let's go back and talk with Glory and Able and see what they think. But first…" He paused as if uncertain how to say whatever it was he wanted to say. "You and Glory… You seem to have gotten closer."

Zane gave a nod. "We have. She's a special person." The words were benign, lacking even a modicum of the depth of what he felt for her, but he couldn't put it into words yet. After last night…

Hunter grinned. "That's good. I'm glad to see you moving on. What happened with Christine was horrible, but you deserve to find happiness."

Zane sucked in a breath, his dream from the night before weighing heavily on his mind. Maybe it meant that he should stay away from Glory, or maybe it was already too late for that. Dubose could be the end of him. Either way he wasn't leaving until she was safe from the madman.

He shrugged and tried to act like it didn't mean anything. "It's not like that, brother. She tolerates me being in her space, and I happen to like being in her space. We both know the future isn't certain."

Hunter frowned, his brows drawing together over his eyes. "Are you certain that's all it is?"

Zane swallowed, very uneasy with the direction of this conversation, especially after what had happened between them last night. "What do you mean?"

Hunter shrugged. "You look at her like you looked at Christine, that's all. I assumed it meant that you had something…well, special."

Zane was very much afraid that they did. No, terrified. He never wanted to feel that way about anyone again, and he'd thought he'd made himself immune to that vulnerability. Despite the omen from his past and his own experience, somehow Glory had found a way in through all of his defenses. He'd be damned if he knew what to do about it.

"It could be, if we let it." His answer was as honest as he could make it.

"But you don't want to let it?"

Zane shook his head. No, Glory wasn't Christine, but his heart was still the same one Christine had torn out and stomped all over that night back on the Reyes hacienda. It wasn't willing to forget or to even believe that love was worth the pain all over again.

"Does Glory know you feel that way?" Hunter asked.

Guilt and anger collided within him, swirling together in a storm that begged to be let out. He knew that Hunter was right. He needed to have a serious talk with her to let her know that whatever was happening between them couldn't go any further. He'd thought they'd been on the same page about that, but after last night… Hell, he'd gone and messed that up last night when he'd held her. The worst part was that he couldn't even regret doing it.

Shaking his head, he said, "Let's go make a plan for dealing with Dubose." He led the way back across the hall, feeling, for the first time in his life, like he was in over his head.

Chapter Seventeen

The rest of the day was a whirlwind of preparations. Glory barely had time to think much less dwell on the fact that Justin was coming for her. She and Charlotte spent the day packing up the women and children in the boardinghouse. The two women and children were booked for the first train out the next morning. Sarah and her mother would be going out to the Jameson ranch with Clara, Emily and Edward. Glory had hoped to get them out on the first night, but everyone had agreed that leaving in the morning was best. No one wanted to travel at night, not with a threat looming over them.

It turns out they needed the extra time to pack their trunks anyway. Glory stayed up late into the night to help Clara get her household packed. Since no one knew how long they'd be gone, it was best for her to pack up everything she might need for the baby. It had been midnight when Able escorted Glory back to her room.

She said good-night at the door and closed it softly, only realizing in that moment how much she'd missed seeing Zane that day. She'd become accustomed to having him shadow her throughout her day. It hadn't made sense today though, with Able needing to help with packing.

The only light in the room came from the streetlamp outside. It cast a soft glow that barely reached the sofa where Zane was lying. A part of her had hoped he'd be awake so they could talk, but she knew that he needed his rest. She'd get the details tomorrow, but she knew that he'd coordinated a round-the-clock watch with the men that had come into town from the Jameson ranch. She'd see less of him now as he took his scheduled shifts. Her heart clenched at the thought, as if she was already beginning to lose him.

"Hey." His sleep roughened voice surprised her. He didn't sit up, but she could just make out his features in the shadows. "Did you finish packing?"

"Yes, but I'm afraid we're going to have to find a buckboard or two to rent. Clara has insisted on taking everything." She kept her tone light because for some strange reason she was feeling very insecure with him. He hadn't been avoiding her. Well, not exactly. They'd simply been too busy to see each other, but no matter how many times she told herself that, she couldn't seem to shake the feeling that something had changed. Even though she hadn't been particularly sober last night, she remembered how gentle he'd been with her and how he'd held her. She could use a little holding tonight, but it seemed inappropriate to ask.

"It must be hard to have to pack up and leave on short notice, especially when she's so close to having a baby."

"I'm sure it is." Glory stood there, wanting to bring back the intimacy of the previous night but feeling too awkward to accomplish it. She was being silly. He was probably as tired as she was, if not more so, and standing here bemoaning the fact that they'd barely touched all day wasn't doing anything but putting her in a bad mood. "Well, good night."

"Night."

She let out a breath, feeling the slightest bit defeated, and walked to her bedchamber. She'd almost closed the door when he called out, "What time do we leave for the train station?"

"Six thirty," she answered, silently chastising herself for expecting anything more.

The next morning was full of goodbyes. Glory said goodbye to the boarders at the train station, only to return home in time to help load the children and Clara off to the ranch. It had taken her carriage along with the Jamesons' carriage and two buckboards to get everything loaded. Hunter and two of his men with big guns strapped to their hips and rifles fastened to their saddles were to ride mounted alongside. She didn't know why it hit her so hard, but as she watched the small caravan pull away she had to blink back tears.

Castillo rode in one of the carriages with Clara, Sarah and her mother. From the other, two pairs of chubby arms waved enthusiastically at her, the twins riding with Emmy, Caroline and Charlotte—Glory had begged her to go at the last minute so the children would have someone with them who was familiar with their routine. They hadn't wanted to leave her, but when she'd told them about the horses and rabbits waiting for them there, they'd become excited and hadn't stopped talking about which horse they wanted to ride. It didn't matter that they'd never seen the horses. They had a whole herd of them in mind.

She was going to miss their whimsy. She knew that this was for the best and that they'd be cared for, she was only sad that she wouldn't be the one doing it. A large hand ran up and down her back in a slow caress. She looked up to see Zane watching the last buckboard as it disappeared around the corner.

"They'll be fine," he said.

"I know." But she sniffled anyway.

Putting his arm around her shoulder, he drew her against his chest. "I know it's hard, but you'll see them again. I promise you that."

She closed her eyes and allowed herself a moment of comfort. "I sent the telegram to their mother yesterday." She'd made herself do it, despite the hustle and bustle of making all the other arrangements. She needed to finally tie up this loose end.

"It's good that you're getting that settled. You need to move on one way or the other."

She nodded and looked up at him. This time he looked down at her and his gaze was as deep and intense as she remembered. His thumb caressed her cheek, giving her chill bumps even though the morning was already quite warm. There were so many things unsaid between them, but she didn't know how to broach them or if he even wanted to. He'd made it clear that he didn't want any permanence in his life. "I have to go. We're taking stock of the cellar today. Do you have watch?"

"Afternoon and early evening. We'll talk tonight about how the men will be stationed. I want to wait for the rest of the men from the ranch to arrive before we finalize things."

"Would you like to discuss it over supper?" She bit her lip, for some strange reason nerves twisted her belly as she waited for his rejection.

It didn't come. He hesitated, but then gave a nod. "In your room. I think we need to keep you out of sight as much as possible."

She didn't like that. She was a fixture at Victoria House. The last thing she wanted was for people in town to become suspicious. She didn't want Justin to know that he'd rattled her. But instead of arguing, she nodded. They could talk about it more tonight. "See you then."

"We have to close Victoria House." Zane sat across from her at supper that night. He'd been a little late and looked tense as he'd taken his seat. She realized now it was because he'd known that she wouldn't like what he had to say.

"We are not closing."

He raised a brow as he picked up his utensils and cut into his mutton. "I knew you'd see it that way."

She shrugged and gave him a smile. "That's because you know it doesn't make good business sense."

Taking a bite, he chewed it slowly as he studied her. She tried not to analyze too closely why the sight of him eating was so appealing to her and looked back down at her plate. She wasn't particularly hungry, and hadn't been since Justin Dubose had come back into her life.

"I suppose it doesn't, but I'm more concerned about what makes sense for your safety."

"I can't let my business fail because I'm worried about my safety."

"Do you really think the House will fail if you take a few days to lay low?"

She honestly didn't know what to think. Aside from the occasional ailment that had her taking a nap during the afternoon before the crowds started, she'd never taken any time away from her work. This past week had been the least amount of attention she'd ever given the place. Victoria House was the focus of…well, everything in her life.

"I don't know. It might." It was a lame argument, but it was all she had.

When he didn't answer right away, she looked back up at him to see a smile pulling at the corners of his lips.

"You find that funny?" she asked.

He shook his head and carved off another bite-sized portion of meat, smile firmly in place. "You wouldn't know what to do with yourself anyway."

Something about the way he said that ruffled her. "That's not true. I have my books." She motioned toward the small corner shelf currently stocked with about a dozen books. She'd already read them, but kept them to pass around to her ladies who liked to pass their time reading. Despite the fact that she'd donated to the local library and had been involved in getting the vote to the ballot to change the library from subscription to free, she didn't feel comfortable walking into the place. She either sent Charlotte or she ordered her books, which could sometimes take months to arrive.

"And…" Her voice trailed off as she looked around her parlor. Even she had to admit that she didn't have much to do. Without the twins and the boardinghouse, her business and her advocacy work, she had nothing. "Fine. You've made your point."

He laughed and she kicked him under the table. On one hand, she could see the humor, but on the other hand, it was a keen reminder of what she didn't have. A fresh ache welled in her chest as she remembered the domestic scene at the Jameson town home from yesterday. She'd probably never have that rich home life with a family. For years she'd been telling herself she was fine with that, but she really wasn't and she didn't know if she ever would be.

"Ouch!" He scowled at her and made a show of rubbing his leg.

"Serves you right." She sniffed and pushed some stewed carrots around on her plate. "You shouldn't tease me."

"Maybe I like teasing you." He said it with that certain timbre in his voice, that soft husk that prickled her skin and made it feel like he was caressing her with his words. His eyes were playful but somehow still held that intensity that she found so alluring with him. It was as if she was the entirety of his focus.

Maybe I like it when you do. That's what she wanted to say, but she didn't, even though the butterflies that constantly swarmed her belly when he was around had started batting their wings. She opened her mouth, but found her throat too dry to speak, so she had to swallow several times.

A blush stained her cheeks. He had her so turned around, and she wasn't sure how he felt about her. He was always teasing and he'd been quick to comfort her this morning when she'd needed it, but he also seemed to keep his distance. A sound on the roof interrupted her before she could respond and make a cake of herself.

"Is that a man on the roof?" It had sounded like heavy footsteps, making her pulse race as she imagined all kinds of scenarios that involved Justin coming into her room through her window.

"That's one of the things I wanted to talk to you about. We've got a man stationed on the roof twenty-four hours a day. He should be able to see anyone coming and going, and he'll sound the alarm if he sees Dubose. I have a man on the roof of the general store down the street too. Able helped me with a drawing of Dubose, and they've all seen it. Obviously he's likely to have aged since Able last saw him, but it's the best we have. As we discussed yesterday, we have someone at the train station and a man at each entrance to the House."

"I doubt a gunslinger hanging outside my front door will be good for business."

"Neither will Dubose getting inside the House."

He made a good point. "Touché."

He grinned and tossed his last bite into his mouth. When he'd finished chewing he said, "Since we've closed up the boardinghouse, Able's moving in here. It'll be easier to keep watch if everyone is under one roof."

The way he paused and stared at her with his brow furrowed made her think there was more. She nodded to encourage him.

"Since Clara is at the Jameson ranch, he could stay here in your suite if you prefer." He said it as if she'd missed the obvious conclusion. "I could go back to my room."

She didn't want Zane to go back to his room. She very much wanted him to stay here, but only if he wanted to stay here. Why was she such a ninny when it came to him? She blinked to break his stare and regain some of her equilibrium. "Would you like to move back to your room?"

There. She'd leave the decision up to him. It would tell her if he saw something for them or if he'd rather go back to how things had been before they'd spent the night in bed, because she, inexplicably, couldn't come straight out and ask him. Annoyed with herself, she took a drink of water.

"Do you want me to?"

She wasn't certain if he was toying with her or if he was as anxious about their arrangement as she was. Either way, she decided it was time to get everything on the table once and for all. She wasn't this wary a person, and she didn't want to be that way with him. Not anymore.

"I want you to stay..." She let her voice trail off to gauge his reaction. She thought she saw a little flare of relief along with something else that she couldn't name. That something else left her wary, but she pressed onward. It was time to confront what was between them. In for a penny, in for a pound.

"In there." She nodded toward her bedroom, gripping her hands together in her lap so hard that she was certain her fingers had probably lost their color, but she couldn't remove her eyes from him to check. And she couldn't loosen her hold, not until he answered her.

He looked from her to the door and back again. His eyes had gone wide but now they narrowed at her, extinguishing any hint of his earlier teasing humor. His jaw was tight, his shoulders tense. "I don't want to rush you, and I can't promise a future."

"I know. With…" She didn't want to say Justin's name. It had no place in this room, not right now. "With the immediate future so uncertain, maybe it's best to live for now." She so wanted to live instead of simply surviving.

His eyes flared and he sucked in a deep breath as his gaze went to her lips. She wet them on impulse. "Are you saying that you want more than what happened the other night?"

Her stomach tilted and whirled, and she couldn't believe they were even having this conversation. The fact of the matter was that she didn't know if anything more than kissing and touching was possible for her. But she'd never even been willing to try before now. A week ago she'd have thought it was impossible, but now anything felt possible with him.

Because of Zane. Because she loved the way he made her feel when he was around, whether he was kissing her or not. Though she especially loved the kissing. She'd regret it for the rest of her life if she allowed this distance to grow between them and didn't at least reach out and try to see what could happen with them. He was special to her. In her whole life she'd never met anyone who made her feel like he made her feel and that was something.

"I'm not sure. I know that doesn't sound fair, but the truth is I'm not really certain what I mean." She shrugged. "Maybe we could see what happens."

He took a minute, sitting there in his chair with his gaze roving over her face. She'd have given anything to know what he was thinking. Thankfully, she didn't have to wait long. Her heart sped up again when he pushed back from the table and got to his feet. He slowly walked around to her and extended his hand.

"I've spent the past week trying and failing to keep myself away from you. I can't do it anymore." One corner of his lips tipped upward and heat flared in his eyes. "Let's go see what happens."

She couldn't breathe as she put her hand in his. Closing his fingers around hers, he pulled her to her feet. "Before we go…there's something I need to tell you." She hadn't mentioned it last night because she hadn't been sure it would matter. Her throat went dry and she swallowed a few times. Her tongue suddenly felt like cotton in her mouth.

He brought a hand to her cheek in a move that had quickly become familiar to her. She loved when he stroked her like that. It somehow managed to say, "You're safe," and "I accept you," at the same time.

Her expression must have been as terrified as she felt, because he said, "Whatever it is, it won't change tonight."

"Promise?"

"Promise. Tell me."

"I have a scar." She did her best to never look at it, because it was a stark reminder of all that had been taken from her. The only reason she was bringing it up now was because he'd probably see it and she didn't want it to ruin anything. Maybe she could hide it from him, but she wasn't sure. It was best to tell him now. If he didn't want to continue, then she'd rather know now than later.

The corner of his mouth tipped up again. "I have several. You can't think I'd care about that."

She shook her head. This wasn't coming out quite right. "It's from that night…" Her stomach churned. This was a bad idea. Why had she ever thought that she could do this? She didn't want to mention the pregnancy, so she said, "The night I was pushed down the stairs."

"Hey." His arms went around her waist, encircling her and making her feel safe. "You're here now. I've got you."

Such a small statement, but it somehow gave her the strength to keep going. She had the memories, but she didn't have to get taken back to that place. She was here. Zane was here. She liked here. The pressure that had started squeezing her chest eased up and she could breathe again. "There was a problem and…well, I have a scar from the procedure the doctor performed to get th-the baby out." It had also ensured that she'd never bear another child. Dubose had seen to it.

She watched his face carefully for some change in his expression, but nothing happened. He must be an excellent poker player. She regretted telling him already. Not because she didn't want him to know, but because she'd completely ruined the moment. Who would want her after that confession? She should've simply tried to keep it hidden. "I'm sorry."

"Don't be sorry." He held her tight against him and dropped light kisses on her cheeks, her forehead, her chin and finally her lips. "But I'll ask you again, did you think I would care about a scar? It doesn't change that I want you."

She *had* thought it would change things. She realized that she'd expected him to pull away. There were plenty of women who weren't scarred, and he could probably have any one of them. She hadn't realized how utterly ridiculous that sounded until she found herself almost saying that to him. "It seems minor when you put it that way."

"I know it's not minor to you, but I want *you*, Glory, you and your scars."

The air around them had changed, charged with an energy that seemed to draw them together. Without even quite realizing how it had happened, her body was against his and he was lifting her into his arms. He was strong and solid, and she was happy that, while she felt anxious because this was new and exciting, there wasn't an ounce of fear in her. Desire left no room for that.

Desire and a sneaking suspicion that she'd allowed her heart into the mix. But as she looped her arms around his shoulders and brought his mouth down for a kiss, it didn't feel wrong or dangerous. It felt exactly right.

Chapter Eighteen

Zane held her tight as he released her legs, letting them slide down his body in a smooth glide that left his blood rushing through his veins. He couldn't stop staring down at her. The elegant sweep of her cheekbones, the perfect fullness of her lips and the intoxicating look in her hazel eyes. He knew that look. Christine had given him that look, which is why her betrayal had ripped his heart out.

He could've better dealt with the fact that she hadn't loved him after all. That their relationship had been built on lust he'd mistaken for love. It would've been easier to handle when she'd left him broken and bleeding in the dirt. But that hadn't been the case. She'd loved him. He'd seen it her eyes and felt it in her touch. The simple truth was that she'd chosen something else over him.

The pad of his thumb traced over Glory's brow as he saw an echo of that look in her eyes. She was falling in love with him. He swallowed thickly, aware that his hand held a slight tremor as he touched her. She closed her eyes and leaned into his caress, a soft sound at the back of her throat letting him know how much she enjoyed being touched by him. They'd agreed not to talk about the future, but he couldn't go further with her until he was certain that she understood.

"Glory?"

"Mmm…" She opened her eyes and there was that look again. Warm and open and trusting and part of him wanted that, reveled in it even; but, with that longing came dread and certainty that they were headed for a cliff and the inevitable fall.

"I need you to know that this…" He broke off and had to swallow again past a tongue gone thick and clumsy with all the things he didn't know how to say. "I can't promise you more than tonight. Hell, we both know I can't even promise you tomorrow."

She gave him a slow nod, her teeth working her bottom lip. "You make me feel like no one ever has, Zane. I don't want to spend the rest of my life regretting not holding on to this moment. We both know tomorrow isn't certain. But tonight can be."

He wanted to crush her against him, but holding her was like holding something very precious. He didn't want to chance breaking her, so he very slowly and with infinite tenderness brought his lips to hers. She opened beneath him, enthusiastically deepening the kiss, and he was lost. All his careful intentions fell to the wayside. She tasted so sweet and good that he drank from her lips, wanting more.

She groaned in the back of her throat, a sound that moved through him, thickening his blood and driving it south. He held her closer, but it wasn't close enough. Suddenly her gown was too much, he wanted her naked and beneath him. His hands tightened at her waist as he held her flush against him, the hard steel of his arousal pressing into her soft belly. Hard where she was soft. Rough where she was smooth. The differences between them begged to be explored.

Breaking the kiss enough to take a deep breath and calm himself down, he looked down at her. To his surprise she gave him a coy smile.

"I want to see you without your shirt again. I didn't get to touch you last time."

He grinned, amazed and in awe of the beautiful woman before him. She was a contradiction of eagerness and hesitancy. His fingers were already on the buttons of his shirt before he'd even realized he'd moved, so he had to remind himself to go slow and let her set the pace. He was the luckiest man alive right now that she was letting him in and allowing him to show her how good things could be between a man and a woman.

Without looking to see where it would fall, he tossed his shirt to the side. His chest swelled with an emotion he couldn't be bothered to name as her gaze raked over him hungrily. Gently taking her hand, he brought it to his chest. Her teeth tugged at her soft bottom lip as she ran both palms over him, making him want to take her lips again. So he did.

Her hands gently squeezed his chest muscles as she opened for him, allowing his tongue to delve inside and taste her sweetness. He wanted to taste her everywhere, but he'd take what he could get for now. As they kissed, she explored him. His chest, his back, the planes of his stomach. Her fingers stopped at the top button on his pants.

"Go ahead." His voice was a breathless whisper when he pulled back.

She hesitated. Her fingers traced over his skin, making everything in him tighten and burn with need. Slowly so that she could tell him to stop if she wanted, he reached for his pants, his fingers finding hers at the button. Very gently he popped it open. She took in a harsh breath, but she didn't draw away. Instead, he felt her fingertips tracing over his belly, playing in the light matting of fur that led down into his pants.

Gritting his teeth against the pleasure, he stood there for her, letting her explore him. He was throbbing, needing her to touch him, wanting to be buried inside her, so he closed his eyes and thought of anything but her soft hands playing over his skin.

"You're so beautiful," she whispered.

He grinned. "I've been called a lot of things, but never that."

She smiled up at him. "Well, then, that's a travesty. It's true." Her eyes roamed over his torso in appreciation and her hands followed as if she couldn't get enough of touching him. The fingers of one hand traced over his shoulder, the one with the scar. "What happened?"

He wanted to shrug off the question, but the way she looked at him as she asked, her eyes so solemn and knowing, he couldn't. She looked at him not as a marvel, but as someone who carried scars of her own. Someone who'd been through the worst life could offer and just might be able to understand. It wasn't even a conscious thought, but he found himself telling her. "It's a lash from a whip."

She gasped, but she didn't pull her hand away. Her fingertips traced it up and down his shoulder before moving up to his face. He'd never allowed a woman to touch his scar before. That horrible night had been too fresh and vivid in his mind for too long. But he found himself leaning into her touch.

"This is the same type of scar," she whispered, her fingertip tracing over his brow.

He gave a slight nod so that he wouldn't dislodge her hand. "It happened the same night as the other. The night the Reyes hacienda was raided by the Derringers."

She didn't seem horrified or upset. There was calm acceptance in her expression, an acknowledgment. They were both survivors. "It makes you look dangerous," she said, a teasing light in her eye. "When you're angry you look downright vicious. And now…"

"And now?" he prompted.

"You look like the big bad wolf, waiting to eat me up."

"Hmm…not a bad idea."

She giggled, the light and happy sound washing over him and filling him up with sunshine and contentment.

"You'll need to take off your dress first."

She nodded and turned so that he could work the fastenings. His fingers, thick and clumsy, trembled as he unfastened each tiny button. He took advantage of her exposed neck and placed an openmouthed kiss at her nape, letting the tip of his tongue drink the salty sweetness from her skin.

She sighed and moved back into his touch. "That's lovely."

He nearly laughed at her description. He'd take lovely. As he unbuttoned her dress, he kissed his way down her spine until his lips found the cotton fabric of her chemise, then he kissed back up, loving the chill bumps his touch raised on her skin.

"Take this off," he whispered in her ear when he'd finished.

She moved away to take the garment off and step out of her shoes, carefully placing the dress in the armoire. He sensed some hesitation in her, so he took the opportunity to sit on the edge of the bed and take off his boots. He'd gone back to his own clothes since he'd been on watch. Well aware that they might not progress past kissing and touching tonight, he vowed to pace himself and ignore the hunger roaring through his veins.

When he was left in his pants and she only in her chemise, she walked over to stand in front of him. His hands were drawn to her, catching her by the waist and pulling her closer. She was smiling a little, but there was fear in her eyes now.

"We don't have to do more tonight." His voice was husky and rough.

"No…it's not that."

His fingers tightened in the chemise and he placed a kiss in the tantalizing dip between her breasts where the fabric met her skin. There was a ribbon holding it together and he wanted to pull it apart. To see her breasts. To taste them.

"You can tell me."

"I want to do more, I'm just…" She shook her head and ran a hand over her face in exasperation. "I don't like that I'm afraid, but I am."

He ran his hands up her rib cage and back down, stopping short of her breasts. "Does it feel good when I touch you?"

She nodded.

He took in a deep breath, taking in her rose scent. In the back of his mind warnings flared, but he ignored them. He ignored everything but the woman in front of him. "You get to set the pace, Glory." To demonstrate his point he brought his hands up again, stopping just under the fullness of her breasts. He met her gaze before he went further, silently asking for permission. She gave him a nod and he took them in his palms. The mounds barely filled his hands. Her nipples were tight against his palms, and her lips parted as he gently tested their weight.

"More?"

She nodded again, and he shifted his hands, circling her nipples with his thumbs. She gasped and bit her lip, leaning into his touch. He could barely make out their shadow in the dim light, which taunted him, making him want to see her even more. Gently, he stroked over her nipple, drawing another sound from her lips.

"When you're ready, untie the ribbons so I can taste you."

Glory felt her nipples harden even more under the skillful touch of his hands and fingers. He continued to gently knead her breasts, playing with her nipples, which were hard little peaks under her chemise. She moved slowly, her fingers trembling, but she untied the ribbon and the fabric gaped apart. Wanting nothing more than to feel his hands on her bare skin, she grabbed them and brought them to the opening. He pushed the fabric aside, his fingers eagerly seeking her skin. His callused palms were slightly rough as they raked over her smooth breasts, sending flares of heated pleasure across her skin. His hand was so large as it closed over her that it encompassed her entire breast.

They were opposites in so many ways on the outside, but on the inside they were the same. He understood her in ways she couldn't explain. He worked her nipples between his forefinger and thumb, tugging slightly. She gasped as darts of electricity shot directly to her belly. Liquid heat pooled between her thighs, making her rub her thighs together to alleviate some of the tension.

"I want your mouth," she whispered.

A soft growl came from his lips as he closed his mouth over one the beaded peaks. The rough hum sent desire spiraling to her center. From his rough hands to the purely masculine sounds he made, she loved every part of him. His gaze never left hers as he tugged with his mouth and teased her with his tongue. The strength went out of her knees, forcing her to hold on to his shoulders to keep upright. She felt drunk all over again, only this time he was her brandy.

Finally he pulled back, placing a kiss on each breast before pushing her chemise down and off her arms so that it fell to the floor. She was left naked before him, completely exposed in a way that she didn't think she'd be comfortable with. And she wasn't. The vulnerability had an immediate dampening effect on her need for him.

The familiar squeeze of panic in her chest made it hard to breathe. Her fingers felt numb on his shoulders, craving his warmth but unable to feel it. This was a mistake. She should've insisted on staying clothed. Her scar was there, between them, and it would always be there no matter what she did.

She meant to step back, but his hands tightened on her hips and he slid off the bed onto his knees before her. He stared up at her as if she were perfect. His hands moved over her skin in a caress far too gentle for their size. Bending slightly, he kissed her stomach, her navel and below to the vertical scar that stopped at her pubic bone. She didn't realize that she was breathing in short pants until he raised his head to give her that hint of a smile that she'd come to associate with him.

"Beautiful." It was one word, but it said so much. She didn't pay attention to the scar or the fact that he could see it. She was so consumed with him that she couldn't see anything past him.

Her fingers gently brushed his black hair back from his face, and he turned his head, placing a kiss on her palm. Then he went back to kissing her belly, her legs, only to place a final one on the russet curls that covered her sex. A shiver went through her body, cold and hot at the same time. A mix of pleasure and anxiety to match the push and pull going on within her.

His large hands moved up her leg, past the bend of her knee to gently knead the muscles of her thighs.

She widened her stance to give him room and he took advantage, taking his touch higher before retreating again. He did this a few times, and each time she held her breath as he got closer to the apex of her thighs. A pleasurable ache had begun to bloom there. The concept of arousal wasn't foreign to her. She'd felt it before, particularly when he kissed her, but she'd never experienced it like this. With a man ready and waiting to stoke the flames higher.

She could even feel the tension coming off him. If she looked down, she knew that she'd see the large bulge in his pants that had pressed against her earlier. He was as aroused as she was, and he was holding himself back, drawing it out to make it as good for her as he possibly could. Tenderness swelled in her heart as she stared down at his face, a face that had become precious to her.

The next time he moved his hand up her inner thigh, his fingers grazed her sex. She gasped aloud at the sensation, the ache became a dull throb, begging for more of his touch. When he brought his hand up again in that slow, teasing caress, she took it with hers. His heavy-lidded stare dared her to go further, so she brought his fingers to her. He grinned, gently moving his fingertips over her, spreading the dampness he found there. She moved her foot out farther to ease his way, and he found her swollen. Waves of need pulsed through her when he touched that particular place. Using her own moisture, he slicked the pad of his finger over her again and again until she was panting aloud. Her cry filled the air when she felt the wet heat of his tongue replace his finger.

He rose to his feet, but didn't stop the delicious motion of his hand. His other came up to tip her head back so that he could claim her mouth in a deep kiss. She liked it. She actually liked the way his hand gripped her hair, the way her naked breasts were pressed against his solid chest, and especially the way his other hand gave her pleasure between her legs. She even liked that she could faintly taste herself on his tongue. Her hips rocked with his movement, needing even more. When he broke the kiss, she actually laughed.

He smiled down at her, but his brow was furrowed at the same time in question.

"I didn't think I would enjoy it this much," she confessed. Relief mingled with the pleasure, giving it sway to coil ever tighter in her belly, asking for more. More of him. More of this. Her own palms moved down his smooth chest to rub over the rough hair that led down into his pants. Hesitant but determined to overcome her anxiety, she moved her hand down farther, stroking over the bulge in his pants. She was rewarded with his rough exhale of pleasure.

"We don't have to do more than this," he whispered. His hands moved to her hips and she got the distinct impression that she'd just made him go weak in the knees. A thrill of power surged within her.

She squeezed gently, testing out the feel of him. She wasn't certain how far she could go with him, but she hadn't reached her limit yet. "I want to see you."

He reached down and finished unfastening the buttons down the front of his pants. She watched his movements with her breath stuck in her throat, anxious to see all of him. Slowly the fabric parted and he pushed his pants down his thighs. His manhood sprang free to stand tall and thick against his belly. He didn't move, giving her the time she needed to study him. She'd been prepared to feel the familiar coldness of fear creeping over her, but she didn't feel that. Or rather it was a faint echo pushed to the far reaches of her mind. Curiosity had taken its place with need following close behind.

She gently took him in her hand, enjoying the way his breathing became harsh in response to her touch. He liked what she was doing and that knowledge somehow fed her own desire, making it burn hotter. His skin felt like silk here and so hot. Her fingers couldn't quite touch her thumb as they wrapped around him. His large hand covered hers and he showed her how to stroke him and bring him pleasure.

As she moved, she was torn between watching her movements and watching his face. His eyes were hooded, mere slits in his face as he stared at her. They were nearly black. Yet, despite the intensity of his expression, he managed to keep his gentleness. He never touched her or urged her further than she wanted. She felt that if she turned away from him in that moment that he would honor her need for time, and that, more than anything, urged her forward. She let him go to draw him down for a kiss. Her tongue stroked his, and the hard length of him pressed hard and eager against her belly. An answering pulse beat between her thighs, and she moved against him, loving how hard and strong he felt against her.

She wanted more, and that knowledge was exhilarating. It spurred her forward to take a leap of faith and go further. "More," she whispered against his lips.

His answering groan reverberated inside her. The heat in her belly coiled even tighter and higher, reaching for something. "Glory," he whispered, placing open-mouthed kisses across her jaw and down her neck. His teeth raked over her skin, sending the flame of pleasure burning in her belly ever higher. She closed her eyes and gave into all the good things he made her feel.

His hands tightened on her hips as he lifted her, setting her up on the bed. She moved back, giving him room and he came down between her thighs. She gasped at the sudden contact of his hard manhood against her open sex, but he didn't make a move to do more. He kept his weight on his knees as he bent over her to take a nipple into his mouth, sucking deep before teasing her with his tongue.

She writhed beneath him, caught up in the pleasure of his hot mouth and the decadent feel of his hardness stroking against her where she throbbed, making her aware of just how empty she felt there. He groaned her name again but this time it was a plea, a request, a need for more that she understood. She instinctively answered, throwing her arms around him and pulling him down, needing everything he could give her.

Except the moment his weight came down on top of her, a subtle change began to happen. The hands that had been so pleasing a moment ago, roughened from years in the saddle, now felt hard and abrasive. The solid strength of his chest wasn't comforting and attractive as it had been moments ago. It now seemed unyielding and oppressive as it pressed her into the mattress. His mouth, once hot and decadent, belonged to someone else.

"Glory?" His deep voice cut through the fog that she hadn't even realized had moved between them. She opened her eyes to see him rise above her. "Are you with me?" he asked.

"What happened?" Her voice didn't sound like it belonged to her.

He gave her a tender look. "You left me."

Her heart fell, but he only smiled, and before she could think of what to say he had flipped their positions. She was sprawled across his chest trying to figure out what he was about as he moved a pillow behind him. Before she knew it, he sat back against the headboard, and she was across his lap.

"Kiss me." His voice was soft, but there was a subtle order in his tone.

She marveled at the contradiction he was and gently pressed her lips to his. She intentionally didn't deepen the kiss because she wanted to know what he'd do. He was grinning when she pulled back.

"Do you trust me?"

She did. He'd sensed that she'd needed to stop before she had regained her equilibrium enough to say the words. "More than anyone."

His eyes stroked down her face to her lips and back up again. "Then watch my hands." He put his right hand through the bronze spindles in her headboard, grasping one tight, and then did the same with his left hand. "I promise to keep them here. You can tie them there if it makes you feel better. Do with me what you will. You're in control. We do only what you want."

She stared at him in shock. "What do you mean?"

"I mean you can curl up at my side and take a nap, explore until your heart's content or climb on. The choice is yours."

She couldn't stop the giggle that escaped her lips. Amusement shone from his eyes, but he was still as hard as ever between them. The heat that had languished a bit inside her, flared back to life, and she squirmed on his lap. "Are you certain?"

He nodded. "I want tonight to be good for you, Glory."

He might live by his gun, but he was the most caring man she'd ever met. How could he be real? But he was real and he was hers. For tonight. She tried not to dwell on the pang of bittersweet uncertainty that shot through her.

She moved slowly, her palms becoming familiar with every dip and swell of his chest. She turned in his lap and straddled his thighs.

His breath came out in a slow exhale as if he'd been holding it. "Thank God. I was afraid you'd choose the nap."

A laugh bubbled up and out of her. Being with him was so easy. He was right. This felt better, like before when they had stood together. She didn't feel overpowered or overwhelmed by him and the need inside her came flooding back.

Holding on to his shoulders for leverage, she moved forward until his shaft was pressed against her belly.

Her swollen sex throbbed as she rocked against his hard length. He groaned deep in his throat and the sound nearly slayed her. She kissed him, his familiar taste drawing her back down into the throes of arousal. She rocked again, loving the sounds he made in response. Who knew that bringing him pleasure would be so addictive? Very soon she wanted more, so she rose up over him, her fingers digging into his shoulders to hold herself steady.

Inch by slow inch she lowered herself over him. She was so slick that the thick head of his manhood pushed right in. He let out a harsh exhale that matched her gasp. The fullness of him inside her felt incredible. She moved to test out the sensation, pulling up to nearly dislodge him before sinking down even farther. His entire body tensed. He kept his word but the muscles of his forearms flexed as he gripped her headboard, and she worried that her bed might not survive him. She did it again and again, working herself onto him until he was fully seated within her. They both let out a cry as he slid home, and she fell against his chest.

He kissed her temple and very gently moved his hips, flexing within her. It was all the encouragement she needed. Wrapping his hair around her fingers, she rose over him, moving slowly at first and then faster as she gained confidence. Flutters of pleasure deep in her belly urged her onward. He felt so good inside her that she forgot everything else but him and what was happening between them. Her entire world narrowed to them, to the way he throbbed inside her.

"So beautiful." His harsh voice rasped across her skin.

Heat spiraled through her, tightening the coil of pleasure inside her tighter and tighter until the tension exploded within her. She cried out and his voice was husky as he urged her higher, so that she was riding the crest of her pleasure. When she started to come down, he followed her over, his hips pumping upward as he pulsed within her, finding his release.

She was able to watch his face as he came. To see his eyes at the exact moment when he fell apart. He was beautiful. Rough and gentle, hard and soft. Perfect. She held him against her as they both came down, all the while wondering if she'd ever experience a more flawless moment in her life.

Chapter Nineteen

Zane woke up with a start. Disoriented, he tried to sit up, but a warm, soft body in the bed next to him kept him where he was. He smelled roses and everything that had happened a few hours earlier came back to him. He closed his eyes and tightened his arm around her waist. She snuggled back against him, her soft bottom making him start to go rigid.

He cupped her bare breast, gratified when she sighed and relaxed into him with a gentle snore. The sound brought a smile to his lips. There were so many things he wanted to know about her, but he wasn't certain he'd get the chance. He'd had that damn dream again. The one that left him questioning his life and mortality. Did it mean that he was destined to die when Dubose came to town? Did it mean that he should leave her anyway, even after Dubose was taken care of? He didn't know.

One thing he knew for certain was that he couldn't disregard it. It meant something.

Knowing he wouldn't get back to sleep after that dream, he sat up and looked down at the woman beside him. Being with her had been different than being with any other woman he'd ever known. Their joining hadn't been only about mutual pleasure. There'd been something more. The only thing that had ever come close was his time with Christine. He didn't like to think about her, especially not when in bed with Glory, but there she was.

He'd loved Christine. Cared about her like he'd never cared about another person, but even in their brief time together, even with his thoughts of marriage, he'd never imagined the contentment of growing old with her. Theirs had always been a relationship rooted in now. That's the relationship he and Glory had agreed upon as well, but this morning he saw more. He saw himself waking up with her every morning for years to come. He saw himself on a front porch holding her wrinkled hand as they watched the sunset and going to sleep with her at his side. They'd agreed not to think about the future, but that's all that he could think about now.

The tread of a boot on the roof overhead brought him back to the present, reminding him that he had more pressing concerns to think about right now. There'd be no future to consider if he couldn't figure out Dubose's plan. He moved to get out of bed, unwilling to wake her with his restless thoughts, but the moment he did she stirred and tightened her arm against his.

"Don't go," she whispered. "It's the middle of the night."

He hesitated. It wasn't that he didn't want to stay, it was more that he knew he'd never want to leave if he did.

She rolled over onto her back to look up at him in

the muted light coming in through the window. Light spilled across her shoulder, one breast was partially revealed. The expression on her face cinched his decision. It was so full of hope and tenderness that he felt himself relaxing back into the bed before he'd even made the conscious decision to stay. It was wrong. There were so many reasons to go, but he wasn't strong enough to turn away.

She went eagerly into his arms and settled against his chest. He'd planned to hold her until she went back to sleep, but she didn't seem sleepy anymore. Her finger drew small circles on his chest. He took a deep breath, trying and failing to keep her warmth from seeping into his heart. He realized then that she was far braver than he was. She'd faced her fear, but he couldn't. He was terrified of loving her.

"I know that you should go back to the sofa soon, but you don't have to go yet."

"Oh?" he asked absently more than from the fact that he had any strong objection to the suggestion. His mind was too busy racing along with his heart to think clearly.

"It makes sense, don't you think? We don't want Able to come early in the morning and find you here." When he didn't answer right away, she rolled her head to look up at him. His face must have reflected his mounting terror, because she asked, "Are you okay?" She rose up a little to see him better.

He nodded and managed to hold on to what she'd said. "Why shouldn't he find us?"

She stared at him as if he should know the answer to that question, before a tremulous smile made her lower her head. "I don't want to put you in danger," she teased. "I haven't talked to him yet. And I know you'll think I'm a contradiction, but I don't want people to know...to talk."

Irrational fear moved over him like a tidal wave, latching onto the scars from his past and refusing to let go. He could recognize it for what it was, but he could no more stop it than he could stop the churning of his thoughts. This hadn't meant to her what it meant to him. She wanted to keep them a secret. To keep *him* a secret. No one could know and the second they did would she turn from him?

He gave her a single nod, unable to do more at the moment.

She sat up, pulling the sheet with her to cover her breasts. "Are you certain you're okay?"

"Fine." His voice came out sharper than he'd intended it to, and she looked up at him a little stunned. "Why don't we make it easy? I'll trade with Able and take my old room back."

"No, you misunderstand. I don't want that." Her voice came from behind him as he sat on the edge of the bed and pulled on his pants. The heat of her hand nearly scalded him when she placed it on his bare shoulder. It was like a siren's call, luring him back to where he knew only pain awaited. He rose to his feet and stepped away from the bed as he worked the buttons.

"Zane, please... I didn't mean to offend you. I'll talk to Able tomorrow, I promise."

"But that won't solve the problem of people *talking*, will it?" He grabbed his shirt and shrugged into it without looking at her. She was silent on the bed. Despite his intention, he couldn't leave without seeing her expression and knowing how she felt.

Her brow was furrowed in pain when he met her gaze. "Can't we talk about this? You even agreed that the future was uncertain. I'd rather there not be talk among the staff until we know if there is even something to talk about."

A cold knife of pain moved through his chest, nearly taking his breath. He was horrible. Here he was deriding her over this when he'd already been fighting his own demons and losing, unable to face his own fears to have a future with her. Leaving his shirt open, he sat back down on the bed. Only a few inches separated them, but it might as well have been miles. She made no move to touch him.

He owed her something, so he said, "I never told you about Christine."

She shook her head, silently urging him on. So he told her, and it felt good to open up to her. He told her about how he'd fallen hard. About how Christine had led him to believe that she felt the same. He still thought that she'd been honest about that, but it hadn't been enough. When her brother found out about them and beat him to within an inch of his life for daring to lay a hand on her, it hadn't mattered.

He took a deep breath and forced himself to meet Glory's gaze head on. It wasn't fair of him not to explain to her. He'd never been a coward a day in his life, but here he was…afraid of her and what she did to him. "That's why I don't know about the future, our future.

The way she hurt me... I don't know if I'm able to open myself up to that again."

As he spoke, her eyes welled up with tears, but they didn't fall. "She's why you've been pulling away from me. I felt it yesterday at the Jameson home and again today. It's because of her?"

"Cas and Hunter swear that she never really loved me if she could do such a thing, but they don't know. I saw her. I held her. I know the way she looked at me. It was love and it was real. But it didn't matter."

She took in a wavering breath, and the sound of it pierced his soul. "I would never allow anyone to hurt you... You must know that?"

He raised a hand but stopped short of touching her knee, instead he let it fall back to the bed. He didn't have that right anymore. "I know that you wouldn't. I don't mean that you'd harm me in that way." He ran a hand through his hair, frustrated with his inability to say what he meant. "I'm saying that love is fleeting. We embrace it when it's convenient and discard it when it's not."

"So you don't even want to try?"

He shook his head. "There's no point."

Her chin dropped down, but she didn't say anything. After a moment, she pulled the sheet around her even tighter. He wanted to pull her against him and damn the inevitable pain, but he couldn't.

Finally, she said, "Thank you for telling me."

He hated that it had to be this way, but deep down he knew that it was for the best. Better to get out now while they were both capable of walking away. He rose, hating himself as he left.

* * *

Glory never went back to sleep. She lay there listening to the sounds of Zane in the parlor. He seemed restless, walking over to the window to stand there for a few minutes only to pace back to the front door. This went on for over an hour, until gray morning light filtered in through her window.

She wanted to cry. She *had* cried but only for a little while, not nearly long enough to quench the burning pain he'd left in her chest. The tears had dried up, leaving her with an emptiness that she didn't know how to handle. She shouldn't feel this bereft. They'd never agreed to any sort of future. In fact, he'd made it very clear before they'd even started that a future wasn't something they could even consider.

Her brain knew that, but her heart did not. Her heart wanted him.

She squeezed her eyes shut and pulled the pillow over her head when she heard her front door open. Able's deep voice was muffled through the wall and the down of her pillow. She let out the breath she'd been holding when her door shut and Able's heavier tread took him to her sofa. Zane was gone.

For some reason, that brought on a fresh wave of tears. She gritted her teeth in an attempt to hold them back, but a few escaped to run down her face. She hated what had happened to Zane. The truth of the matter was that she didn't know what if felt like to give your heart to someone only to have them turn on you, but she did know a little about how he felt. Her own family had given her to Justin. Didn't Zane see how alike they were? Didn't he realize that if anyone could understand him it was her?

It wouldn't matter if he did know those things. She knew it as soon as the questions had floated through her mind. He didn't really think that she was like Christine, so he didn't care if Glory would be able to understand. He thought that love wasn't binding, and she didn't know how they were going to overcome that.

He thought that when things got rough, she'd leave and go looking for greener pastures. Isn't that exactly what he had just done to her? He'd been fine to flirt and tease, but the moment things had gone deeper...he'd fled. If he didn't think love would last, then he wouldn't be around long. Even if she could convince him to stay now, something would drive him away later.

She'd been right about them from the beginning. He was the wind, and she was rooted firmly in the ground. Shame on her for forgetting that.

She tossed the pillow across the room because it smelled like him. Everything smelled like him. Even her skin. Wiping any lingering tears from her eyes, she rose and grabbed her dressing gown. Somehow she'd make it through the day, God knows that she'd made it through worse. A long hot soak in the tub would help, and then she'd have to figure out how to avoid Zane for...well...forever.

A lump welled in her throat, forcing her to swallow it down. Somehow she didn't think that her usual work ethic and diligence was going to get her through this.

She was right. The day passed in a fog. Mercifully, the sharp pain of their argument had gone to be replaced by a dull ache. It was compounded by the fact that the house itself had changed seemingly overnight. A hush had fallen over the place. Business was slow because a few of the girls had left with Sally for a short holiday. Glory had encouraged the trip knowing they'd be safer there than anywhere near Justin.

It was as if everyone was simply waiting. Able kept vigil at the front door but made frequent trips through the house every hour. Penelope polished the bar so much she'd likely rub a hole in the wood if she kept it up. And Glory paced. It was all she could do. She went from window to window, each time thinking that she might catch sight of Justin. But there was only the usual Helena traffic.

If she was honest, she was also hoping to catch a glimpse of Zane. She heard his voice once midmorning when he'd been out in the courtyard talking with his men, but she hadn't been able to bring herself to go see him. What was there to say anyway?

He didn't believe in them.

Finally night fell and they shut down the house. Able followed her to her room, but she couldn't ask him if he'd switched with Zane. She couldn't bear to hear it. Instead, she'd bade him good-night and had fallen into her bed early. She was exhausted and emotionally drained. This was one day she was happy to end.

Zane awoke with a start. For a moment he thought he might have had that damned dream again, but then he heard a voice. A man yelled something indistinct from the roof. His heart pounded as he pushed up off

Glory's sofa and ran to the window that overlooked the front of the house. Nothing was out of place. Everything looked normal.

He frowned and wondered if he'd imagined things. A quick glance toward her door confirmed that Glory hadn't been disturbed. He tried to ignore the almost painful squeeze of his chest. He probably should've asked Able for his room back, but he hadn't been able to bear the thought of not being here with her. If something happened and he wasn't here to protect her, he knew he'd never be able to live with that. In the end he hadn't asked, and when he'd arrived to take Able's place the man hadn't said anything to him, making Zane think that Glory hadn't told him what had happened.

The faint scent of wood smoke stung his nostrils. Dubose? Another shout broke through the silence. Someone yelled, "Fire!"

Dammit. He grabbed his holster and strapped his gun around his waist as he rushed to her room. He knocked, but threw it open to see her sitting up in bed, sleepy but alarmed.

"There's a fire. We have to go."

She was already moving. "I heard someone yell. Do you think he's here?"

"It's possible." Zane rushed to her armoire and pulled out the first garment he grabbed. Pulling it over her head, he quickly did up some of the buttons in back. "Get your shoes on." He rushed back into the parlor and shoved his feet into his boots, not taking the time to lace them up. When he finished, she ran into the parlor. "Go downstairs. I want you outside," he said.

"I have to make sure everyone knows!" She shouted back over her shoulder as she made for the door.

He followed her and they both pounded on every door on the third floor, shouting for people to get out. There was a window at the end of the hallway and he could see thick clouds of smoke floating past it, which spurred him to move faster. He had no idea where the fire had been started or how long they had to get out of the building.

Once every third-floor occupant had been accounted for, he followed the group of women down the stairs to the second floor. Glory tried to break from the crowd to start knocking on those doors, but he grabbed her arms to stop her.

"I have to go warn them!" she shouted.

"I'll do it. Get the women outside and grab who you find on the first floor."

She looked down the hallway and then back at him. Her eyes were bright with fear. He hadn't been thinking past his next move, but he suddenly realized that he had no idea how this scenario would end. He'd been inside her only the night before, and then he'd foolishly pushed her away. Now this could very well be the last time he touched her. He pulled her close and tightened his arms around her, burying his nose in her hair one more time. The scent of roses was only barely discernible over the smell of smoke. To his amazement, she hugged him back, her small hands tightening in his shirt. When he pulled back, he realized smoke was coming in through the open window at the end of the hallway.

He pressed a quick kiss to her mouth. "I love you,

Glory." If he never saw her again, he wanted her to know that. "Go!"

She nodded and turned back to continue herding the women down the stairs. The night was filled with cries of panic. He ran down the hall, pounding on doors while sending up a prayer that Glory got out safely.

The next few minutes were a blur of activity. The servants who lived on the second floor were already evacuating, so he helped the last ones out and hurried down the back stairway. He wasn't prepared for what he saw. Out of the first-floor windows that looked out over the courtyard, he saw that the boardinghouse was engulfed in a blaze. He was glad they'd had the foresight to close it down. At least everyone who lived there was safe at the Jameson ranch. Except for Able who had stayed in Zane's old room on the second floor, but that room had been empty when he'd opened the door to warn everyone.

The kitchen area was clear of people, so he made his way through the hallway toward the front. For some reason there was smoke here and it appeared to be getting heavier. He inhaled and coughed when it burned his nose and chest. There must be a second fire somewhere, but he couldn't seem to find it.

Chapter Twenty

After getting the women and servants who had filed out with her across the road to safety, Glory hurried around the block to the boardinghouse. A line of men were already carrying buckets of water, but it was clear that their efforts were no match for the fire. It already reached the second floor. Chaos had taken over as people screamed and fled from the surrounding buildings, fearful that the fire would spread. Glory felt helpless as she watched.

There was no doubt in her mind that someone had set the fire. No one had been in the boardinghouse to set it ablaze on accident. Who would do such an awful thing? Had it been Victoria House, she might have understood. It was no secret that many in town didn't like the business. But the boardinghouse had only ever helped people, women and children with nowhere else to go.

Accepting that it was too late to stop the fire, she rushed back around the block to Victoria House. They needed to get water ready so that the fire wouldn't spread across the courtyard. Some of the women had already run for help, but the rest were huddled in a group. She caught sight of Able organizing the servants who stood huddled at the far end of the street. Checking that the women were fine, she hurried past them to talk to Able.

"Able, we need to get a line formed so it doesn't spread."

He shook his head and pointed. "There are already flames from the first floor toward the back."

She saw that he was right. One of the windows in back had been broken out and flames could be seen within the room. What was happening? It was like the world had turned in just a few hours.

"Have you seen Zane?" She realized he wasn't standing with everyone else.

"I thought he was with you. Is he still inside?" Able asked.

"Yes!" she called over her shoulder, already running inside to find him. The sound of thunder shook the night. She drew up short, because it couldn't be thunder. There was no rain and somehow it had come from inside the house.

An explosion rent the air. Before she realized what had happened, someone pulled her back, and right before her eyes, half of the house went up in a roar of flames.

"Dynamite!" someone yelled, and everyone screamed and started running.

All she could think about was Zane trapped inside. She fought the hands that held her, trying to get free so that she could go find him. Half the house was unaffected and she hoped that's where he was, but the hands wouldn't let her go.

"No, Glory! There could be another explosion!" Able yelled.

She didn't care. She had to make sure that he was safe. The entire time she fought them she kept her eyes on the front door, willing him to come out. All of a sudden the hands let her go and she ran as fast as she could toward the house. She had to see if Zane had survived. Dear God, he could be dead now!

"Dammit, I'll go. You stay here!" Able's voice was harsh in her ear as he pulled her away again. Letting her go, he rushed around her and disappeared inside.

There was no way she was standing here by herself while the two people she loved were inside. She'd pull them both out with her own two hands if she had to. Faintly, she was aware of a horse nearby. Its frantic whinny entered the haze of her consciousness, but she didn't dare look away from the house in case she caught sight of Zane through one of the windows.

Someone stopped her again. A strong arm went around her waist, but instead of simply holding her back, it lifted her and her feet came off the ground. Something heavy and dark went over her head, blocking out the light. She screamed, but even she could tell it was muffled in the cacophony of sound around them. She felt herself falling and then landing on something hard. The floor of a carriage she figured out as the door slammed behind her and a male voice yelled, "Go!"

The horses whinnied again and took off at a run. She

could feel the momentum as they rushed through the streets. Someone grabbed her roughly and, although she fought as best she could, they tied her wrists behind her back and tossed her onto the bench seat. She landed on her hands and pain shot through her arms as she tugged at the bindings. What she suspected to be a burlap sack was still over her head, threatening to suffocate her. When she opened her mouth to scream it seemed to cling to her lips, making it difficult to take in air.

"Good evening, Anabelle."

It had been over a decade since she'd last heard that voice, but she recognized it immediately. Her blood chilled in her veins. A sense of weightlessness settled over her, as if she was in a dream and none of this could be real.

"Cat got your tongue, darling?"

"Justin." The hated word crossed her lips in a whisper, but loud enough to carry through the burlap and make him laugh. She knew that laugh. She hated every condescending note of it. Reality came crashing into her, settling over her with a heaviness that moved through her limbs, making her feel as if she were moving through a thick fog.

"That's better."

"What do you want?" Justin had set that fire to lure her out. He could've killed them all. Maybe he had killed Zane. Sorrow and anger opened a hollow within her. If he was dead she knew that she'd never be whole again.

He laughed again. "Why, you, of course. You're my wife. I want you home."

Wife. That word tore through her, savaging the

edges of a wound that had never healed. She had never been his wife. Yes, her parents had given her to him in exchange for him paying off her father's debts. Yes, there had been a signing of papers and words spoken before an officiant. But there had never been a marriage. Glory—Anabelle—had never spoken a word to bind herself to him. She'd never pledged one vow to the loathsome man everyone had called her husband. It hadn't mattered to them that she hadn't participated in the wedding.

But it mattered to her. Justin had never been her husband as far as she was concerned.

"I'll never go with you anywhere."

He laughed again. Dear God, how could he be so nonchalant about it all? He sounded as if they were in a parlor having tea while discussing the latest gossip out of Charleston. Cold fear moved through her veins. If she left town with him, she knew that she'd be dead soon. He'd kill her.

The creak of the leather told her that he was leaning forward, and then she could sense him over her. Her heart pounded as she tried to figure out what to say to him that would make him release her. Suddenly, the burlap sack was removed and she could make out his form across from her in the meager light from the streetlamps that seeped in around the edges of the curtains. He'd aged quite a bit in the decade she'd been gone. He was over fifty now and he looked it. His hair was streaked with more gray than brown, and the lines on his face had deepened. He was still handsome, though now it was as if his true nature had been revealed. Not only was his mouth twisted with a permanently cruel smile, but his whole face seemed to carry the look stamped on his features.

She opened her mouth to scream, hoping that someone would hear her, but as soon as she did he drew back his arm and slapped her with the back of his hand. Her ears rang from the impact.

"Let's not stoop to dramatics, shall we, darling? I've amused myself the past week imagining you scurrying about trying to find me, but I'm done now. It's time to go home."

Heavy curtains blocked her view of the street, so she couldn't see where he was taking her. She struggled against her bindings and kicked out at him with her feet. "I won't go anywhere with you." She was gratified when one of her kicks hit him in the chest, but it only infuriated him.

He drew back again and she screamed and lunged for the door. She'd open it with her teeth if she had to even as they were driving fast down the road. He yanked her by the hair and pulled her back, shoving something between her lips. He tied the strip of fabric behind her head and then pushed her away.

"You're feistier than you used to be," he said, retaking his seat on the opposite side of the carriage. "I can break you again. I did it once." He leaned forward and touched the cheek he'd hit. "I must say, you're more beautiful than I thought you'd be. At fourteen you were like a precious little doll. Now you're a woman. A whore, but all woman." He tightened his grip in her hair, sending pain shooting through her skull. "I never thought I'd find you in a whorehouse." He laughed. "Not only in a whorehouse but running the damn thing. How do you think I can bring you home now? Word will get out about what you are."

She shook her head to dislodge his hand and tried her best to speak through the gag. "Leave me alone. Leave me here."

"What's that?" He made a show of leaning forward even more. "You want me to leave you?" He gave his head a sad shake. "I wish I could, darling. Believe me, I stopped looking for you long ago, but I hope to be the next lieutenant governor of South Carolina. Politics have a way of bringing the past to light." He sat back, grinning at her. "Now you probably don't know this, but there was gossip when you left. Some people said that I'd killed you in the middle of the night and buried you in the swamp. Some people said that you'd run off with Hiram, since he'd disappeared at the same time. As you can imagine, both of those are a detriment to my chances in the election."

She didn't know what he was up to. He couldn't honestly think that she'd go home with him and play the dutiful wife. Could he? There was no way he would trust her to play that role. Something else was happening here.

The carriage drew to a sharp halt, making her neck jerk and her head bang against the seat behind her. The door swung open and a man she'd never seen before appeared in the opening. He was big like Zane, but mean-looking with a snub nose that was crooked, as if it had been broken and not reset properly. The worst part of him were his eyes. They were cold when he looked at her, as if he didn't care who she was or what part he was playing in destroying her life.

"Get her inside, Jenkins," Justin said and put the burlap sack over her head again.

She struggled but the man's hands were unyielding as he tossed her over his shoulder. Before the burlap sack had gone on her head she'd noticed they were at the train station. The early train usually departed well after six in the morning. She had no idea what time it was or how long they had before Justin took her away.

They walked down the wooden platform that ran next to the cars, but she could feel when Jenkins took the steps down to the dirt along the tracks. His boots crunched on the gravel. That probably meant that he was taking her to a private car. Those were hooked on in the back to make it easier to connect and disconnect them when they reached their destination. Her last hope of escape faded away. No one would even know she was on the train if they didn't check. The conductor would have no reason to check the private car for tickets. Private cars paid per car for passage, not per passenger.

Panic spurred her to resist even more, but it didn't seem to help. Jenkins only tightened his grip, and then they bounded up some steps and a door closed behind them. When the burlap sack came off, she was sitting on a narrow bed facing the window. An orange glow lit up the sky in the distance. She knew it was the fire from her home. Despite herself, tears burned her eyes as she realized she might not get away from Justin before morning.

She ran for the door that would lead her into the main part of the car, but Justin stood in the way and Jenkins jerked her back before she even reached him. The ominous clink of metal drew her attention and she saw him grab one end of a shackle that was attached to the bed frame.

"No!" She screamed the word over and over but it was muffled against the gag. The cold metal tightened around her wrist. Jenkins tossed her down onto the bed so roughly that the breath was knocked from her chest. She gasped through the cloth in her mouth, and he was able to tighten another shackle to her ankle. The rope tying her wrists together was cut, but it was too late to do anything about the shackles. She grabbed at them with her free hand, but they were locked tight.

"We don't need to tie her down just yet." Justin intervened and Jenkins stopped short of strapping down her other ankle. He glared at her though, silently daring her to kick him.

Justin opened a cabinet set into the wall, temporarily blocking him from her view, but when he came around it her blood ran cold. He grinned as he held up a hypodermic needle. A drop of brown fluid oozed from its tip.

"It's like this, Anabelle. We see if this can work its magic and make you a biddable wife. If yes, then we'll have some interesting years together. If not, then one day soon I'll find your body at the base of the stairs dead of an apparent suicide. You see, I've told everyone that you spent the past twelve years in a sanitarium in France. They know you're touched." He tapped his temple as he walked over toward her.

He nodded toward Jenkins, who leaned over her, pressing his weight into her thighs to keep her still. He twisted her free arm so hard that she was certain she'd hear the bone crack in a moment. It didn't, but she felt the prick of the needle as it broke through her skin and the burn of the drug Justin injected her with. She closed her eyes, desperate for some way to escape. Instead, she only saw Zane as he'd been the moment he'd told her that he loved her.

She screamed against the injustice of it all. She screamed so hard that her throat felt raw, and the shackle bit into the skin of her wrist. Her body felt heavy, as if her blood had become too leaden to make it all work. Still she screamed.

Chapter Twenty-One

Zane coughed as he pushed out from under the bar in the dining room. He'd dove behind it the moment he heard the blast that came from the large pantry off the kitchen. Plaster fell from the wall as he pushed a hunk of the wooden bar back into it in his attempt to pull himself out.

"Pierce!" Able's deep voice was unmistakable.

"In here!" Zane kept trying to get himself out and got to his feet as Able came through the open doorway.

"Come on." Able led him through the smoke and dust to the front of the house.

It was like they were in a dream. Zane could feel the coolness of the night air blending with the heat from the fire in the distance and realized that half the house was gone. He coughed again, nearly doubling over, and Able helped him the rest of the way out. When he looked back, he could see that the back of the house was rubble. The front might be salvaged if they could work fast enough. Fire blazed in the back and he figured the boardinghouse was a lost cause.

It was chaos outside. People scrambled around them running in all directions. A group of women who worked at Victoria House stood in a huddle, watching it all come down. He expected Glory to be there taking care of them, but he didn't see her anywhere. Able was running off to help when Zane caught up to him. "Where's Glory?"

He shrugged. "I don't know. She was going in to find you, but I told her to wait here and let me go."

They both looked around. Zane's stomach churned with the knowledge that something very bad had happened. What if the fire had been set to lure them out? What if she'd been taken?

"Glory!" He screamed her name. Turning in a circle in the middle of the street, he couldn't see her anywhere. She should be there with her ladies or at the very least with the people who'd formed a bucket line. He searched them all for her face, but she wasn't there.

He ran over to the women and asked, "Where's Glory?"

They all looked at him with blank faces. He turned back around to see Able doing the same thing, walking down the street and asking every person he saw. Everyone shook their heads. Dubose had her. He knew it with a certainty he felt deep in his bones.

It was utter chaos. Everyone was so consumed by the fire, and stopping it from spreading to the other buildings, that he had no hope of finding his men in the crowd. Miraculously, they found him. Two of them came out from behind Victoria House, covered in soot and smoke.

"It was dynamite," one of them said. "Probably thrown through a window in the back of the house."

He nodded. It wasn't what he was concerned with at the moment. "Where's Glory?"

"I kept my station over the general store after the fire broke out," Raul said. Zane had stationed him on top of the building diagonally across the road from Victoria House. "I saw a carriage stop and take her. They were headed toward the train station."

They hadn't had her long, but he couldn't shake the thought that Dubose might want her dead more than he wanted her back. It wouldn't take long to accomplish that task. He caught up to Able, and the four of them made a mad dash across town on foot. The sun was starting to crest the horizon to the east. As they turned the corner that would bring the depot in sight, a black carriage pulled away going in the opposite direction.

"Is that the carriage you saw?" Zane asked Raul.

"Looks like it. The curtains were drawn like that one," the man answered.

"Odds are she's on that train," Able muttered, his narrowed gaze scanning the platform.

The station hadn't yet woken up. The train would leave in about an hour, but with the fire Zane figured everyone was caught up in the excitement. They had no way of knowing if Dubose had men staked out watching for them to attempt to rescue her, but Zane couldn't stand here while she was possibly being hurt.

"Stay here," he said. "Get your guns ready. If someone starts shooting at me, shoot back." He started to step out of the shadows of the building, but Able grabbed his arm.

"You're not going without me," said Able.

Zane nodded. "All right. Once I get to the platform, I'll take cover and you cross."

Able nodded his consent and let Zane go. No shots rang out as Zane crossed the road and in a few minutes they were all safely hidden in the shadow of the station. They made their way through the gap between two cars in the same way, one at a time and as quietly as they could until they were on the side facing away from town and the road. If the carriage happened to come back by, they'd be hidden by the train.

On silent feet they passed by each car. It was unlikely Dubose would take her to one of the public cars, so they focused their attention on the private cars in the back. There were three in all. Each of them identical black lacquer and without markings except for numbers on the side, meaning they were owned by the rail line and leased to elite clients. The men stood at each one, listening for sounds coming from inside before moving on to the next one. It was from the last one that they heard the muffled sounds of men talking.

Zane brought his finger to his lips and stepped away from the car. It only took a minute to form a plan. There were four of them. Two would get on the roof and come in through a window on each side. One would come through the door that faced town, and the last one would come through the door in the back. He hoped it was a good sign that he didn't hear her. Maybe it meant she was simply tied up and gagged, not hurt and unconscious… or worse. He couldn't allow himself to think of that possibility. Every time he closed his eyes he saw her sitting on her bed, tears in her eyes as he'd callously left her.

If he could go back to that moment, he'd have stayed and wrapped his arms around her, keeping her safe. What did his notions of love not lasting matter in the face of never seeing her again?

He shook his head, determined not to think of that now when they had a nearly insurmountable task ahead of them. He walked slowly toward the front of the car so that his boots wouldn't crunch on the gravel, while Able walked quietly toward the back door. They were both too broad to go in through the windows. They waited until Raul and William had pulled themselves up onto the roof and then took their places crouched at the doors. He counted to ten and kicked the heel of his boot against the lock, forcing the door open. The sounds of the back door crashing open along with broken glass from the windows filled the air.

Zane hurried inside with his gun drawn and fired at the first man he saw with a gun. The man fell but another stepped forward to replace him. The flash of a shot rang out and the hot bullet grazed Zane's shoulder, but he managed to hold his aim and fire. The man went down. William tussled with another one, but seemed to have the upper hand, so Zane kept moving toward the back of the car and Raul fell in line behind him.

There was a short hallway with a sliding door on either side. He nudged each door open to find the sleeping compartments empty. He raised his gun as he came to the final door that separated the back room from the one they'd come in through. It was probably a bedchamber.

He and Castillo had taken the Jameson car to Boston back in the spring, so he was familiar with the typical layout of these private cars.

All was eerily quiet inside.

"Able?" Zane called out.

"Come on in, Pierce." It wasn't Able's voice that answered. It was the cultured tone of a Southern aristocrat.

Zane opened the door to find a gun trained on him by the ugliest son of a bitch he'd ever seen. His snub nose was almost twisted to the side by an old break that hadn't healed properly.

"Put your gun down." This came from the Southern voice he'd heard. A second man that he recognized immediately from Able's description as Dubose held Glory in his lap.

She wasn't precisely unconscious, but she couldn't sit up on her own and her sleepy eyes didn't seem to focus. Her gaze flitted from one thing to the next as if it was unable to fix itself on anything. His heart squeezed in his chest at the sight of her. She wore the dress he'd helped her put on, but it was torn in places as if she'd struggled. One side of her face was swelling and a bruise was forming. She wasn't tied up, but he honestly didn't know if she'd be able to walk on her own.

He pushed the door open wider with the toe of his boot and saw Able standing inside the doorway that led to the outside. His gun held before him.

"This is your last chance, gentlemen." Dubose's hand came up to lie threateningly against her pale throat. She sucked in a breath but didn't pull away. "I will kill her before I let you have her back. Don't you think it's best to spare your own lives? I'm willing to let you go free, Hiram. Let me have Anabelle, and we'll call it even."

"Go to hell," Able said.

Dubose jeered. "You first, my friend."

"Let her go, and we'll let you leave," said Zane. The sound of his voice drew Glory's attention, and she turned her head, as if struggling to find him.

Dubose laughed. "I don't believe you." Then he let go of her neck and reached for something. He was partially blocked by the ugly bastard sitting on the chair next to him, so Zane couldn't see what it was.

Everything else happened in an instant. Glory lurched and rammed herself into Dubose. The man holding the gun on Zane fired, but Zane had already dived to the ground, ramming his shoulder into the man's legs. The bullet lodged into the side of the train car. The man fell and Zane punched him in the face. The man fought back, but they broke apart when a gun fired.

Dubose fell off the side of the bed, clutching his chest. Able had shot him.

"Pierce!" Able called.

Zane lurched to the side in time to get out of the way as Able shot the man Zane had been fighting. He'd dropped to pick up his gun and had been about to shoot Zane.

That was the last of them. Zane walked on his knees to the bed and pulled Glory into his arms. She held on to him, but most of her strength was gone.

"What did they do to you?" he asked.

She shook her head and said, "Don't know. Something in my arm." Her words were so slurred that he could barely distinguish what she said.

"Laudanum or opium straight, I'd guess." Able walked up beside them and put a hand on her forehead. "The coward used that when anyone got out of line."

Zane closed his eyes and held her closer. The nightmare was over.

Glory awoke to a pounding in her head and her mouth felt like someone had stuffed it with cotton. She rolled onto her back on a soft mattress. Her limbs were heavy but nothing felt out of place or injured. She brought a hand to her face and winced at the pain it caused. It hurt so badly that there was bound to be a big ugly bruise on her cheekbone.

What had happened to make her feel so badly?

Zane! She forced her eyes open and managed to croak out his name. The room was lit by a single lamp across the room. It wasn't her room.

"I'm here." He took her hand and brought it to his face.

He'd been sitting on the bed next to her all along, she realized. He moved over her, smiling down into her face. He was wearing pants, though he wasn't wearing a shirt or boots. A white bandage was wrapped around his upper arm. She was tucked into a bed, the covers up under her arms, and she wore a clean, cream silk dressing gown.

The fire could've been days away. Or maybe it had all been some kind of strange dream, though she doubted that because she could still smell the smoke, and this wasn't her room at Victoria House. Could they be at The Baroness? She looked back up into Zane's deep brown eyes and knew that whichever it was, they were safe now and she was with him. He was alive. That's all that mattered.

"How are you feeling?" he asked.

"I think I'm fine. I could use some water." She wanted to hold him, but with the way they had left things, she wasn't certain that she should.

He looked down at her mouth, hesitated and moved from the bed to get her a glass of water from a pitcher on the table. When he came back, he helped her sit up in bed and handed it to her. She drank it gratefully, the cool liquid sliding down her throat and making her feel immediately better.

"What happened to your arm?"

He glanced down as if he'd forgotten about it. "A graze. It's nothing. Do you remember what happened?" he asked when she handed him the nearly empty glass.

It was starting to come back to her. She remembered the fire, the carriage ride, the terrifying sight of Dubose's face, but then everything went hazy. "I remember Justin took me to the train, but I'm not certain. After that everything seems like a dream."

"Able and I found you soon after. Dubose drugged you. We sent for Caroline and she thinks its laudanum."

"How long have I been out?" Some light peeked in through the curtains of the fancy room, but she couldn't tell if it was dawn or dusk.

"Since this morning when he drugged you. The sun's going down now."

A horrible thought came to her. "What about the twins and Clara? Justin didn't find them?"

"No." He was quick to reassure her. "They're fine. Dubose never went to the ranch."

She breathed a sigh of relief.

"No one at the House was seriously injured. I want you to know that Dubose is dead, Glory, and so are the men he hired. The sheriff has identified them all as men wanted in other parts of the territory. We think he hired the investigator to find you and then hired men to bring you back with him. He made everyone think he had gone to France, so we believe he didn't want anyone from South Carolina to know the truth."

She remembered that part of their conversation. "He planned to tell them I was in an asylum in France for all these years. He wanted to run for public office and apparently a missing wife wasn't helping his plans." He'd been prepared to kill her if she didn't go along with his vision of domestic bliss. She shuddered at the thought.

Zane took her trembling hand in his. "How are you?" he asked again, his dark eyes solemn and full of concern. "We brought you to The Baroness. Caroline's waiting in the next room. Do I need to get her so you can talk to her alone?"

Her heart twisted as she realized what he meant, and she squeezed his hand. "He didn't hurt me." Her memory was spotty, but she was certain she'd remember if Justin had forced himself on her. "Not that way. I'm glad he won't be around to hurt us anymore."

She stared up into Zane's eyes, hoping that his concern was a sign that he'd had a change of heart. Perhaps she should be angry with him for walking out on her, but she couldn't find it in her. Not after last night. He could've spared himself and not come after her. He might've even saved himself from the fire, but he hadn't. He'd stayed behind to help everyone out, putting himself in danger to do it. Then he'd wasted no time in finding where Dubose had taken her.

Zane was a good man. He would've done those things whether or not he'd meant it when he'd told her that he loved her. Had the words said in a moment of crisis actually meant anything to him?

He leaned forward. "I'm sorry, Glory. I told you that he wouldn't hurt you anymore and then I let him take you." Shaking his head, he added, "I'll never forgive myself for that."

"Please, don't be sorry." Her fingers were shaking when she brushed back the hair that had fallen over his forehead, needing to touch him. "It wasn't your fault. No one expected him to start a fire."

"I should've expected it."

She sat up, taking his face in her hands. "No, Zane. You did everything you could. Please don't let him take any more from us. He's gone. It's over."

"I thought I'd lost you," he whispered, his voice breaking.

She swallowed past the lump in her throat. "I thought so too. When the house exploded and you were inside… I was so scared, Zane."

He closed his eyes as he dropped his head so that his forehead rested on hers. "Forgive me for being a fool.

I let my fear push you away, but I want you, Glory. I want to live the rest of my life with you."

She made a sound that was half laugh, half sob. "I never should have wanted to keep us a secret. What do I care if the staff knows about us? Sally accused me of always making excuses for not living my life, and she was right. I do it because I'm afraid too. But I don't want to live in fear anymore, Zane. I want to live with you. Every day. I love you."

He pulled back enough to look down into her eyes. He kept looking at her as if he couldn't believe she was whole. His eyes were soft and sweet as his gaze stroked her face. "Marry me, Glory. I love you, and I don't want to spend another day without you. I want you to have your own house with your own rose garden. I want to see Emily and Edward grow up with you as their mother."

She could barely see him through the tears in her eyes as he offered her everything she'd ever wanted. "I do want that, but there's something you should know first." Her breath stuck in her throat as she tried to figure out how to say the words. It was the last obstacle in front of them, but it wouldn't be fair of her to accept without giving him the choice. "I can't bear children. When I lost the baby, he made the doctor do something that would ensure I wouldn't get pregnant again." She said it fast to get it over with.

His face was a mixture of pain and rage. "That bastard. I'd kill him all over again if I could."

Uncertain if this had changed his feelings on marriage, she hurried to say, "I know that I should've told you before. I knew that I should, but I couldn't find the words or the right time—when is it appropriate to tell someone that?—so I waited. And then you said what you said about love, so I thought it wouldn't even matter—"

He took her face in his hands and covered her mouth with his. She fell into the kiss, needing the affirmation that they were together. That they'd survived. When he pulled back, he looked down at her and his face was so full of love that her chest ached. "I want *you*, Glory. As long as I get to be with you nothing else matters."

She did cry then. Relief made her weak, but it didn't matter because he held her. She wrapped her arms around him and he climbed into bed beside her, holding her against him. He brushed kisses along her hairline and down to her jaw, so she turned her head and took his lips again. He groaned and deepened the kiss.

When they pulled back for breath, she asked, "Are you sure, Zane? I know that you think love is fleeting."

He groaned again, laughing at his own words. "That was a stupid thing to say. I know that my love for you isn't fleeting. It won't go away, not as long as I have breath in my body."

She smiled and brushed away a tear. "And I'll make sure every day that you know how much I love you."

He smiled and wrapped his arms around her. "Then we'll get married as soon as you're better. Wherever you want."

She didn't care where, as long as it meant she'd be his forever. But it made her think of her home. "How bad is Victoria House?"

"It's mostly gone, Glory. I'm so sorry."

She nodded, having already expected that to be true. After the explosion and the fire, whatever was left would probably have to be torn down. Her heart should be breaking. Her life's work was gone. The boardinghouse she'd struggled to make into something that would help people was gone. And yet, she felt strangely free. She'd spent so many years hiding within the walls of Victoria House that she almost felt giddy with the prospect of not having to hide anymore.

"What about the staff? Where have they gone?" she asked.

He explained that Able had found rooms for them at hotels and boardinghouses for the time being. She knew it was only a matter of time before they scattered to other parts of the world, because she didn't plan to build Victoria House back. She had a very different future in mind.

As if he read her thoughts, he said, "I have some money saved up from my years with the Jamesons. Enough to build a small house. Hunter offered me a portion of the ranch at a good price. We could raise horses. You could rebuild your boardinghouse."

She smiled up at him. "That sounds lovely."

He grinned. "It does?"

"Yes, every bit of it."

"You won't miss the fancy lounges or your fancy chef?"

She scoffed. "Who says I can't keep my fancy chef? He can move with us and cook for our family."

He chuckled and then kissed her softly. "You really mean yes?"

"Yes!" She laughed, and he tightened his arms around her and rolled, bringing her across his chest.

"I love you, Glory Winters. Get used to hearing that every day."

"Except maybe change it to Glory Pierce. I love the way it sounds."

He groaned and pulled her down for a thorough kissing.

Epilogue

Five years later

Summer picnics had become a tradition at the Jameson Estate. They'd spend the afternoon fishing, playing in the wildflowers and napping, while the evening was spent chasing fireflies and listening to stories under the stars.

Glory ate up every moment of it, thankful for every day that she spent with her family. In the wilds of Montana, her life in South Carolina seemed to have happened to someone else.

"Momma, look!" Edward called from the rock he stood on at the edge of the river. He held up his fishing rod and Emily squealed as she tried to reach out and grab the fish, but kept getting scared off by the flopping of the poor fish. Zane laughed as he helped her.

The twins had been with them every day of the past five years. Their mother kept in touch, but the papers to make them her and Zane's had been filed after their marriage. Today was their wedding anniversary, and they celebrated every year with their family around them.

She waved and called out encouragement before turning her attention back to Caroline and her baby. The girl babbled up at them both.

"She's going to be a talker," Clara predicted, her own daughter sat gurgling on her knees as Clara bounced her up and down.

Able's deep laugh drew her attention as he tossed his nearly five-year-old son over his shoulder. "No one can talk more than this one." The boy giggled and shrieked as Able pretended that he was going to toss him into the river.

Hunter and Emmy walked in the wildflowers with their own children in tow, while Emmy's younger sisters, both teenagers, dipped their feet into the cold water.

Castillo drew Glory's attention as he sat down beside his wife and pulled her into his arms. They'd moved back from Boston after Caroline had finished her studies. Castillo worked with Hunter and Zane, building up their horse ranch, while Caroline had built a clinic in Helena. She and Glory had joined forces. The women Glory helped in her boardinghouse were able to gain work experience at the clinic.

Now that the boardinghouse wasn't attached to a brothel, she'd even found a schoolteacher able to work full-time to teach the women other skills. The boardinghouse had become a secondary training school that women in need could attend free of charge. Glory hoped to expand the courses offerings even more in the future. She still had her real estate which earned them a comfortable annual income in rents, and the horses had started to pay off. People all over the country had heard about the Jameson stock. Orders for foals came in often before the horses were even mated.

Emily squealed as Edward chased her with a worm, her laughter carrying across the field. Emmy's children joined in. Zane came down beside Glory on the blanket. His arm moved around her waist, tucking her back against him.

"What are you thinking?" he whispered against her ear.

There'd been a time when she'd thought that good things rarely came along unexpectedly. She'd been right, but Zane was definitely one of those good things. He'd changed her life in a million different ways, all for the better. "That I love you."

He smiled and kissed her shoulder, his mouth warm through the fabric of her dress.

Life was better than she'd ever imagined it could be.

* * * * *

If you enjoyed this story
check out the first two books in the
Outlaws of the Wild West miniseries
by Harper St. George:
The Innocent and the Outlaw
A Marriage Deal with the Outlaw

COMING NEXT MONTH FROM

HARLEQUIN®

HISTORICAL

Available September 18, 2018

All available in print and ebook via Reader Service and online

A WESTERN CHRISTMAS HOMECOMING (Western)
by Lynna Banning, Lauri Robinson and Kathryn Albright
Come home for Christmas in these three feel-good stories of festive romance in the Wild West!

A PROPOSITION FOR THE COMTE (Regency)
Gentlemen of Honor by Sophia James
Threatened by her late husband's enemies, cautious Lady Violet Addington needs the protection of the dangerous Comte de Beaumont. But what can she offer him in return...?

HIS RAGS-TO-RICHES CONTESSA (Regency)
Matches Made in Scandal • by Marguerite Kaye
Conte Luca del Pietro needs Becky Wickes, London's finest cardsharp, to help catch his father's murderer. But as their chemistry burns hotter, the stakes of their dangerous game get higher!

THE WARRIOR'S BRIDE PRIZE (Roman)
by Jenni Fletcher
Gambled away by her intended bridegroom to centurion Marius Varro, Livia faces a difficult choice as a barbarian rebellion strikes: her Caledonian roots or the husband she's falling for...

A MOST UNSUITABLE MATCH
Sisters of Scandal • by Julia Justiss
While trying to find a man of impeccable reputation, Prudence Lattimar must avoid Lieutenant Johnnie Trethwell—his family is as notorious as hers, no matter how charming and unfailingly *honorable* he is!

THE MAKINGS OF A LADY
The Chadcombe Marriages • by Catherine Tinley
Just as Lady Olivia thinks she's found a suitable match in suave Mr. Manning, charismatic Captain Jem Ford, the subject of her childhood infatuation, returns. Dare she hope he'll notice her as the lady she's now become?

YES! Please send me the **Home on the Ranch Collection** in Larger Print. This collection begins with 3 FREE books and 2 FREE gifts in the first shipment. Along with my 3 free books, I'll also get the next 4 books from the Home on the Ranch Collection, in LARGER PRINT, which I may either return and owe nothing, or keep for the low price of $5.24 U.S./ $5.89 CDN each plus $2.99 for shipping and handling per shipment*. If I decide to continue, about once a month for 8 months I will get 6 or 7 more books, but will only need to pay for 4. That means 2 or 3 books in every shipment will be FREE! If I decide to keep the entire collection, I'll have paid for only 32 books because 19 books are FREE! I understand that accepting the 3 free books and gifts places me under no obligation to buy anything. I can always return a shipment and cancel at any time. My free books and gifts are mine to keep no matter what I decide.

268 HCN 3760 468 HCN 3760

Name   (PLEASE PRINT)

Address   Apt. #

City   State/Prov.   Zip/Postal Code

Signature (if under 18, a parent or guardian must sign)

Mail to the **Reader Service**:

IN U.S.A.: P.O. Box 1341, Buffalo, New York 14240-8531
IN CANADA: P.O. Box 603, Fort Erie, Ontario L2A 5X3

* Terms and prices subject to change without notice. Prices do not include applicable taxes. Sales tax applicable in NY. Canadian residents will be charged applicable taxes. This offer is limited to one order per household. All orders subject to approval. Credit or debit balances in a customer's account(s) may be offset by any other outstanding balance owed by or to the customer. Please allow 3 to 4 weeks for delivery. Offer available while quantities last. Offer not available to Quebec residents.

Your Privacy—The Reader Service is committed to protecting your privacy. Our Privacy Policy is available online at www.ReaderService.com or upon request from the Reader Service.

We make a portion of our mailing list available to reputable third parties that offer products we believe may interest you. If you prefer that we not exchange your name with third parties, or if you wish to clarify or modify your communication preferences, please visit us at www.ReaderService.com/consumerschoice or write to us at Reader Service Preference Service, P.O. Box 9062, Buffalo, NY. 14240-9062. Include your complete name and address.